BAZAAR GIRLS

KERRIGAN BYRNE
& CYNTHIA ST. AUBIN

OLIVERHEBERBOOKS

Author's Note

Spoiler alert: this is NOT a "not like the other girls" book.
At several points while writing it, we asked ourselves how much
ADHD is too much for a character to have and still remain
relatable? But then we asked ourselves, relatable to who(m) (Also
spoiler alert, parentheses, em-dashes, and italics are totally a
neurodivergent thing so, buckle up, kids). In embarking on
representation romance, we're writing about people who don't just
have the quirky, adorable traits of their various traumas, medical
conditions, or psychological diagnoses. We don't get to put this away
when it stops being "cute" and "endearing." Because sometimes it's
"hard" and "weird" and deeply isolating. Which is why "not like
the other girls" isn't a punch line or a criticism to be leveled at a
story where the heroine is a person with disabilities or
neurodivergent. Because we are like the other girls. So many girls
who would like to be represented more in the mainstream. Girls that
deserve a happily ever after even when it arrives messy, perpetually
late, with an empty tank and desperately in need of a snack.
Townsend Harbor is full of characters some might call odd, wrong,
queer (in every sense of the word), and (the word that hurts the most)
"difficult" but what they are is real. We all come with flaws, kinks,

diagnoses, red flags, traumas, and tastes. In our romantic fantasies, those things are part and parcel of the whole human experience. Our deepest hope is that someone sees themselves in the way we always want them to be seen.

As worthy of the deepest, truest love.

Contents

Procrastiknitting

KNITTING WHEN YOU SHOULD BE DOING SOMETHING ELSE BUT ALL YOU WANT TO DO IS KNIT.

GEMMA MCKENDRICK RUSHED AROUND HER COZY BUT cluttered craft boutique, fluffing pillows, swiping dust from the knickknacks, and jamming a mental knitting needle into the balloon of panic swelling against her ribs. Twice already, she'd had to swap out her sweater as damp rings darkened the pits. Hyperhidrosis—just another of ADHD's delightful bonus body betrayals.

In exactly twelve minutes, the biweekly Stitch 'n Bitch club would commence, and she was running late.

Per usual.

The detailed list of necessary preparations she'd gone to the extra trouble of neatly typing out in a burst of rare and blessed motivation at the ass crack of dawn this morning sat languishing on her counter at home. Most likely marked with a coffee ring from one of the mugs that tended to gather in herds on every available horizontal surface of her kitchen. The mental checklist she'd hastily assembled in its stead bore only a marginal resemblance.

1. Hide-y up: shove everything in the store that resembled extraneous clutter in any available hiding place
2. Charcutercheat: put out the preassembled trays she'd bought because she'd run out of time after having watched two hours of TikTok tutorials and dirtied every champagne glass she owned attempting to make sheet of cured meats into perfect pork roses
3. Maid of Dishonor: quickly skim the magazines Cady left over a week ago and weigh in on the centerpieces she'd helpfully marked with an elaborate color-coded system of sticky notes

With the googly-eyed cat clock behind her fabric cutting counter conspicuously counting down the seconds, Gemma realized item three was a no-go. Better to risk her best friend's always-gentle censure by asking for just one more day (again) than to half-ass her responsibilities.

Just once in her life, she'd love to be serenely standing next to the vintage Chesterfield that ate up a good third of Bazaar Girls' wood-floored lounge area, welcoming the attendees in a soothing, Martha Stewart-esque monotone, a tray of hors d'oeuvres that didn't already look half masticated balanced on one perfectly manicured hand.

Instead, she was blotting the sheen of sweat from her upper lip and railing the ice bucket with a bottle of Prosecco when the front door swung open to reveal the first attendees.

Myrtle Le Grande and Vivian "Vee" Prescott sailed in as a mournful mechanized dirge that *used* to sound like the enthusiastic bleating of sheep intoned their arrival. Septuagenarian life partners and proprietresses of some of Townsend Harbor's most iconic businesses, their presence made Gemma acutely aware of her own shop's neophyte legacy on picturesque Water Street.

They were as different but complementary as salt and pepper shakers—Myrtle was the zany Lucy to Vee's steady Ethel. Their outfits, like their observations, often reflected the disparate nature of their general approach to Life, the Universe, and Everything.

"What on earth is wrong with your doorbell?" Vee asked, whisking her bakery box over to the table where Gemma was frantically trying to chill the wine.

"Sounds like the poor things are dying of the dysentery," Myrtle added, reaching into an oversized bag to produce a pitcher of poison-green liquid. "When an animal makes a sound like that, you better hope you've got good reflexes or well-sealed wellies."

Gemma looked into the wiry woman's watery blue eyes beneath the shock of perpetually porcupine-like ash-gray hair. Below it, her outfit was an enthusiastically haphazard assemblage of prints and fabrics.

"I need to change the batteries." Yet another item on her endless list of assorted and oft-neglected chores.

"You got a ladder?" Myrtle asked, shrugging out of an oversized windbreaker. On the back, a cartoon logo version of the elderly woman perched atop a towering poop emoji—pixelated flies and all—above bubble letters spelling out "Fertile Myrtle's Manure." *We're the shit!* appeared in feminine cursive beneath. "I'll get that little bastard licked pronto."

"I do." Gemma sighed. "But the safety hinge is broken."

"Don't give it another thought." With its silky Sussex syllables, Vee's voice was like a cool palm pressed against Gemma's clammy forehead. "What else can we help with?"

It was a question Gemma heard often, and usually with this exact flavor of kind concern. Because despite her consistent efforts to the contrary, she always looked like she needed it.

"Um, you can set out the pattern printouts for tonight's project if you want," she said, tipping her head toward the stack of papers next to the cracked iPad that served as her register.

"On it." Myrtle's knobby knees made the wings of the butterflies printed on her leggings bulge into a beetle-like shape as she shuffled over to the patterns. Lifting one of the sheets, she squinted through the thick lenses of her sparkly pink reading glasses. "Spicy bean dip?"

Heat rose to Gemma's already glowing cheeks. "The pattern's on the back. I sort of had to reuse some paper."

Because she'd completely forgotten that the printer in her small office cubby was out, and no way was she running down to the Copy Cat even *if* she hadn't been completely and totally out of time.

She'd successfully avoided her former boyfriend's parents for the last three years in a town with a population that barely cracked the quadruple digits. Damned if she was going to besmirch the only perfect record she had because she couldn't remember to order a goddamn ream of printing paper.

"Better for the environment anyway." Vee relieved Myrtle of the stack and began dealing them out pattern-side-up along the couch cushions and folding chairs set out around the old coffee table that served as the center of their knitting circle.

"What's on the agenda for tonight, anyway?" Myrtle asked, dipping one of the clean mugs Gemma set out into the ice bucket and topping it with her toxic-ooze-colored cocktail.

"A certain knit halter top that everyone and their parrot have been coming to the store asking for ever since Cirque de Café."

Myrtle's eyes brightened. "Did you hear that, Vee? She's finally parting with the pattern for that tit sling we liked so much."

Vee's elegant patrician face creased in a smile redolent of long-suffering affection. What Myrtle was hauling around beneath her splashy blouses these days could probably be covered by a Starburst wrapper.

The front door whooshed open, and the mournful lowing that followed deepened into a range that sounded distinctly demonic.

"Jesus." Darby Dunwell shot forward as if zapped by a cattle prod. Her hot-pink coif tipped back as she glanced up in the direction of the sound. "That sounds like hell's intercom."

Her strawberry print halter-top sundress flared as she spun to greet them, a smile that still made Gemma's guts go all buttery spreading across her pinup-perfect face. The hottest prospect in town, and vanilla-cone-eating, future-Velcro-shoe-wearing Ethan Townsend had gotten to her first.

Gemma's flush deepened further when Darby caught her in a quick hug, trailing the tantalizing scent of coffee in her wake. The owner of a vintage coffee camper the same iconic shade as her hair, Darby tended to steep in a concentration of the heavenly aroma.

Darby turned to add her contribution to the table just as the door opened and the unholy sound croaked out again.

"That's it," Gemma's best friend said with a harried smile stretching her rosebud mouth. "I'm calling Fawkes to come fix that thing."

Gemma swept forward to help Cady with her bundle of bags, biting down on the knee-jerk need to nag her about carrying such a heavy load. Despite a debilitating back condition, her best friend had been doing better than ever lately.

With Fawkes overseeing her treatments—and probably quietly intimidating doctors and specialists into ponying up the primo care—Cady had been accepted into a trial for some hot new wonder drug.

Information Gemma had received secondhand through the wedding planner she was shocked her best friend had hired.

Cady's thick blonde braid swung between her shoulder blades as she winced. "Bro. You still haven't changed that battery?" she teased.

"I was totally going to, but I'm pretty sure the ladder I stole from my parents' house was made around the same time Homo sapiens were first inventing tools."

"Why didn't you tell me?" Cady asked. "Fawkes could take care of that lickety-split."

He wouldn't even need a ladder.

As if the burly, mostly monosyllabic walking brute squad should be the answer to all of Gemma's problems as he had been Cady's.

"This looks amazing," Cady said, giving Gemma a side hug as they approached the table.

"Thanks," Gemma said, some of her anxiety easing in the proximity of her best friend's presence.

Only to return abruptly when the front door swung open in the key of dying ruminant.

As she turned to welcome what she assumed was one of the Stitch 'n Bitch regulars, Gemma's words died on her lips.

There, in the doorway of her store, stood Gabe "The Babe" Kelly. An old—relatively speaking—friend of Darby's from Boston, he'd made his Townsend Harbor debut in a duet on aerial silks that left neither eyes nor panties dry.

Gemma's very much among them.

"Hey," Darby said in a tone that conveyed more than a little pique. "Everyone, you remember Gabe."

Remember?

Remember?

If she lived a thousand years, Gemma was quite certain the man's image would remain indelibly seared in her mind until her last second.

And not just because she was pretty sure he'd broken several laws of physics during the Brewbies benefit. Gabe Kelly also happened to be the most soul-crushingly beautiful man Gemma had ever met in person.

Met being a somewhat generous term for Gemma's stammering, twitchy-faced, dart-eyed performance when they'd been introduced.

"Hey," Gabe said, giving their small company a perfunctory nod before lasering in on Darby. "Talk to you for a minute?"

In private being heavily implied.

"Sure," Darby said.

"You can use the—um—the—" Gemma snapped her fingers as if the sound of it could reconnect the cognition and speech centers of her brain scorched by Gabe's presence.

"Office?" Vee suggested.

"Right." Gemma's cheeks flamed. "The office. Behind the curtain on your left."

Gabe's gaze swiveled to her directly, and Gemma promptly forgot how to breathe.

"Thanks." Motioning for Darby to walk ahead of him, Gabe pointed his boots in that direction.

Gemma waited for what she hoped was the proper suspicion-reducing amount of time, then excused herself to get a nonexistent ball of Alize Diva Stretch yarn from the storage room.

Helpfully adjacent to the office.

"...can't keep doing this, Darbs," Gabe was saying, his Southie accent making it sound like *Dahbs*. "You keep stuffing envelopes full of cash through the mail slot and the feds are gonna think I got myself into the family business."

"Until you pull your head out of your ass and take the money, I sure as shit can," Darby insisted.

"You think I can't run a legit shop, is that it?" The question was barbed with a defensive challenge.

"What I think is that I'll be damned if I'm just going to let you sleep on that sad little cot in your shop and shower at the gas station until you have enough stashed away to get yourself a place to live."

"I appreciate your concern, but I'd rather sleep with my dick in the fucking dirt than take money from you. I know how hard you worked to get where you are, and I didn't move to Townsend Harbor to siphon off you like some kind of leech."

When she spoke again, Darby's voice had a gentleness Gemma didn't often hear when she was addressing her customers. "But did you know that was a private seed loan from your father that got me started in the first place?"

"Figures," Gabe grunted. "Meanwhile, if *I* asked my old man for money, he'd tell me to pound sand."

"Which makes it all the more satisfying for me to give it to you," Darby said.

Gemma held her breath through the tense silence that followed.

"Look," Darby continued. "If it makes you feel better, you can pay me back whenever. Just take the goddamn money."

Another beat of silence. "All right," Gabe said. "But I *am* gonna pay you back. You know that, right?"

"Duh," Darby said, followed by a muffled impact that Gemma could only assume was them hugging.

She took that as her cue to hightail it back to the shop, where Myrtle, Vee, and Cady had finished setting up the snacks table.

Darby and Gabe emerged moments later.

"You ladies have a good evening," Gabe said. And then, for no reason she could possibly imagine, he grinned at Gemma before pushing through the door and out into the night.

"All right." Darby rubbed her palms together, looking both flushed and pleased as she addressed Cady. "I want to hear all the wedding drama."

"You guys," Cady said, dramatically slumping onto the couch. "I've got so much to tell you."

After they'd all settled in with their drinks and their yarn, Cady regaled them with the various horrors of the wedding-planning process that Gemma had been only loosely involved in thus far.

Gemma tuned back in as Cady described her latest dress fitting. "The lace bodice is stunning, and the skirt is the perfect amount of poufy. I can't wait for you all to see it!"

"Will the ruggedly handsome groom-to-be be wearing a kilt?" Vee asked with a sly wink.

A blush stained Cady's cheeks. "Roman will be wearing a suit, like a normal person."

"There's nothing normal about that man," Myrtle said. "Did you see the size of his—"

"Shoes?" Darby suggested with faux innocence. "I'm sure Roman has *very* large feet."

Peals of laughter filled the room as Cady swatted at the voluptuous coffee aficionado with a plastic ruler used for determining the yarn gauge.

Gemma smiled despite the brief pang of jealousy, the familiar teasing banter easing her worries. She loved seeing Cady so happy, even if talk of weddings made her own perpetually single status seem glaringly obvious.

Shaking off the thought, she forced her attention back to the conversation, only to realize the topic had shifted to the budget of the upcoming nuptials.

The dreaded B-word caused an instant and violent twist in Gemma's gut.

It had been weeks since she'd last logged into the spreadsheets bearing Bazaar Girls' profit and loss statements, despite the fact that she had four weeks to send them along to her father.

The very thought of it set off a wave of the same panic that had been the cause of Gemma's waking drenched in a cold sweat that morning.

An icy fist clutched at her heart as she surveyed the shop. Gemma's passion for her business was evident in every detail of the store, from the whimsical knitted tea cozies to the hand-painted signs announcing upcoming workshops. She had spent months selecting every last item in it. Each ball of fine merino wool and designer crochet hook. She had poured her heart and soul into Bazaar Girls, determined to create a cozy, welcoming space where people could come together and share their love of crafting. And wine.

But as much as she loved her store, the sidecar of intense dyscalculia that came with her neurodivergence made tracking the money side of things a bit like juggling flaming torches while riding a unicycle.

She could clearly envision what needed to happen. Familiarize herself with the principles using every available tutorial. When it came time to put her notes into actual practice...

Disaster. And several small fires.

She hadn't realized just how far into the tangled terrain of her own mind she'd wandered until Vee stood up with an apologetic look.

"Well, I hate to call it a night already, but I'm afraid I have an early appointment with a vendor making hand-cast dildos out of recycled plastic."

The assembly took this as their cue, the women making short work of the clear-up.

Myrtle, Vee, and Darby exchanged hugs before departing with the leftovers Gemma insisted she didn't have room for.

Cady hung back.

Gemma's heart began to thump hard between her shoulder blades as she felt her friend's eyes boring into her back.

At last, the inevitable question came. "Everything okay?"

Gemma waved a hand, refilling Cady's glass with the last of the Prosecco. "Totally fine. Just busy with the shop. You know how it is."

Cady's eyebrows rose in a silent challenge.

Gemma sighed, setting her own glass on the table with a clink. She should have known Cady wouldn't buy it.

"Dad's been on my case again about the profit margins." Gemma twisted a loose thread on her sweater, frustration simmering. "Basically, I have until a week after your wedding to demonstrate that Bazaar Girls is on track to be profitable, or he feels that I should consider a 'more stable career path.'"

Cady was silent for an extended beat. "Do you think that maybe, possibly, you might have just a little much on your plate?"

The instant jolt of irritation Gemma felt was a dead giveaway that her best friend was most assuredly right.

Per usual.

"I'm fine," she said automatically. Cady shot her a look, and she relented. "Okay, maybe I'm a little overcommitted. What with the Harbarian Field Day, Canna-cake Bake-off, Townsendites for Sane Parking..." She trailed off, the complete list being way more than she wanted to try to remember. "And someone has to make sure the Townsend Harbor annual mackerel-wrestling contest isn't a disaster."

"The only disaster would be my best friend working herself into the ground." Cady bumped Gemma's shoulder playfully. "Seriously, do I need to plan an intervention?"

"Intervene all you want," Gemma said. "As long as there's wine and snacks involved."

Cady laughed, the sound bright and joyful. "Deal. Now, best friend duties aside, you have to relax and enjoy this. It's my wedding, not yours. Let me worry about the details."

Gemma swallowed hard against the lump in her throat.

"You're right," she said softly. "This is your wedding. I just really want to make it special for you."

Cady smiled, eyes shining, and Gemma's heart swelled. "If you're there, it will be."

GEMMA WAVED GOODBYE TO CADY AND LOCKED UP THE boutique as fatigue settled into her bones. She'd stayed up late the night before working on wedding plans, and today had been a long day of customers and classes. All she wanted was a glass of wine and her couch.

She'd made it about halfway there when her Fiat made a sound that rivaled her dying doorbell, sputtered, coughed, and went silent.

Gemma's knuckles were white on the leather steering wheel as she guided her car to the shoulder and shifted it into Park.

On one side of her dashboard, a slim white needle dipped into the red tick marks nearing the E on the gas gauge. On the other, the orange SERVICE ENGINE warning glowed accusatorially.

As it had for the past month.

Now she was stranded, the boutique her only source of light against the encroaching darkness.

Panic bubbled in her chest as she fumbled for her phone.

Whom could she call at this hour? Her parents were out of town, and she didn't want to bother Cady so Fawkes could come to her rescue.

- Roadside assistance.

Pawing through the pile of unopened mail in her passenger seat, she found the "we're definitely cutting you off if you don't pay us within a week, you lazy motherfucker" notice and located the 1-800 number listed at the top. Taking a deep breath, she dialed and reached a wildly enthusiastic operator who promised to have someone out to her within an hour.

As luck—or lack thereof—would have it, help arrived sooner and in a form that made her feel like someone had turned her seat heater up to the taint-toasting setting.

Gabriel fucking Kelly.

TWO

Dipstick

THE DEVICE TO CHECK YOUR OIL LEVELS.

GABRIEL'S GRIP TIGHTENED AROUND THE WORN leather steering wheel as he spotted the cherry-red Fiat stalled on the side of the winding coastal road, hazard lights blinking in the darkness.

Of course it was Gemma *fucking* McKendrick.

In the months since he'd moved to Townsend Harbor, he hadn't been able to get the image of her out of his head—all creamy skin and an entire storm cloud of wind-tousled, dark hair. The way she'd laughed that night at Darby's benefit, head thrown back and eyes crinkled, had haunted his dreams.

As did how her tits looked in a knitted bikini halter.

Which was exactly why he couldn't get tangled up with her.

Gabe shook off the thought, jaw clenching. He didn't need the trouble that came with a high-minded woman like her. Not when he was still clawing his way up from the gutter.

Gemma was sweetness and light, the girl next door with a heart of gold. Gabe was darkness and danger, Southie trash with a rap sheet to prove it. Her family would throw a shit fit if she brought him home for Sunday dinner.

And she wasn't the "fuck buddy" kind of girl. Everything about her screamed monogamy.

He pulled up ahead of the Fiat and killed the engine with a sigh, adjusting his jeans. This was gonna be torture. Luckily, he grew up with a handful of older brothers in an Irish Catholic crime family free of normal boundaries or any women, so...he'd been waterboarded in kindergarten, and the torture only got more serious from there.

Like when Johnny had promised the pinky nail on his left hand would grow back.

He scowled down at his naked finger, a constant reminder to trust no one.

When Gabe hopped out of the tow truck, Gemma stumbled out of her car, shivering without a jacket.

How the hell did she look even sweeter—and sexier—than he remembered, in that prim, cat-themed sweater vest and pleated skirt? Like a sexy librarian fantasy come to life.

If this were a porno, he'd be paid in trade...

After snagging an initial glance at him, she widened her eyes, a blush blooming on her cheeks as her gaze ricocheted around the shadows of the trees that surrounded the narrow lane. "Where's— um—where's Jim?" she queried warily as he approached.

"Jim?"

"Jim Conter? You're driving his truck?" Alarm whitened her face.

"Oh." He shrugged. "Don't know Jim. I just bought this truck as part and parcel of the Jim's Auto Body Shop estate."

Oh shit. He slapped his trap shut. If someone had an "estate," in his experience, it was because they were European nobility.

Or dead.

"You and Jim know each other well?" he asked, crossing himself against the dead out of habit.

People in this town seemed to know and love each other. It was wicked weird.

Suddenly Gemma found her shoes very interesting as she muttered, "He's rescued me sever—a few— He's towed my car before."

"Sounds like you need a new ride," he teased.

Instead of a witty rejoinder, she shrugged and shuffled to the driver's door. "I don't know what happened to it. Usually, I can get it home and back to town when it's like this without a problem."

Gabe swallowed hard, trying not to stare at the way the breeze molded the dress to her curves. Without thinking, he unzipped his hoodie, peeled it down his shoulders, and had her wrapped in it before she had the chance to protest.

"Pop the hood," he said, cutting off any other conversation. "I'll take a look."

"The hood." Flustered, she wiped at a few tendrils of dark hair escaping from her ponytail to frame her face as she sank into the sweatshirt still warm from his skin. "Okay. I can do that. I can pop the hood."

Folding back into her toy-sized car, she pulled a lever. The trunk unlatched. She pushed a button. The mirror moved. Then the gas door clicked open. Finally, she found the hood lever and pulled.

Damn, she was cute, he thought as he put everything but the hood back where it needed to be.

"How long you had this car?" he asked.

Her forehead wrinkled like he'd asked her to solve a quadratic equation in her head. "Like, two years? Or three?"

That long and she didn't even know how to pop the hood?

Uh oh.

"Is that bad? Your face said it was bad," she fretted as she shuffled to where he lifted the hood and propped it up.

"No need to panic," Gabe drawled, voice dipping low. "I'll make sure you get where you need to go."

A blush stained Gemma's cheeks as she looked away, fiddling with the strap of her purse. Gabe bit back a groan, heat pooling in his gut and lower. He had a weakness for a girl in trouble. Not to mention a girl wearing his oversized clothing.

He was playing with fire here, but for the first time since he'd left Boston behind, Gabe might not mind getting burned.

Do the job, he reminded himself. *Then get the fuck out of here.* To a girl like this? *You* are the *trouble.*

As he inspected the engine, he caught Gemma sneaking glances at him from under her lashes, cheeks still flushed. His mouth twitched. He should *not* be noticing her noticing him.

At all.

When he straightened, grabbing the grease rag hanging from his back pocket and wiping his hands, her gaze flickered to his arms, exposed in a black ribbed tank.

He smirked and couldn't help flexing his triceps. "See something you like?"

She sputtered, scarlet cheeks deepening to rash-y. "What? No. I just—"

"Relax," he drawled with a chuckle. "I'm messing with you."

Gemma cleared her throat, turning her attention very studiously to the engine. "So, uh, what exactly seems to be the problem?"

Shaking his head, Gabe leaned against the side of the car. "Aside from your gas gauge sitting on E? When's the last time you filled up?"

"Yyyyesterday?" Gemma winced, looking to him for a moment as if he could help her with the answer before it skittered away. "Or maybe the day before. Was that a weekend?"

"It's Wednesday." Gabe cocked his head and assessed her. Was she on something? Or did time just have no meaning when you were that pretty? "Jesus." He huffed out a laugh, shaking his head. "You're lucky you made it as far as you did. The fumes probably carried you here through sheer will alone."

Gemma's shoulders hunched and her cheeks flamed impossibly brighter. Irritation flickered in Gabe's chest at the sight. He hadn't meant to make her feel stupid.

"Hey." He nudged her shoulder with his, voice softening. "I

was just teasing. Everyone makes mistakes sometimes, yeah? It's an easy thing to forget."

Gemma glanced over at him, eyes searching his face.

Gabe held her gaze, willing her to see he meant no harm. She broke eye contact immediately, but after a moment, the tension eased from her shoulders.

"Good news is I can get you back on the road," he said. "Bad news is, it'll take a second to make sure nothing in the engine seized. Hop in—I'll give you a ride to the shop."

"Oh, no, I couldn't inconvenience you like that," Gemma protested.

Gabe slanted her a look as he opened the passenger door, keeping his smile pasted on as he said, "Wasn't asking, lady. It's the middle of the night and you're not safe. Get in the damn truck."

Her mouth pressed into a hyphen, but she ambled over and slid into the seat. He took a slow breath, steeling himself for the drive ahead as he finished hooking the front of her car to the tow truck.

Gabe slid into the driver's seat, acutely aware of her beside him. A floral scent flooded the cab, mixing with the leather interior to create something intoxicating. Her light cotton skirt brushed his jeans, sending another spike of heat through his body.

Trouble. This was trouble with a capital Fuck.

Yanking the truck into drive, he pulled back onto the road as Gemma fiddled with her seatbelt. A glance at her from the corner of his eye and he almost groaned. Up close, she was even more distracting—all rosy lips and long lashes and soft curves he was dying to get his hands on.

He cleared his throat. "So, uh. How's the yarn shop doing?" Small talk. He could do small talk. Even if the only thing he wanted was to pin her to the seat and devour her mouth.

"Good, good." Gemma fussed with the hem of her dress. "We've had an increase in sales the past few months. I think the marketing strategies I put in place are helping."

He didn't know dick about marketing strategies. Growing up in a chop shop taught a kid that word of mouth was the only way to find clients. And even then, if word of mouth became too, well...mouthy? The Kelly family tended to do something to the owner of the mouth. Something that would keep him from talking any more.

Not the kind of conversation one had with the girl next door in a cat sweater.

Luckily, Townsend Harbor's peninsula was only seven miles across, which meant no one was ever very far away from anything in this town.

The rest of the drive passed in a blur. By the time they arrived at the shop, Gabe's restraint was fraying. He swallowed a groan as Gemma unfolded from the truck, the hem of her dress riding up her thighs.

Tonight was gonna be a long fucking night.

In the shop, Gabe parked himself beneath the hood of Gemma's Fiat for several minutes, pulling off covers and caps, checking fluid levels, assessing the level of wear and tear. Buying time to get his shit together, mostly. The ache in his jeans wasn't going away anytime soon, not with her hovering at his elbow.

"So, what's the diagnosis, doc?" Gemma asked with affected drama. "Am I gonna live?"

He slanted her a look, noticing the nervous twitch of her fingers. The way she gnawed at the inside of her cheeks. "Your car, you mean?"

Her nose wrinkled adorably. "Unless you've got some bad news about my health I should know about."

Gabe snorted. "Your health seems fine to me." Too fine. "Your car, on the other hand..." He scratched his jaw, smearing grease from his fingers. "It's not looking great."

"Oh, no. What's wrong with it?"

"When's the last time you had it serviced?"

"I..." She worried her bottom lip. "It's been a while."

"A while," Gabe repeated. "Your oil is sludgy as shit and your fuel filter needs to be replaced. Like, yesterday." He remembered the gauge on her dash, the needle buried below E. "I think your brake fluid is leaking, and this hose needs to be replaced. You're gonna destroy your engine if you keep driving like this."

"I didn't realize..." She flushed, backing away from the engine lest it take some oily sort of revenge. "I'm not great with...cars. With life, really."

Probably had Daddy Dearest or some guy to take care of this stuff her whole life. Guys liked to take care of their girls' car sometimes. It was a love language. He heard there was a book about that.

"I can fix it up, get you back on the road," he offered.

She bit her lip, nodding profusely as if fighting back strong emotion that the situation didn't warrant.

Gabe wanted to reach for her again, reassure her with his touch. But he'd already pushed his luck, and the last thing he needed was to get carried away and do something he'd regret.

Like kiss her.

"You can pick it up tomorrow," he said gently.

Gemma nodded, her cheeks still pink. "What do I owe you?"

"Don't worry about it. Consider it a favor." He turned back to bend over the engine.

"I can't just *not* pay you."

"You can and you will." The thought of her owing him anything left a bad taste in his mouth. "Just promise me you'll knit me a Red Sox sweater."

She moved around the new auto repair shop using her fingertips to discover everything. The smooth, scuffed desk, the graze of the polished tools, the cold steel of a wrench.

He'd thought all this new stuff too shiny. Too nice for hands as dirty as his own.

"Do you want to move in with me?"

Gabe hit his head on the open hood of the tiny car as he straightened and turned to blink at her with *What the fuck?* poised on his lips. She was joking. Right?

Uh oh. Why didn't she look like she was joking?

"It's just that I can tell you're not comfortable here on that cot." She pointed to what had effectively been his bedroom since he landed in Townsend Harbor. "The basement apartment of my house is empty, with a couple of bedrooms that aren't being used. You'd have your own kitchenette," she rushed to add, only taking a breath when the exhale ran out. "The house doesn't smell like engines and creosote, and you're much less likely to get mesothelioma if you don't sleep next to cars. I read that somewhere."

Gabe stared at her, torn between suspicion and temptation.

Living in Gemma's house, being so close to her...it was a dangerous idea. His past wasn't one he wanted catching up to him, because it would catch up to whomever was in his life, as well.

And yet...he *was* tired of living in the garage. Tired of the isolation, of never quite fitting in. He'd promised himself that this was his chance at normalcy, stability...

Home.

And if he was honest with himself, the thought of seeing Gemma every day sweetened the pot.

"I don't know," he said slowly. "I wouldn't want to impose."

"You wouldn't be." Gemma smiled then, bright and earnest. "Friends help each other out, right?"

Friends. The word was a balm, easing the wariness in Gabe's chest. He could do friends.

Taking a deep breath, he nodded. "All right. Let's give it a shot."

Gemma's answering grin was like the sun breaking through the clouds. "Great! I'll get it cleaned up and ready for you to move in. We can work out the details about rent and stuff later."

She turned on her heel abruptly, already chattering to herself about getting supplies to make the apartment homier.

Gabe just watched her go, shaking his head.

He was in deep, deep shit. But for the first time, trouble had never felt so good.

THREE

Knitty Litter

THE KNITTING RELATED DETRITUS THAT
COLLECTS ALL OVER THE HOME WHEN ONE
KNITS (OR CROCHETS).

GEMMA BURST INTO THE KITCHEN, HER HEART
pounding as she surveyed the disaster zone that was her morning
coffee stop. Empty mugs were strewn across the counter, a
month's worth of mail was piled haphazardly on the dust-coated
dining table, and her latest experimental knitting project had
unraveled into a tumbleweed that hunkered beneath one of the
empty chairs.

She groaned, mentally cursing her ADHD for derailing yet
another plan. She'd meant to spend the whole day deep-cleaning
the house to prepare for Gabe's arrival, but between fantasizing
about leaping onto his lap in the cab of his tow truck and trying
to finish ordering the winner's ribbons for the annual Harbor-
Que and Pumpkin Carving Contest, the hours had magically
evaporated.

Glancing at the clock on the microwave that hadn't displayed
the accurate time since the power outage that accompanied
winter's last coastal windstorm, she reminded herself again to sync
it to her phone.

Which was...somewhere?

Pausing dead center in the sprawling chaos, she counted the sonorous tolling of the city hall clock tower.

Eight. Nine. Ten...

Eleven.

Gabe was due to arrive in half an hour.

"Shit! Shit, shit, *shit.*"

Galvanized by the pure panic that served as one of her only reliable forms of motivation, Gemma at last launched into a frenetic flurry.

Yanking a large black lawn bag from the cabinet under the sink, she began sweeping the non-breakable clutter into its cavernous throat with a judicious forearm. Each hastily denuded surface was then treated to the most superficial of passes with a damp handful of bleach wipes.

The best invention since the Rabbit, in her opinion.

Never mind that *that* sparkly purple bastard had cost her an extra half-hour in the shower this morning.

Because damned if she hadn't woken up in such a lather that she'd needed to buzz out a couple—before commencing with her proscrasti-cleaning.

As the shower's steamy spray pelted her naked skin, she'd mentally replayed—with some artistic edits—the trip back to the auto shop Gabe had bought from Hot Rod Johnson with the seed loan from Darby Dunwell.

The graphic images floated into her mind once again as she scrubbed stained mugs and attacked crusty pans with far more force than was warranted. Gabe's callused hands grasping her waist, his musky scent enveloping her as she straddled him on the front seat. The truck's horn emitting intermittent beeps as she bounced up and down on his hard, throbbing—

Startled by the "Baby Got Back" ringtone she'd set to full volume in case Gabe called, Gemma lost her grip on the cauldron-shaped mug she'd impulse-bought on the trip she and Cady had taken to Salem for Gemma's twenty-second birthday. The mug plunged into the copper pot she'd been soaking for the better part of a week, splattering soap bubbles onto the window.

"Oh, please don't be broken." She shuddered as hot water leaked down her wrist and into the glove but exhaled a sigh of relief when the ceramic emerged unharmed.

Using her forearm, she pushed hair back from her sweat-damp forehead and nudged off the tap, scanning the kitchen with her wet hands held aloft like a freshly scrubbed surgeon.

A muffled Sir Mix-a-Lot inquired about itty-bitty waists from somewhere in the region of the dining room table.

Sure enough, nestled beneath an avalanched pile of mail, she found the phone. When she saw *Dad* on the screen, her pulse leapt into overdrive. The gloves left a luminescent smear on the screen as she silenced it. Gemma so wasn't in the mood for one of his patented guilt-inducing lectures thinly veiled as concern.

Grateful for the silence, she glanced around the kitchen. How the hell did it look exactly the same despite the fact that she'd been cleaning for the better part of an hour?

Ish.

At this rate, she'd be lucky to have the place halfway presentable before—

The rumble of a motorcycle engine outside overrode her thoughts. Gemma's heart leapt into her throat as she squinted through the suds-flecked window overlooking the street.

Gabe Kelly sat astride a vintage Harley, looking like he'd stepped from the pages of a bad-boy biker romance novel. Black leather jacket. Intricate tattoos climbing his smooth, tanned neck from beneath the collar. Faded jeans clinging to the sloping muscle of his powerful thighs. Battered motorcycle boots. Aviator shades. Wind-tousled dark chocolate hair. Crooked grin.

Gemma's knees went weak as he killed the engine and swung off the motorcycle in one graceful movement. She swallowed hard, transfixed by the play of muscles under the ribbed tank clinging to his torso as he made his way up the walk.

Toward her front door.

"Shit!"

She hurriedly shoved a stack of dirty plates into the sink. A tsunami of dishwater slopped over the edge, soaking the bleach-speckled, oversized Townsend Harbor High t-shirt she routinely wore as part of her cleaning ensemble.

More choice words escaped her as she peeled off the yellow rubber gloves and shot them at the dish drainer bulging under the weight of pots, pans, and flatware that had been in it long enough to collect a fine coating of dust.

Gemma pulled her hair off her neck and piled it into a messy bun with the elastic ever-present on her wrist just as the doorbell tolled a merry note through the foyer.

Quickly twisting the soaked t-shirt fabric into a knot at her navel, she kicked off the Baphomet slippers she'd stolen from Myrtle at the annual Bare-Naked Book Club White Elephant gift exchange last Festivus. Better to answer the door in second-day socks than with her soles jammed into the plush belly of a minor demon dedicated to child sacrifice. Gemma was pretty sure she'd read that on one of the So Now You're a Landlord websites she'd mined for something resembling a basic lease.

Pausing in the foyer, she snatched the framed family portrait on the entryway table and shoved it in the drawer before pasting a smile on her face and opening the door.

And there the fuck he was.

The most beautiful man Gemma had ever seen, standing on the porch of her childhood home with a duffel slung over his shoulder and a smirk that made her feel like someone had stuffed a lit road flare down her T-rex print lady boxers.

"No sheep?" The corners of Gabe's hooded eyes crinkled behind the sepia filter of his lenses.

Gemma felt her heart knocking against her ribs as she forced herself to meet his gaze. She blinked like a woman who'd accidentally looked directly into the sun's retina-frying rays.

Sheep?

Was it a reference to something he'd said last night? An inside joke? The rapid scan of her Swiss-cheese memory returned exactly dick in the way of usable data.

"I'm sorry?"

The grin widened, revealing a row of straight white teeth with canines just pointy enough to send her inner emo tween into a belated sparkly-vampire-worshipping swoon.

Did he *have* to look like every single adolescent fantasy rolled into one swaggering package?

A package like the one you could totally see nestled to the left if you snuck a peek at his jeans right now?

And damned if her eyes didn't flick directly to the subtle bulge in the crotch of his buttery soft, perfectly worn denim.

Goddamn intrusive thoughts and their brain-hijacking bullshit.

"Sheep," Gabe repeated. "Like your doorbell at Bazaar Girls?"

Hearing the "r" in Bazaar licked into a soft "ah" by Gabe's Southie accent had Gemma's nipples tightening against the stretchy fabric of her sports bra. A sports bra only separated from Gabe's smoldering gaze by the fabric of a t-shirt that hid about as much as tissue paper even when it *wasn't* liberally moistened with Dawn-laden dishwater.

Because damned if she could buy any other brand as long as their advertising touted the soap's miraculous ability to purify oil-slicked ducklings.

Her thoughts, not so much.

"Oh," Gemma said, crossing her arms over her chest and emitting a shrill little giggle. "Right. I forgot you'd heard them—er, it. The doorbell, I mean." A single bead of sweat crawled down her ribs like a sluggish insect.

In the distance, the eleven-thirty Kingston ferry blasted its departure in a distinctly flatulent key.

"So." Gabe tugged off his sunglasses and tucked them into the pocket of his jacket. "You gonna show me the basement, or should I just bunk down on the porch swing?"

Heat flooded Gemma's face for the second time in as many minutes.

"Right. Sorry, come on in." She stepped aside to let him pass, catching a whiff of leather and soap that made her head go all swimmy. She watched helplessly as Gabe crossed the threshold of her parents' house like he owned it. Which he kind of did. Five feet and eleven inches of easy confidence and a rooster's loose-hipped swagger transforming every inch of the space he occupied.

And her body chemistry right along with it.

Gabe glanced around the mess of a living room and kitchen, his full lips twitching in what she dearly hoped was amusement and not disgust.

"I'm sorry it's such a mess," she said, feeling a sympathetic twinge in her abdomen as he flicked the blade of a wooden windmill her parents had recently sent back from Tulipfest in Amsterdam with the tip of his finger. "Things have been a little crazy lately. But I swear to God—"

"Don't." The sudden intensity of the word brought her up short. Gabe's Adam's apple bobbed with a conspicuous swallow. "Don't worry about it, I mean. I grew up with four Irish brothers. I promise you, I've seen worse."

"Four?" Gemma asked, attempting to regain control of the conversation and her racing pulse simultaneously. "That must have been...chaotic."

"That's a friggin' understatement." Gabe's chuckle felt like warm honey sluicing down Gemma's spine. "But it taught me how to handle messes, if you know what I mean."

His dark eyebrow arched suggestively as a dimple flickered at one corner of his mouth, and Gemma nearly had to grab the doorframe to keep from sliding down it like a cartoon floozy.

"For sure," she said, attempting a smile she suspected to be totally unconvincing. "I meant to finish cleaning up. I just..." She trailed off with a helpless shrug.

"Got distracted?" Gabe asked, a knowing glint in his eyes.

"Something like that." Her teeth sank into her lower lip as she stole a glance at his perfect ass while his broad back was turned. From memory, she reconstructed the dense field of muscle beneath the buttery leather. She'd gotten to the dangerous taper of his waist above the waistband of his jeans when she noticed that he was looking at her expectantly.

Had he said something? Asked her a question? Politely requested that she stop ogling his gluteal area?

Gemma swallowed sand and took a steadying breath, shifting on her bare feet. "So, the thing is, the basement isn't exactly ready for you to move in yet." She tried to make it sound breezy, but the words fell like a brick between them. "If you maybe want head to the shop, get your workday started—"

"No problem," Gabe said with an easy smile. "I'm not in any rush." He cocked his head and regarded her with something that could have been pity or confusion, depending on the angle of the light hitting his angular jaw through the grubby living room window.

"Gotcha," Gemma said, feeling small and fragile under the weight of his gaze. "But I really need to get it finished up before I can even think about letting you see it."

"Haven't gotten rid of the bodies?" Gabe's mouth twitched, and the flash of a dimple deep enough to hold a dime sent her train of thought careening into a fiery crash.

"What?"

"Bodies," he repeated. The floorboards squeaked as he closed the distance between them. "Dead bodies? Because if that's the case," he said, dipping into a confidential tone that deepened his voice to a panty-melting purr, "I know a guy."

She blinked at him.

A crease appeared between Gabe's dark brows. "That was a joke."

Gemma fought the urge to cringe at the forced laugh that escaped her. Were it not for the pile of assorted yarn bits and hair she'd recently swept under the area rug, she might have been tempted to crawl under it. "I totally knew that."

Kind of.

Between Gabe's recent release from prison and Darby's hints at the Kelly family's less-than-legal connections, she couldn't swear it under oath.

"Here's what." Gabe's voice cut through her thoughts with a gentle tug. His gaze held hers for an extended moment before he reached down to grab his duffel bag. "How about I give you a hand?"

Gemma's breath hitched in her chest, and she had to work to keep her face from splitting into a horrified grimace.

"Really, you don't have to—"

Gabe didn't wait for her reply, and was already heading for the basement door. Gemma hurried after him, pulse racing as she pulled in a lungful of earthy air several degrees cooler than the daylight they'd just left.

"Wait," she called after him.

But it was too late.

There, bathed in the bright blue-white glow of the energy-efficient LED bulbs her father had installed to save a whole forty-four dollars a year, was the source of Gemma's shame.

The ADHD hobby hyper-fixation graveyard.

Boxes overflowing with half-finished projects. Bolts of fabric. A precariously tall stack of tatting thread and cookbooks poised to tip at any moment. Dusty cobwebs clung to the ceiling and corners, betraying how long it had been since she last ventured down here.

An entire eternity passed as Gemma stood welded to the bottom step, holding her breath as she braced herself for Gabe's declaration that he actually didn't mind sleeping at the shop after all.

He merely slung his duffel down at the base of the stairs and turned to her. "Where do you want to start?"

"Seriously," she said, "you don't have to do this. I know it looks like a lot, but it'll only take me a couple hours." And perhaps a small miracle.

"And with me helping you, it'll go even faster." Gemma bit back a whimper as Gabe shucked off his leather jacket. "Already closed the shop for the day."

Guilt lanced through her. "So you're saying that I'm now costing you money in addition to time," she pointed out.

Tossing his jacket over the stair railing, Gabe angled his broad shoulders to face her head-on.

"I'm saying that I've got nothing else going on today and I could use the distraction," he said, a shadow briefly flickering behind his eyes.

Distraction from what? she wondered.

"Unless," he continued, "having me here is making you uncomfortable, in which case, I can fuck off immediately, no harm done."

"No!" Gemma said hastily. She cleared her throat, trying for a casual tone. "Not at all. I just...need to put on some shoes."

They both glanced down at her bare feet, at the toenails still sporting the mostly grown-out fire-engine red she'd selected last time she and Cady had gone for a pedicure together.

Gabe's dark eyes took their time making their way back upward by way of her ankles and calves. When they reached her face, he gave her a lopsided grin that sent her stomach into a death roll. "All right."

Before Gabe could add anything else that elevated her blood pressure, Gemma bolted up the stairs, gently shutting the door behind her before collapsing against it.

She took a deep breath, trying to steady her jangling nerves.

What the ever-loving fuck was wrong with her, anyway? He was just a man, after all. An average, everyday dude who put his pants on one leg at a time.

Before pulling them over an ass that would have made Michelangelo weep bitter tears of jealousy down his marble-dust-caked cheeks.

And those arms...

Sir Mix-a-Lot started up again.

"Shit!" Gemma sprinted toward the kitchen to silence the phone that had somehow become eighty-seven times louder in the last ten minutes.

When she saw the name on the screen, it nearly slid from her sweat-slicked fingers.

Lyra.

Though she felt a heart-clenching stab of longing for the cooling balm of her twin sister's even, eminently sane voice, Gemma sent it to voicemail.

There wasn't a snow cone's chance in hell's foyer that Lyra would hear even a single syllable of her breathless greeting without knowing something was up.

Tucking the phone into the pocket of her shorts, she stalked to her bedroom closet and quickly threw on her usual uniform of a skirt, cami, and cardigan before sliding her feet into a pair of chunky Mary Janes. That it would magically restore some semblance of respectability was too much to hope for, but being less naked around Gabe felt like a formidably beneficial idea.

She had made it back to the top of the stairs and was getting up the nerve to descend when her phone chirped within her pocket.

Despite knowing she'd regret it, Gemma lifted the device to glance at the screen.

Two words in Lyra's ever-understated, never over-punctuated, always emoji-less text.

Talk tonight?

Sure, Gemma texted back. *Seven?* she added, knowing her sister would suggest a time if she didn't.

A thumbs-up reaction zipped back almost immediately. The technological equivalent of a lukewarm shoulder pat.

Gemma descended, her heart as heavy as her steps. It wasn't like this civil remove between them was a recent vintage.

Talented as she was in the art of self-deception, she couldn't even pretend it was Harrison Lynch's fault.

Nope.

Choosing a terrible romantic partner who managed to alienate the person Gemma had once been closer to than any other human on all the earth had been the lone mirror-twin-centric milestone Gemma had managed to reach first.

She forced the thought out of her head, reminding herself that she had bigger problems at present.

Like Gabe Kelly's V muscles.

With a box parked on one shoulder, his shirt had ridden up to expose a strip of tanned skin above the waistband of his jeans. Gemma froze in place, transfixed by the sight of the dangerous curve above the sharp shelf of his hip, marveling at the warmth gathering at her middle and unfurling tendrils as softly as spring roots.

"There she is," he said, dusting his hands off on his jeans as he shouldered the box onto a stack bordering the path he'd already begin to clear. "I thought maybe you up and left."

"Left?" Gemma asked with a nervous giggle. "Why would I leave?"

Gabe dusted his hands against his jeans and pushed a dark lock of hair back from a forehead that Gemma couldn't help but wonder if it was as smooth as it looked. "Because I scare the shit out of you?"

"What? No. Not even." The hysterical giggle returned, but this time, it brought a carpool of the charming nasal/esophageal spasms she often resorted to when her brain short-circuited.

Pffft, and *phhllbbt*, and *shhhhht*.

Gabe's grin only deepened along with his dimple. Goddammit.

"Maybe we oughta get something out of the way right up front."

Gemma's breath caught in her throat and her fingers curled around the stair railing as he approached.

Stopping a good few feet away this time—saints be praised—he reached into his pocket and held out an envelope to her.

Brow furrowed, Gemma took it, unable to stifle the tiny gasp at the sheaf of bills she glimpsed inside.

Gabe stuffed his hands into the pockets of his jeans as a flush crept up his neck.

"I know you said you didn't want a deposit, but I thought it was only fair to give you a little insurance. I mean, sharing a home with a guy like me is a risk a lot of people wouldn't take. Especially in a town this nice."

A guy like me.

The resignation embroidered with gratitude made Gemma feel like she'd been mule-kicked in the chest.

"Gabe—"

"Don't bother telling me you won't accept it," he interrupted, looking at her from beneath the fringe of obscenely long lashes. "Because you can't make me take it back."

Indeed, she doubted if anyone could make Gabe Kelly do anything at all.

And, as much as she was loath to admit it, she was thinking about the triumphant Venmo memos she would send once the cash was safely deposited in her pitifully naked account. The relief she would feel at crossing names off the list of People I Owe Money to and Need to Avoid at the Organic Farmers' Market.

"You win." She shrugged, tucking the envelope into the pocket of her skirt.

"I usually do." A strange light flickered in the depths of his eyes. "Mind if I use your bathroom?"

Gemma made herself look him full in in the eye, counting three whole Mississippis before she spoke.

"You mean *your* bathroom," she said, lifting an arm to point past his mounded deltoid. "Down the hall to the left."

"Thanks."

Gemma bit her lip as she watched him disappear down the hallway, her eyes landing on a sight that was strange when liberated from the visual candy that was her new tenant.

Recognition tingled through her like a live wire at her sister's familiar, neatly lettered handwriting.

Gemma and Lyra's Magic Manifestation Box...absolutely positively do NOT open until our twenty-second birthday!!!

Or else!!! had been added in Gemma's loopier, lazier red marker postscript.

A pang of longing rose in her like smoke for the version of Lyra that was enthusiastic enough about anything to commit the now-egregious sin of multiple punctuation.

She'd been searching for it for over a year now, thinking it lost to the sprawling entropy of the basement. When asked, Lyra had only the vaguest memories of its creation. Part time capsule, part hope chest, they'd sealed it at exactly eleven past eleven p.m. on their eleventh birthday, their pinkies linked as they applied the final piece of glittery purple duct tape.

Deciding to forgo searching for the stepladder, she tested the stability of a giant rubber tub and stepped onto it. Her fingers grazed the box's edge as she stretched up onto tiptoes. After several false starts, she managed to catch a corner and bat it closer to the edge of the gently swaying stack.

"Gotcha!"

Only, she didn't.

No sooner had she sandwiched the dusty cardboard sides between both hands, the entire configuration began to slide, corners poking her chest, ribs, and hips as she attempted to body-block everything back into place.

And she might have succeeded if the sweaty sole of her foot hadn't slipped inside her shoe.

She felt it all beginning to go, the terrible, inevitable physics that would lead to her untimely death by debate trophies and mead-making supplies, when a blur in her peripheral vision became a solid wall of body against her back.

Gabe.

His body was pressed to hers, all hard muscle and warmth. His arms sandwiched hers, his much larger hands miraculously landing in precisely the right place to shore up the wobbling tower.

"Whoa." The syllable rumbled through her back by way of his chest, and his breath tickled the fine hairs at her nape. "You okay?"

Okay?

Okay?

Had she not been hopelessly distracted by the sensation of his hips branding her lower back, she might have been able to assemble a coherent answer. Gemma was melting, her muscles liquifying to better mold every available molecule to this warm, solid man.

"I...needed a box," she blurted.

"Next time maybe pick one that *isn't* on a pile that makes the Leaning Tower of Pisa look plumb."

The smile in his voice was as contagious as the rhythm of the heart beating wildly against her back.

"Duly noted," she said.

"Got it?"

"I think so?"

Gemma felt an odd sense of loss as his hips pulled back from hers. "Now slide it off onto that shelf while I hold the rest."

For perhaps the first time in her life, Gemma did exactly as told.

"Good."

The word rolled off his tongue like a lullaby, with just enough gravel to make the hairs on her arms stand up.

His hands were surprisingly gentle as they guided her back onto terra firma, but his smoldering gaze did nothing to squelch the raging fire inside her chest despite the fact that they were both covered in dust and sweat.

Her fingers curled into his shirt of their own accord, clinging for balance.

Or maybe just clinging, period.

Gemma licked her lips nervously and saw his eyes drop to follow the movement, sucking all the air from the room.

Gabe's mouth opened, then closed again as he stepped back and cleared his throat. "Let me—" He gestured vaguely at the box. "You know."

"Thanks," she breathed, quickly averting her gaze lest he see the heat in her cheeks and guess the images in her mind. "For... Yeah."

"Don't mention it."

Gemma felt strangely bereft when he turned away, her body a tingling constellation of the places he'd touched.

"Should we..." He trailed off, gesturing toward the pile where he'd been working before she nearly became the *Townsend Harbor Leader's* next bizarre headline.

"Definitely."

Gabe made a beeline for the biggest box and hefted it with a grunt that tightened Gemma's pelvic floor like a snare drum.

What the actual fuck had she been thinking?

At this rate, she was going to spontaneously combust before the day was through.

FOUR

Torquing the Nuts

USING A MANUAL TORQUE WRENCH TO TIGHTEN LUG NUTS

GABE'S FINGERTIPS TREMBLED AS HE HEFTED ANOTHER box, grateful for the work.

The basement air was charged with the electric promise of incredible sex. Stepping away, he pulled his nonchalance around him like a winter coat.

This was no big whoop, right? Just a bit of chemistry. Easily diverted into something else.

Someone else.

The memory of their previous social encounters lingered, a reminder that any romantic entanglement between them would only lead to a metric fuck-ton of regret. Especially on her part.

With a sharp clearing of his throat, Gabe turned on his heel and gave Gemma a chance to root through the box she'd opened and gather herself. He scrubbed a hand over his face, cursing himself for giving in to temptation. The feel of her soft curves pressed against him and the scent of lavender in her hair—it had been too much.

Thank fuck they didn't kiss.

That would have been a mistake, no matter how badly he wanted it. Because he'd always been a "mouthy little shit-fuck," according to Father O'Leary and basically everybody else, he gave in to his own tendency to say something rather than repress awkwardness.

"Ah, sorry about that. I didn't mean to...bodycheck ya back there."

Gemma blinked once, then twice, her dark eyes wide and vulnerable.

When a photo slipped from the box and fluttered to the floor, he leapt on it as the savior of a conversation.

"WHO'S THIS?" HE ASKED, EXAMINING THE IMAGE OF two identical smiling women who dressed so incredibly different, but had the exact same face. Yep, there was that tiny mole under Gemma's left eye, but beneath the other woman's right. "The fuck outta here—you have a twin?" he realized aloud.

The tension in the basement dissipated somewhat, replaced by a flicker of nostalgia on Gemma's face. "Lyra. We're mirror twins." She tucked the photo into her pocket and shrugged.

"She live around here?" If Gemma was hot enough to give him a daily heart attack, two women looking like her in this tiny town was basically the universe taking a giant shit on his sanity. "You guys got that weird twin magic where you know if she breaks her arm or whatever?"

"Noooooooooooooo." Gemma's drawn-out response would have been wicked insulting had her twin been in the room. "We're not even close."

It was Gabe's turn to blink. They'd jumped right out of awkward moment and into awkward-as-fuck history. "You guys competitive or something?" he asked, drawing on his own sibling issues.

"Or something," Gemma muttered. She blew a strand of hair out of her eyes and straightened, dusting off her hands. "Lyra's always been the 'good' twin, you know? The one who excelled at piano and aced her classes. The one who is going to marry a successful East Coast lawyer." Her mouth twisted wryly. "Our parents always said we balanced each other out. Lyra's the paragon of perfection. And I'm..." She visibly grappled with emotion before summoning a smile from somewhere that broke his heart. "I'm everything else." She motioned around with a self-deprecating wince. "All this chaos."

"Hey, there's nothing wrong with a little chaos," Gabe reassured her, handing back the photograph. "I'd take creativity and passion over order any day."

A faint grin tugged at Gemma's lips as she ducked her head, tucking a loose strand of hair behind one ear. Her cheeks didn't turn red like other people when she blushed, but dusted a peachy pink that was quickly becoming his favorite color.

Gabe carefully lifted a dusty box labeled "Bedding" and set it on the floor, sneezing as the particles swirled around him. Gemma stifled a giggle and handed him a tissue from some hidden magic pocket.

"Thanks," he said, watching with a detached but amused sort of alarm as she attempted to lift a box full of vacuum-sealed mason jars of dried legumes over her head.

Gabe grabbed it before she realized she'd done so without opening the closet first.

"So let me lift all these boxes and put them in the back of this closet over here," he suggested. "And you tell me why I already know your twins' old man sucks a bag of ripe shit."

She glanced at him askance. "We...we have the same father. He's actually pretty great."

Lucky.

Also, not what he meant. "Sorry, East Coast motorhead speak for her—uh"—what did nice girls call them? —"her partner."

"Ah, Harrison Lynch." Gemma sighed dramatically, rolling her eyes as she pulled out a fitted sheet with a vibrant floral pattern. "He's a lawyer from old-money New York. They met at a charity auction where she was bidding on some antique furniture for her law office. He swept her off her feet, or so she claims."

Ew. Yuppie trash. "Sounds like quite the catch," Gabe said, trying to suppress a twinge of physical desire as he helped Gemma stretch the sheet over the mattress.

"Maybe for her." She shrugged, smoothing out the wrinkles. "But I think he's a bit too slick for my taste. He's manipulative. And controlling. Lyra's changed so much since they started dating —she's harsher, more cynical. Half the time she parrots his opinions like they're her own." Her mouth twisted unhappily. "Dad's so impressed with Harrison's money and status that he doesn't see it. But I do."

"Dads can be blinded by that stuff." Gabe raised an eyebrow, matching the pillowcases to the sheets as if he'd ever been the kind of guy a dad didn't clean his shotgun in front of.

"Yep," Gemma confirmed, tucking in the corners. "He has a habit of scaring away any guy who shows the slightest interest in his daughters. I'm pretty sure he keeps a baseball bat by the front door just in case. But one look at Harrison's net worth and his walls came all the way down."

Her disappointment in her father was palpable. Gabe did what he always did—tried to help. "I don't know. I think it's a kindness that I never had a sister for just that reason. I don't think a guy exists that would have survived my dad and brothers." He squished down a rise of masculine rage at the very hypothetical mistreatment of his nonexistent sister. "Yeah. It's for the best."

Their "baseball bats" were tire irons and switchblades and the very non-hyperbolic willingness to curb-stomp a motherfucker for looking at someone sideways.

Gemma looked over her shoulder, dark eyes wide with alarm. "You don't have to worry, though. My father isn't a violent man. Like, at all."

His was.

He was.

Cute that she worried he would be afraid or intimidated. Almost made him wish he were the kind of guy who could be.

"Good to know," Gabe muttered, his internal conflict deepening as he envisioned himself facing off against Gemma's protective father. It wasn't in the realm of possibility, because he wasn't in a romantic relationship with her.

She was a friend of a friend who'd offered him a place to crash. That. Was. All.

"Hey, don't worry about it," Gemma reassured him, sensing his unease. "Not applicable, right? And besides, you've got bigger things to worry about—like finding a place for all these boxes I forgot to move out of your new house." She grimaced in a way that told him her lighthearted ribbing of herself covered a deeper source of painful truth.

Not that he knew anything about that mire of bullshit.

Luckily, he'd played a lot of Tetris while waiting for his father to do crimes as a kid, so he found organizing boxes strangely comforting, like finding a missing puzzle piece he hadn't even realized was lost. Besides, he didn't hate the idea of being nosy and learning more about his paradox of an open-hearted but enigmatic landlady.

"I suppose I should let you settle in," she said.

"Yeah. Sure."

They stared at each other for several heartbeats, something strange and very possibly dangerous stretching across the space between them.

"Would you like a tour of the rest of the house?" Gemma offered in that chirpy way she had when she was nervous. "I can show you around."

He wasn't ready to be without her—and was also not ready to examine why—so he shoved his rough-skinned fingers in his pockets so they wouldn't reach for her. "Lead the way."

Gabe trailed after her, glancing around the cozy space with interest. The kitchen was cluttered but homey, with granite countertops, oak cabinets, and appliances that had seen better days. Framed photos of Gemma and her sister at various ages lined the walls, along with artsy prints and a corkboard crammed with recipes, coupons, and a haphazard collage of fabric swatches. Yarn fibers gathered in corners and beneath furniture like pet hair, and something glittery had recently lifted its leg and marked the entire butcher block, which... How the fuck?

"It's usually not like this," she said, again evoking her favorite sentence as she bustled around wiping everything and cleaning nothing. "Things have been nuts, and my living space usually reflects how my brain is looking, so...it's in disarray at the moment."

Though she gave a genuine giggle, a soft sheen of moisture crept over her eyes before she blinked it away.

"I mean, I've been to prison, so nothing in your home could possibly shock me." Not even the sheer amount of unpaid bills stuck to the fridge.

"Is that a challenge?" Gemma teased, arching an eyebrow as she wiped the glitter onto the hardwood floor before realizing what she'd done. Frowning, she bustled to the pantry and extracted the broom. The scent of lavender and cinnamon wafted through the air as the soft glow of the afternoon sun filtering through the lace curtains threaded her hair with a spectrum of dark.

Even if he paid six months in advance at the market price, he'd still only make a dent in her business credit card.

"We haven't really discussed the long-term lease," he said. "How much do you need me to pay per month?" What she didn't know was that in a small amount of time, he'd earned enough to afford the rent (or maybe even a mortgage) out here but hadn't wanted to pull the trigger unless he got comfortable enough to take his shoes off without feeling like he'd track his shit all over this entire town.

"Oh." She stalled as if walking and digesting his question was too much in her present condition, and he'd nearly bowled her over. Again. "Well, what do you think is fair?"

His gaze snagged on a stack of unopened mail teetering precariously near the edge of the counter, and he frowned. "That's really up to you," he said, realizing they really should have talked about this earlier. "I mean, I'm here to help out with your business expenses... Do you need help catching up on bills or anything?"

"What?" Gemma squeaked, slamming the cupboard beneath the sink. "No, I'm fine. Why?"

Gabe jerked his chin at the landslide of mail waiting to happen. "Just looks like you've got a lot going on, that's all."

"Oh." Gemma flushed, hastily scooping the mail into a drawer. "I've been meaning to sort through that. Things have just been so busy lately..." She trailed off with an embarrassed laugh.

"Hey, it's okay," Gabe said gently. "I get it—life gets crazy sometimes." He didn't miss the flicker of relief in her eyes, and the appearance of a smile that made his chest feel tight. Must be another pang of guilt for invading her privacy.

What was *with* this...this...urge to take care of her? Why did he even consider himself in a place to do so? Because he wasn't. He still needed to get his own shit together.

He followed her into the living room, taking in the cozy, cluttered décor—an eclectic mix of hand-knitted throws and vintage memorabilia. It was like stepping into another world, one where the lines between past and present blurred together in a beautiful dance of color and texture. Instead of showing him valuables and style, she pointed out family photos and knickknacks along the way, her voice growing more relaxed with each room.

"Nice place you've got here," Gabe said, running his hand along the back of an overstuffed armchair. "It's...cozy." Cozy. One of his favorite words. Something as foreign to him as Mandarin.

"Thanks," Gemma replied, her eyes twinkling. "Most of this stuff used to belong to my grandparents. Mom and Dad couldn't bear to part with it, so we all just keep adding to the collection. You must think we're hoarders."

"I've seen *Hoarders*," Gabe reassured her, picking up a particularly garish crocheted throw pillow to avoid mentioning it was his favorite show during a stint in prison. "This doesn't look like that at all."

Gemma smiled at him, and for a moment, the tension

between them seemed to dissipate. They wandered through the rest of the house, Gabe occasionally stopping to examine various knitted creations, while Gemma filled him in on the colorful history behind each piece. Her parents' room was off-limits, hers a tempting closed door at the end of the hall. The upstairs bathroom was tidy and smelled of fresh showers and lavender soap.

By the time they'd circled back to the kitchen, she was chatting easily about Townsend Harbor's history, and he was doing everything to listen and not watch the way each of her round ass cheeks made her little skirt bounce as she walked.

Jesus. How many times was he going to fuck her in his head before this was over?

Reaching for something, anything, that made him forget how thirsty he was becoming for her, he idly allowed his fingers to wrap around the fridge handle and pull.

The smell hit him first, preparing him for the sights. Suppressing a cough, he quipped, "So I know where you grow your penicillin—where do you keep your food?"

His laughter died at the sight of her face.

Gemma froze mid-sentence, color suffusing her cheeks with a tomato red. She slammed the fridge door shut by throwing her entire weight against it and flattening herself against a second look. "Oh God, I fucking forgot! I haven't had a chance to go grocery shopping in weeks. I'll clean it, I swear."

"Whoa, hey, it's no big deal," Gabe said, holding up his hands. "I'm just messing with ya."

But Gemma was already scrubbing at her eyes, breath hitching. "You must think I'm a complete mess. I can't even keep my own house clean—how am I supposed to run a successful business? I'm letting everyone down, all the time. No matter how hard I try, I'm throwing together all this medium shitty wedding stuff for my best friend, and my dad thinks my business is about to fail, so I can't look at the accounts because I'm afraid he's right—"

Gabe watched her struggle to swallow with a rising sense of panic. He'd really shit and fallen in it this time. One probably couldn't rib pretty PNW-raised girls like you could the bad bitches of Boston who considered it a love language.

"Like I'm spending all my time pretending I'm not drowning, but what do I give up? I can't abandon my business! It's everything to me!"

"Of course not; that wouldn't—"

She forged ahead as if he'd not spoken. "I'm an elected official on the city council and have already missed my maximum meetings for the year."

"Can't be that serious—"

"It's only September!" she wailed. "And the worst part is, the more I fail, the more likely I am to fail bigger! Harder. And more spectacularly. My ADHD makes it nearly impossible to stay on top of everything, and stress activates the most stressful symptoms, which is just the meanest cycle I can think of right now. I feel like I'm letting everyone down, and my life is just one big mess. Now, I'm inviting you into this mess as if I'm doing a good thing, but probably you're just going to get poisoned by my fridge. They'll make a true-crime documentary about it." By this point, a couple of tears had escaped her spiked lashes, and she dashed them away before they could anoint her cheeks with salt.

Welp, Superman had kryptonite, and Gabriel Malachy Cathal Patrick Kelly had the stress tears of dark-eyed beauties with ADHD.

Good to know.

So, he rushed to do the only thing he ever had control to do.

Fix the fuck out of the problem.

"Listen," he said in his best *calm a woman down without telling her to calm down* voice. "Everyone gets overwhelmed, regardless of their...um...of what else they have to struggle with in their brain. I know you feel like you're letting everyone down, but I mean...has anyone actually told you that?"

If they did, he'd go have a conver-*fucking*-sation with them ASA-*fucking*-P. See if they could hurt her feelings with a fewer teeth.

"No one says stuff like that out loud." She sniffed.

She'd very obviously never been to a big city in New England.

"It's not like that. It's in all the stuff they're trying not to say," she explained, distress tightening the features of her upturned face. "It's in the pity while they watch me struggle. The 'helpful' suggestions. It's in the way they forgive me before I can even apologize. In the way they try to be useful that makes me feel like..."

"Like you're a turd floating in the gutter on its way to the sewer?" he finished for her, realizing too late that he'd thrown his own crude spin on things, spicing it with his personal issues.

However, it had a somewhat positive effect in that her next blink didn't produce tears, but confusion. "I mean, not so much that as, like... They pity you, you know? I can just hear everyone thinking at me all the time... *Can't you just be different?* And I'm trying. I'm trying so fucking hard all the time."

The tears returned, this time with prejudice, spilling down to her chin and soaking into her sweater. Goddammit, a man couldn't be expected to go through this without doing something about it!

Despite himself, he reached for her and pulled her into a very, very gentle, brotherly hug and never even thought about angling his hips in her direction. A top-half hug. As if she didn't have very soft tits that pressed ever so sweetly against his chest.

"I think being hard on yourself is really exhausting, too," he said. "But just think of all the stuff you do so well. You juggle more responsibilities than a one-armed carny, and no one has any idea that you're struggling with it other than the two of us. And that's only because I can still smell the war crime that happened to that kimchi in there."

"It used to be coleslaw," she sobbed into his chest.

Yikes. He'd need a HAZMAT suit to fix this. Luckily, he knew where to get one. He knew how to get a lot of things. How to do a lot of things. How to fix a lot of things.

He couldn't communicate effectively. Couldn't keep himself out of trouble. Couldn't sit still for very long, commit to a relationship, raise a family. Escape his own family. He couldn't save himself from himself.

What he could do? Make Gemini McKendrick's life a little less stressful.

And didn't that seem like a worthy endeavor for once?

"Hey now." Gabe ran his big, rough hands down her arms, and the calluses snagged in the soft knit. "You're doing better than you think. Look at all you're pulling off. You're there for your friends. You show up every day ready to work. Ready to help. You give this town life, and you give your life to this town."

Her shoulders stopped jerking with the silent war against her sobs, and she was concerningly quiet for a second. "You really think so?"

"Absolutely," he replied, sliding his hands beneath her shoulder blades and charting the lithe columns of muscle beside her spine. "I've heard nothing but good things about you from Darby. She loves the shit outta you, and she's one tough sell, trust me. She knows quality people, and still keeps me around for some reason..."

Pulling her head back, she sniffed in a way that'd be unattractive on any other woman. "You're quality people!" she insisted, making his shriveled heart grow two sizes, like the Grinch or some shit. "Or Darby wouldn't keep you around!"

"Bah." He forced himself to release her again before he got them both into old-school amounts of trouble by kissing her tear tracks down to her lush mouth. "I just used to sell her quality weed beneath my pop's nose—that's why Darbs keeps me around."

"I don't believe you," she said, a genuine smile breaking through the storm of her tears.

"Now you're getting the right idea." He winked in a way that'd been unlocking knees since he was fifteen, reminding himself he wasn't trying anything with this woman.

Even though a shift in the atmosphere, and her gaze, told him the wink had worked.

Fuck. Friend zone! Go find the friend zone and bury your goddamned boner in it, you piece of trash! he screamed at himself.

Putting the marble island between their bodies felt almost safe enough. "You know, I can't think of one other person that could keep up with all you try to do," he said. "And regardless of how it feels, the struggle doesn't show. Not like you're afraid it does. You are really something else, Gemma. Something extra impressive."

She blinked up at him, her eyes searching his for sincerity. "You don't know me that well," she breathed, her voice having lost several octaves and the moisture replaced with a glint he couldn't believe was there.

"Don't have to," Gabe replied, running his palm over what used to be a fauxhawk. "You're like a superhero or some shit, juggling knives while riding a unicycle. Who can remember to clean out the fridge with all that going on?"

A hint of a smile tugged at the corner of her lips as she leaned over the counter on her elbows, which would have given him so much cleavage to look at if not for that fucking nun's collar on the shirt beneath the cardigan. Good thing he couldn't see that skirt riding up the back of her thighs and could still pluck a thought out of the mush of his brain.

For a man who'd always been called *sharp* or *quick*, the sight of her 180-degree turn from freak-out to an almost feline pleasure at his compliments sure made him feel like he'd stalled on the side of the road for once.

"You busy now?" he asked.

She cocked her head at him. "I mean... No."

"Then why don't we tackle some tasks around here together? I'm trash with mail, too, but I've cleaned out the deep freeze at the Boston County Juvenile Detention Center, and I'm pretty sure that some of the freezer-burned meats were from before the war."

That touched her trembling lips with a half-smile. "Which war?"

"The fuckin' Revolution."

Her next hiccup was accompanied by a laugh as she rubbed

the last of the tears from her eyes. "I would never ask an enemy to clean out that fridge, let alone someone I'm beginning to— Not by a friend."

She didn't need a friend right now. What she needed was help. What she needed was to know she was okay. That her mess was okay. That her everything was okay.

If *okay* secretly meant *magnificent.*

"My middle brother, Mark, he's had ADHD from the get-go," he said. "Not your kind, either. The one that marks you a behavioral issue because you can't sit still through a five-hour school day. His nickname around the house was dumbass."

Her eyes went cartoon-sad wide. "Which one of your dad or brothers did that?"

"Our mom." He laughed, then wondered why she'd stopped laughing along. "Don't worry about him—it was better that stick than what Pops, Mikey, Luke, Johnny, Matt or I would call him. You can trust that." Noting she seemed more troubled than amused, he quickly added, "Point is, Mark, though still a dense dumbass, is actually wicked smart at numbers. I'm talking the kid who flunked out of every math class since Mom skated out with a bench-warming hockey player when he was five and I was three. I'm talking a Rain Man wonder kid mothafuckah who left the family business to work with the real criminals on Wall Street."

She was looking up at him as if he'd sprouted horns and told her he was the devil's bastard.

"Point is, you're a genius at so many things. Like, this place is just littered with the proof of your talent, skill, ambition, and general awesomeness. I'm just hoping you don't hang how you feel about yourself on how good your fridge smells. Doesn't really matter that much, at least in my book."

"I want to read your book," she whispered.

At least, he thought she did.

"What?"

"Nothing. I— I just— I should probably get to work." She straightened quickly and pushed away from the kitchen island to open the pantry and stare into its depths, very obviously *not* looking at him.

Gabe watched, transfixed, as she leaned on the pantry door. Smoothed her hair. Glanced at him. Smoothed the other side of her hair and pretended to have something to look at in there, which was apropos of exactly nothing. She picked up a foot and rested it on her knee as if doing yoga or some shit. Chewed her lip. And still couldn't fabricate anything to cover up the fact that his words of praise had bloomed color into her skin that hadn't been there before. That if she was one of the kitties on her sweater, she'd be purring at his praise and rubbing that lithe, graceful body up against him.

Begging to be petted.

Her next glance caught him watching her, and she gave him a shy smile that sent warmth tingling from the tip of his scalp to the soles of his feet.

And here he'd thought he'd left the dangerous ground on an entirely different coast.

"Welp, I guess I'll start downstairs, and you start here and we'll meet in the middle. Unless we fall asleep first, then I'll catch you in the morning."

"Sure. Yeah. I'll see you in the morning, Gabe." Gemma closed the pantry door without touching a single thing inside of it. She returned his gaze with one he couldn't decipher. Something a douchebag would interpret as an invitation glimmered in the depths of her eyes.

"Bright and early." He forced a smile and headed for the basement stairs, cursing himself with every step. Of course, the girl that caught his eye was the one he shouldn't be looking at. So what did he do? Fucking moved in with her.

He was the Kelly dumbass. Everyone knew that by now.

Once he'd cleared himself a decent path, he threw himself onto the lumpy mattress with a groan, staring up at the slightly cobwebbed ceiling. Closing his eyes didn't work. All he could see was Gemma.

When the shower on the floor above switched on, he almost grabbed his shit, climbed on his bike, and roared out of town forever.

She was upstairs. *Naked.* Steamy and creamy and slippery naked. Bubbles sliding down her skin as she scrubbed her long, heavy hair. Soaped her breasts. Her thighs. Her—

"Fuck."

In that moment, Gabe hated every part of himself. Especially the incredibly hard, aching part he found gripped in his hand.

His life had always been one big joke, it seemed. Well, the joke was on him this time.

Didn't stop her name escaping on the harsh whisper in the dark as he came.

FIVE

Frogging

RIPPING OUT STITCHES WHEN YOU'VE MADE A MISTAKE

Gemma stood in the doorway to the kitchen, blinking eyes still bleary with sleep. Drawn from her bed by a seductive tangle of savory aromas, she'd gotten as far as the dining room before her slippered feet shuffled to a stop.

Something looked...different.

Scratch that.

Everything looked different.

Lighter. Brighter. More hopeful?

Was that even possible before her brain had received its morning chemical goosing of caffeine?

Then again, was anything about the scene before her remotely possible?

On her long-neglected stove, a pan she hadn't gotten the chance to wash before Gabe showed up yesterday boasted bacon quickly becoming the perfect golden brown. Atop the gleaming granite counter, the coffee maker emitted a friendly hiss as rich, dark brown brew dripped into the waiting carafe. And was that a stack of fluffy pancakes piled atop the glazed red *You're Special* plate she and Lyra had traded back and forth on their birthday each year?

A plate that, only yesterday, had lain broken in half on a shelf in the pantry after an unfortunate incident involving an ill-timed verbal invective from Samuel L. Jackson in *Pulp Fiction* startled it from her hand?

She really needed to re-evaluate her choice of ringtones.

A thought that coincided with her identification of the source of at least part of the golden glow making her kitchen look like a Vermeer painting.

Someone had changed the light bulbs.

Plural. Not just the one that had sat dark for the last four months.

All of her father's clinical blue-white bulbs had been traded out for a version that rinsed everything in a warm, storybook glow.

Taken together, she felt like she'd gone to bed regular old Gemma McKendrick but woken up a Disney princess.

Until she attempted a freshly roused full body stretch and felt the unfortunate consequences of yesterday's basement exertions. She was pretty sure Rapunzel never dropped an F-bomb when her thighs burned just from shuffling toward the solace of coffee. Snow White, *maybe*. Waiting on seven diamond-obsessed miners afflicted with a catalog of now-diagnosable disorders had to play hell on your sciatica. Fun-sized or not.

"Morning."

Gemma snapped her head around with a gasp that sucked strands of hair into her mouth.

Gabe leaned in the doorway connecting her kitchen to the walk-in pantry like an Adonis-like fairy godfather. He was barefoot and shirtless in nothing but a pair of low-slung gray sweatpants, his bare chest boasting pecs that would make an Abercrombie & Fitch model-bro weep steroid-laced tears into his macro-smoothie bowl. Below them, twenty-seven-pack abs narrowed into the iconic V-cut disappearing beneath his waistband. Dead center, his small, flat belly button topped a column of sparse, dark hair threaded with ginger that Gemma could all too easily imagine connecting with the thatch at the base of his thick, hot—

"Coffee?"

"Please," she croaked in the ten-pack-a-day rasp that always plagued her until her vocal cords had been baptized by a hot beverage.

"How'd you sleep?" His voice was several octaves deeper, too, edged with a rasp that made her toes curl inside her Baphomet slippers.

Because once you'd had a four-alarm cabbage-related meltdown in front of a guy, it pretty much trumped any concerns about footwear of questionable religious origins.

"Pretty good," she lied.

Gemma was reasonably certain she'd never had a good night of sleep in her entire life. Having come across the concept of sleep chronotypes, she instantly recognized herself when she'd gotten to dolphin. The deceptively clinical words "unihemispheric sleep" blandly characterized the state of only one half of her brain experiencing restful REM, while the other did the vitally important work of anticipating her imminent and most likely violent death at the hands—or teeth—of a predator.

Or parent, if her recent activities ever came to light.

"How about you?" She edged around the corner of the counter, careful to keep her distance, lest his raw animal gravity turn her into the sexual equivalent of one of those face-hugger things from *Alien*.

"Like a fucking rock. That mattress could help a nun sleep through an orgy."

Gabe opened the cabinet above the coffee maker, and his callused hand went straight for the handle of a soup-bowl-sized mug bearing the words *Knitting: because murder is wrong*.

Her favorite.

Steam curled from the mug's thick rim as he poured.

Gabe set the mug on the table, and she caught a current of what she instantly knew was his post-sleep, pre-shower scent.

Fabric softener. The ghost of shampoo. Warm, salty skin. Earthy, a little dirty, and impossibly sexy.

"That smells amazing," she sighed, curling her fingers around the handle still warm from his grip.

"Darby's Mean Bean dark roast," he said. "Pretty sure it could juice an eighteen-wheeler if there's ever a shortage of diesel." He grinned, and it all came back to her in a knee-weakening blast.

His words.

His arms.

His heart.

His—cock piercing?

Gemma wasn't entirely sure *when* her eyes had drifted from his face to the crotch of his sweatpants, but lo, sometime during her vivid mental reverie, it had most definitely come to pass.

And despite her tearing them away ASAFP, the image remained burned into the backs of her eyelids—the telltale oblong bulge ending in the hint of ye olde unmistakable ridge, flanked by two small but exceedingly distinct spherical buds.

For that level of detail to be present, Gabe would have to be boxer-less.

Dear Christ on a Wheat Thin. Gabe Kelly rolling commando. In her *kitchen*.

"Cream and sugar?"

"I'll do it!" She shot out of her chair as if someone had wired hydraulics to her ass. Half because most people of her acquaintance were horrified at the amount of each she routinely dumped into her coffee, and half because she needed to shove her face in the refrigerated air before Gabe decided to fry an egg on her burning cheeks.

She tightened her fingers around the handle of the refrigerator door as a burst of cold air hit her face—a welcome change from the bulb of body heat that had seemed to follow her around like a personalized storm cloud in Gabe's presence.

As she reached for the familiar carton, an unfamiliar sight tugged at the periphery of her vision.

The crisper.

Empty of several varieties of organic produce slowly turning to sludge after an impulsive attempt at going vegan (again), it now housed a neat stack of Tupperware containing pre-prepped ingredients.

Celery, peppers, and onions for a stir fry. Mushrooms, zucchini, and carrots for a soup. Tomatoes and cucumbers for a salad.

Gemma's heart expanded against her ribcage as she imagined him carefully washing, slicing, while her sleep-creased face was still buried in her pillow.

He'd even lopped the base off the bendy stalks of celery she'd intended to donate to Myrtle for composting and stuck them in a glass bouquet vase.

"Little trick I learned at McCool's," Gabe said, obviously having noticed her noticing his handiwork. "The kitchen manager was a massive tool, but he knew his shit."

"Is that where you learned to cook?" she asked, pouring enough half and half into her mug to turn her coffee the color of sand.

"Pretty much."

Seeing his wilted smile, Gemma was tempted to slam her head in the refrigerator door.

It sure as hell hadn't been his mother.

Until she'd met Cady in the tenth grade, Gemma had been so blissfully ignorant, so painfully naïve, when it came to the reality of what it was like for people who had grown up with shitty parents.

But now, here she was, looking at Gabe and imagining the boy he must have been at five. Tears filmed her vision, blurring her coffee mug as she pictured him wandering into the kitchen in the aftermath of his mother's departure. Sleep-rumpled and saucer-eyed. Hungry and confused as he searched the pantry for some-thing edible. Not yet comprehending that he'd been hugged, or held, or kissed by her for the last time.

"Bacon's almost ready."

Gemma jumped at the intrusion of his adult voice into her heart-shredding mental movie. Tawny, pale liquid sloshed over the rim of her mug and onto her stretched-out sleep shirt.

"Sorry," he said, sounding not sorry at all. The corner of his mouth curled as he reached around her to grab his own mug. "Didn't realize you startle so easy."

"I don't," she said, a little too quickly. "I'm just not used to encountering other humans until I leave the house."

She turned her back to him and busied herself locating the maple syrup in the pantry before setting out the butter dish and getting plates down from the cupboard. Anything to keep her traitorous gaze north of Gabe's navel. Physically and psychologically speaking.

Officially out of menial tasks, she concentrated on the deft swing of the spatula between the pan and paper-towel-lined plate.

"Ladies first," he said, stepping back to grant her access and gesturing to the taste-bud-tweaking spread with a flourish.

Gemma took a single fluffy pancake and exactly two strips of the perfectly crisped bacon. Had she been alone, she likely would have ditched the plate, slapped the bacon directly on the pancake, splashed everything with syrup, and rolled it up like a burrito while eating with gusto parked right in front of the counter.

Just her luck that the one time in recent memory she set herself up to dine like a goddamn lady, her phone began to ring the precise second when she lifted the first forkful of pancake from the plate.

The jaunty bass line of her ringtone seemed to fill the entire kitchen. Gemma groaned, dropping her fork and nearly knocking over her coffee in her rush to silence her phone.

A bonus wave of adrenaline sizzled through her as she saw her father's name flash across the screen.

Twice in the past two days, she'd sent it to voicemail without answering. Twice her father had left voice messages, the second discernibly chillier than the first. Risking a third time could earn her a drop-by from one of the neighbors.

Which would be bad. *Very* bad, she thought, glancing at the shirtless man across the table, a jewellike drop of amber syrup adorning one corner of his grin.

With a deep breath, she pressed the green icon and reluctantly answered the call.

"Hey, Dad," she said, attempting to sound cheerful but unable to hide the quaver in her voice.

"Hello, Gemma?" His surprise at having actually reached her made the end of her name curve up like a question.

"Hey," she said again. "How's it going?"

Please don't answer that.

"Fine. Just fine." Pause. "I'm sorry to interrupt your morning, but we hadn't heard from you in a bit, and we wanted to check in."

Check *up,* more like.

"Yeah," she said, eyeing her bacon longingly. "I've just been super busy. With the downtown zoning project for the city council, and Cady's wedding—"

"And the with the store, I hope, *ha ha.*"

Her father was the only man—or woman, for that matter—who actually *said* the syllables instead of laughing.

"Well, yeah. Of course I'm busy with the store."

Longer pause. "And how are things going?"

Thing: 1. Noun. any person, place, object or event that one need not, cannot, or does not wish to give a specific name to but that has the potential to affect the profit of the failing business I was foolish enough to invest funds to help my irresponsible daughter launch.

"Good," Gemma said, sounding more than a little manic. "Really good."

"Yeah?" An obvious invitation to elaborate that Gemma flatly ignored.

"Yeah. In fact, today is the annual MOTO sale, so I really

better finish my coffee and get going," she said, slurping for emphasis.

"MOTO?" he repeated.

"Make one, take one? It's where customers can come knit something in the store and trade it for an item of their choice." Not bad, she thought, for something she'd made up on the spot.

"Trade? As in, without making a purchase?" he asked with the same disdain usually reserved for terms like *liability* and *bad debt.*

Both of which she identified with just a little too strongly at present.

"As in offloading pieces I haven't been able to sell while teaching customers a mood-enhancing and life-enriching skill."

"For free."

Her knuckles whitened on the mug's handle. "For *fun.*"

In the silence that followed, Gemma heard the unmistakable honey-sweet lilt of her mother's cajoling voice but couldn't make out the words.

Her father cleared his throat.

"It seems I have to run as well. Your mother signed us up for a stroopwafel-making class."

Longest pause yet.

"Is there anything you need?" He always managed to ask this question like he really hoped she didn't have an answer.

"Nope. Not a thing." *Beside a block of ice to sit on,* she thought, glancing up just as Gabe's tongue flicked out to swipe the syrup from his lips.

"Call you again soon. Take care."

"You too."

He disconnected before she'd finished pronouncing both Os.

Gemma set her phone face down on the table and thumbed off the ringer.

"Everything okay?" Already half finished with his four-stack, Gabe sat back in his chair.

"Uh, yeah, just...family stuff," she managed, forcing a tight-lipped smile. She took a sip of her coffee, hoping it would provide some comfort amidst the storm of emotions brewing inside her.

"I got a family, and holy shit do they have some stuff," he said, wiping his mouth with the paper towels they'd co-opted as napkins before balling it in his fist and tossing it aside. "Chances are I'd understand."

What surprised Gemma even more than the warmth and understanding in Gabe's eyes was just how much she *wanted* to tell him. Wanted to unload the burden of her fears and responsibilities onto his broad shoulders. Which wouldn't end well for either of them.

"Really, I'm okay," she insisted. "I mean, I have coffee, carbs, and bacon that I didn't even have to make sitting in front of me. How could I not be?"

His eyes flicked to her plate, where the bacon fat had begun to resume its opacity. "Want me to heat those up?"

"It's fine, I promise," she said, lifting a bite of pancake. She chewed mechanically, working the damp, sweet mouthful past the knot in her throat.

Gabe's eyes narrowed, frankly assessing her.

Gemma bit down on the inside of her cheek hard enough to taste copper.

She would not, *could* not, cry in front of this beautiful man two days in a row.

Just as she couldn't let him become yet another distraction steering her eager engine off course.

Bazaar Girls had to turn a profit this quarter, or her father would insist on her giving up the lease. Kindly. Politely. Practically.

But certainly.

The thought sent a fresh flurry of panic spiraling through her. She couldn't fail at this.

Not this.

Not this, *too*.

~

OUT OF BREATH AND SOAKED TO THE BONE, GEMMA
pushed her way through the door to Nevermore Bookstore, her
sodden bags damn near cutting ladders in her arms from the
seven-block sprint from Townsend Harbor City Hall.

What was supposed to be a thirty-minute brainstorming
session led to a ninety-minute argument when someone made the
suggestion of moving the Welcome to Townsend Harbor sign
eighteen inches to accommodate a bigleaf maple that had sprung
up since last season.

Watching the minutes tick by on her iPhone, she'd sent at
least three apologies and no less than five assurances to Cady that
it should be only about fifteen minutes more.

And now here she was, rolling in just as all the Bare-Naked
Book Club guests were rolling out.

Well, *almost* all.

From her puddle in Nevermore's moody, maximalist master-
piece of a foyer, she heard a cheerful tangle of familiar voices.

Cady, Darby, Myrtle, and Vee.

Her chest gave a squeeze of gratitude. They'd waited for her.

After dropping her Judas of a broken umbrella in the plastic
tub of outgoing recycling so as not to drench the carpet, Gemma
peeled off her wet jacket and draped it over one of the old building's ancient radiators. She had always loved the Pacific Northwest's blustery, darkly romantic autumn, but some nights still fell
with a chill that would gladly creep into your bones. Feet first.

Her Mary Janes were next to go, tucked under the radiator's
base. As for the waterlogged box of key lime tartlets and tote of
downy merino wool, she was too afraid to look, lest the carnage
tip the tears that had been threatening to spill from her lids all day
if she so much as cocked her head.

Passing by the ornate mirror in the entryway, Gemma did a
comical double take.

She looked like something that had been chewed and spat out.

Her hair was plastered to the sides of her face, mascara raccoon-ringed her eyes, and the perfect ruby lipstick she'd applied that morning had all but dried down to a dull brick hue.

She hadn't looked so bedraggled since she'd taken an involuntary late-night dip in the sound during high school camporee.

Finding a sodden wad of tissues in one pocket of her damp plaid skirt, she swiped away as much as she could, shot her reflection the double bird, and headed toward her friends.

"...still say a spa day is just what the doctor ordered," Vee suggested in the charmingly posh accent that could make a trip to the county dump sound like a day at the derby. "If surviving three weddings taught me anything, it's that the one thing a bride truly needs before tying the knot is quality pampering."

When she heard a wedding-related reference, Gemma's clammy feet inexplicably froze to the stair landing just out of the group's eye line.

"Boooring," Myrtle moaned in a singsong lilt. "And besides, who wants to pay two hundred dollars for a facial when I could just stick my face in a vat of cucumbers for nine ninety-nine?"

"And a lifetime ban from the all-you-can-eat pizza and salad bar at Piggy Pie," Vee added.

"Big whoop," Myrtle retorted. "I've had Pop-Tarts with better crust."

"Ladies," Darby interrupted in her smoky sex-kitten purr, "I am *horrified* by the utter lack of respect for tradition in this conversation. Whatever happened to getting bombed and ogling donkey-dicked dudes?"

This suggestion was met with a murmur of enthusiastic interest.

"I'm all for getting bombed, but I'll pass on the donkey dick," Cady's soft, sensible voice insisted.

"Why go out for hot dogs when you've got kielbasa at home, am I right?" Myrtle clucked.

"Or a reasonable facsimile made from sustainable and ethically sound platinum-cure silicone."

The warm swell of raucous laughter at Vee's perfectly timed punch line failed to prevent the cold knot from forming in Gemma's cavernously empty stomach.

They were talking about a bachelorette party.

A bachelorette party Cady had said—nay, *insisted*—she neither needed nor wanted. Had she changed her mind?

Feeling uncomfortably like a rat in a glue trap, Gemma peeled her feet from the stairs, forcing herself forward.

And immediately regretted it.

They looked so pretty. So warm and cozy and convivial in outfits chosen for both the company as well as the context. Leggings and boots. Duster-length cardigans; colorful scarves and silvery bangles. Even Myrtle, whose sartorial sensibilities ran to the *capricious*, looked like puckishly smart Super Mario in a cranberry-red beret and linen overalls.

Even before Gemma had a chance to open her mouth, all four women twisted their necks to an improbable degree and stared at her with expressions of bewilderment and horror.

"Oh my God," Cady gasped. "What the shit happened to you?"

Gemma shifted on tingling toes, feeling weirdly like an intruder.

"I got caught in the rain," she mumbled self-consciously. "It was pouring when I got out of the city council meeting, and—"

"And you forgot your umbrella?" Cady asked.

Again, being the unspoken coda.

"I actually brought one today," Gemma said, disproportionately defensive at having remembered to both check her weather app and accessorize accordingly. "But one of those asshole wind gusts that dick-punches you when you turn the corner of city hall turned it inside out, and my arms were full, so—"

"Never you mind," Vee said, tugging off her pashmina shawl and rising to wrap it around Gemma's shoulders before ushering her into a chair. "You just come sit by the fireplace and warm yourself up."

Gemma complied despite the tide of guilt rising in her chest for hijacking the conversation. Before she had a chance to apologize, Darby was already pushing a warm mug of tea into Gemma's chilly fingers.

Myrtle plopped down in the empty chair beside her and, pulling a paisley print flask from the pocket of her sweater, dribbled a generous, tawny stream into the steaming amber liquid with a wink.

"That'll put some lava in your lungs," she said, her voice somehow just as soothing as the scent of lemon and wood smoke wafting from the mug.

Gemma sipped gratefully, feeling her joints loosen as she sank back into her chair.

"So, what are we talking about?" she asked, cutting through the awkward silence following her dramatic arrival as deftly as a spork.

"Cady's bachelorette party," Myrtle answered, ever the straightforward soul.

Gemma darted her gaze to Cady, who returned her curious look with a sheepish shrug.

"Darby asked what we were planning," she said hesitantly, her smooth cheeks flushing a hectic pink. "And I told her that we *weren't*, but Myrtle sort of insisted."

"Bet your bearded bits I did." The flask made an encore entrance and was passed from Myrtle to Vee. "How many nights of unabashed debauchery do you think a woman gets in her life?"

"Depends on the woman," Darby said, her fuchsia lips curving in a saucy smile.

"Hear, hear," Vee echoed.

"All I know is, Darby and I aren't letting this one walk down the aisle without at least raising a little hell."

Darby and I?

Gemma's guts clenched as the realization finally hit her.

They weren't just slapping together random ideas as a collective. Darby and Myrtle were actually *planning* this. Together.

Cheerfully taking on a task that *should* have been within *her* purview as maid of honor.

With Cady's blessing.

Cady cleared her throat. "Is the bride allowed to make one request?"

"Does that request involve hot wax or nipple clamps?" Darby asked.

Cady's cheeks deepened to a color that Gemma had only seen on one other occasion, involving a certain pair of panties mysteriously ending up taped to the front of Ethan Townsend's locker as a pep rally prank their freshman year. She couldn't help but wonder if Ethan's ears still turned the same atomic cherry now that he was with a woman who was basically sex on wheels.

"Could we maybe just keep it the tiniest bit classy?" Cady held up a hand with thumb and forefinger pinched together. "It's not Fawkes I'm worried about." She set her mug aside and sat forward in the overstuffed chair the others always left her in lieu of lumbar support. "It's his mother. She's coming into town a week from now, and the last thing I need is her thinking her son is linking up with some kind of shot-guzzling crotch jockey."

Darby shot Myrtle a pointed look. "I think we can manage that. Don't you?"

"Roger that." The flask having made its way back to her after a brief round trip, Myrtle lifted her pinky as she tipped it back. "Classy as fuck."

"Now that we have a plan in place," Vee said, shifting to the edge of her seat, "I suppose we ought to get going. Let you enjoy your final nights with your fiancé before family descends?"

Cady shrugged her thick blonde braid over her shoulder. "I do need to go over the seating charts one last time."

"That reminds me." Darby lifted a beautiful, beaded vintage bag onto her knees and clipped it open. Her slim hand disappeared inside, returning with a beautifully wrapped giftbox.

Cady's blue eyes brightened behind the lenses of her glasses. "For me?"

Darby nodded. "Just a little something for the bridal shower I missed."

Gemma's chest expanded at the mention. She *had* managed that, at least.

Barely.

Cady's smile widened as she ran her fingers over the ornate wrapping paper. She tugged at the knot of ribbon, lifting the lid off the box.

Her mouth dropped open, her cheeks going from pink to white in shock.

"Oh, Darby! No." Cady lifted a beautiful eggplant-purple robe with intricate lace trim from the box. Standing, she held it against her body, admiring its draping lines and delicate stitching. "This is almost too beautiful to wear. You shouldn't have."

Darby's eyes gleamed. "Luckily, that's never stopped me before."

"La Perla?" Vee asked Darby sotto voce.

Darby nodded enthusiastically. "I wore a corset by one of their most temperamental designers in a burlesque show attended by the president of Iceland, who bought one in every color for his mistress. They've been very generous ever since."

"Isn't this beautiful?" Cady gushed, twirling over to Gemma, who gave the buttery silk a perfunctory pet.

"*So* beautiful," she echoed, her throat tight with a bittersweet stew of emotions. Delight on Cady's behalf, ugly envy on her own.

No way could she afford to give Cady a gift like this in her current predicament, no matter how genuine her excitement that her best friend now had something so lovely.

"That come with matching split-crotch panties?" Myrtle asked, beginning to gather up their discarded mugs.

And damned if, at the mention of the C-word, Gemma didn't flash back to her kitchen. Back to Gabe.

Back to Gabe's sweatpants.

Six months ago, she and Cady would have exchanged an

entire thread of text messages by the time the book club rolled around.

Six weeks ago, she wouldn't have offered a lame excuse to leave before Cady could pepper her with very valid questions. About her store. Her parents. Her life.

Six years ago, it would have been her sister, not a tempting, tattooed mechanic whose face she quietly longed to see at the end of a long, defeating day.

SIX

Tunnel RAM

A HIGH-PERFORMANCE INTAKE MANIFOLD

GABE SPRAWLED UNDER THE 1964 PLYMOUTH convertible on his mechanic's creeper. He barely noted the scent of motor oil and rust, creosote and carburetor fluid, for the memory of lavender and fresh soap. His hands moved over the greasy metal by rote, familiar with the contours of hoses and manifolds, while his imagination explored the soft curves of Gemma's body.

Gemma.

"Damn," he muttered, appreciating how her presence ignited a spark in him, much like the engine he tinkered with. He allowed himself to indulge in a graphic fantasy, picturing her flushed face, her breath hitching as he traced his callused fingertips over her soft skin. A shiver raced down his spine as he imagined Gemma whispering his name, an invitation for more. Her floral perfume haunted his senses as she straddled his lap in his fantasy, her soft thighs gripping his hips. Her hair creating dark curtain for their kiss and—

"This car is so sexy!" exclaimed a familiar female voice. "Isn't this car sexy? I would have feelings for this car. Like, the kind of feelings I had for Optimus Prime before I got old enough to realize why it wouldn't physically work between us."

Gabe's wrench slipped, rapping his knuckle. "Shit!" He jerked his hand back, smacking his already smarting knuckle on the undercarriage. "Son of a motherfuck me all to—"

"You all right down there?"

"Jesus, Darbs, ever heard of knocking?" Gabe grumbled, nursing his throbbing finger as he rolled out from under the car, his irritation warring with a genuine smile at the sight of his old friend, Darby Dunwell. She stood there, hands on her hips, an impish grin plastered on her pretty face beneath her signature bright pink pinup-girl hair.

He'd known Darby since they were kids. She was one of the few who knew about his stint in prison, but he wasn't keen on her knowing the depths of his pathetic infatuation with her friend.

"Where's the fun in that?" she teased, sauntering over to him. "Besides, I figured you might need a break from all this grit and grime. Or is this your idea of a spa day?" She smudged a grease smear on his face.

"Ha, you're hilarious," Gabe shot back, unable to suppress a chuckle. Darby's presence had always been a refreshing contrast to the intensity of his work—and a colorful addition to the Kelly franchise before she tuned in to the fact that she lent the building an air of legitimacy and a place to launder money.

Still. The banter between them came easily, and their friendship, built on years of shared experiences and mutual understanding, was a comfortable platonic relationship he hoped never died. He'd never let the fact that she was more than a handful of years older than him stop him from appreciating her extensive hotness.

He just liked her. He liked her when he didn't like anyone. And sex ruined shit like that, so it was off the table before he even became legal for her to hit on him.

Which she never did. He liked that about her, too.

"You should probably put some ice on that." Former Sheriff Ethan Townsend made his presence known in the same douchey way he always did.

By being right.

Gabe's finger was already swelling, the skin split over his knuckle threatening to bleed all over. Shaking it a little didn't fix the swelling or the smarting, so he shouldered past Darby's fiancé, sniffing at the taller, wider man as if testing for a foul scent.

"What?" Ethan's wintry-blue eyes narrowed, but he kept the hands curling into fists to himself.

"Still smells like bacon," Gabe said, selling every hard syllable of his Southie accent. "Underscored with,"—sniff, sniff—"vanilla and fifty shades of beige."

Before the big man could react, Darby stepped between them, her eyes glinting a friendly warning. "He's a *reformed* sheriff, Gabe. He doesn't get in trouble for kicking your ass anymore."

"Good." Gabe and Ethan shared a look that made it clear just how eager they both were to meet in a dark alley someday and test their antipathy with their fists.

Sure, Ethan was maybe three—okay, five—inches taller and a bit wider, but that and the gigantic, metal rod up his ass slowed him down. Besides, Gabe fought like he did everything else.

Dirty.

His father would shit an entire building full of bricks to hear Darby Dunwell—one of the most famous cabaret performers along the Eastern Seaboard—ended up with a strait-laced sheriff from the PNW.

Life was wicked weird sometimes.

Darby stood with her hands on her hips like she meant business. Her coffee shop apron was dusted with flour, a sure sign she'd been baking that morning. "Aren't you charming today?" She arched a brow and set a white bag and a to-go cup on the fender of the Plymouth. "Here's a muffin, and drink your coffee. You're cranky when you're hungry."

"I'm not hungry," he bit out, snatching up the coffee and shoving half the muffin in his mouth. The hot, bitter liquid helped ease the throbbing pain in his finger, and he took a swig to wash down the huckleberry-laden carbs.

"Don't you have a coffee shop to run?" he quipped around a singed tongue.

"Don't you have an engine to fix?" She laughed, undeterred by his surliness.

"You didn't come by with your muscle to share coffee, and you know it." He pinned her with a pointed stare and the tilted eyebrow the Kelly family was famous for. "Spit it out, Darbs. What are you after me to do for you?"

She almost had the grace to look abashed. "I just thought I'd let you know the girls and I are planning a bachelorette party for Cady at the end of the month. I'm in charge of entertainment."

His guts knotted as his gaze sharpened on her. "What kind of entertainment?"

"Oh, you know." She shrugged, all casual innocence.

He knew. He already fucking knew.

"Some drinks, music, maybe a little..." She slid her eyes to Ethan and then back, raising her perfectly shaped brows. "Strip-tease action."

"Are you insane?" he blurted out. "I'm trying to build a repu-tation here, Darby. Dancing at Cady's bachelorette party is not exactly the way to do that."

"Come on, Gabe," Darby wheedled. "It'll be fun. Remember how you bought your first bike from the proceeds of that one Storm from Southie show we did when—"

"I was eighteen," he said, examining the weird flap of skin scraped off his knuckle. "I don't do that anymore."

"You literally came out and did your arial routine for my breast cancer benefit. Just do something like that, but, like...on a pole and without your shirt on."

His gaze flicked to the classic Plymouth, a symbol of the respectable life he was trying to build. Stripping at bachelorette parties wasn't conducive to being taken seriously as a small busi-ness owner in a tiny town with a population dominated by rich, aging boomers, hippie artists, and tourism.

But he needed that fucking hydraulic lift, and he'd paid ten percent of his savings as first, last, and deposit to a very reluctant Gemma before leaving for work.

"I'll pay you double your going rate," Darby added.

"It's not about the money," Gabe ground out, making certain her trust fund fiancé heard him loud and clear.

"Triple, then. And a case of Raven Creek's best Irish stout. It's almost as good as Guinness."

Gabe shot a glance at Ethan, a budding beer brewer, whose stony expression revealed he'd clearly been unaware of this sexy detail of Gabe's past and was grappling with the fact that his fiancée might have seen Gabe's dick.

She did, and she liked it, you silver-spoon-fed fuck.

Gabe looked away, an old shame rising beneath his evergreen confidence.

"That was a long time ago," he muttered.

"And you were great at it!" Darby said. "The ladies will love it, and I swear in this town it'll make you more friends than enemies."

Images of himself, half-naked and gyrating for a roomful of small-town gossips, flashed through his mind, followed by the even more unsettling thought of Gemma witnessing the spectacle. He swallowed hard, trying to find the words to express the maelstrom of apprehension and intrigue swirling inside him.

The only thing he truly wanted at the moment was to be naked in a room with Gemma McKendrick.

"Come on, Gabe, it's just one night," Darby cajoled him, her expression softening as she regarded him with earnest hazel eyes. "Besides, it's not like anyone will think less of you for it. If anything, they'll be impressed by your...talents." She raised an eyebrow suggestively, causing heat to flood Gabe's cheeks despite his best efforts to remain impassive.

With a sigh, he ran a hand over his face. "When and where is this party of yours?"

The aggrieved look on Ethan's face almost made the coming torture worth it.

Almost.

"One more thing," Darby added with a sly look. "Cady told me once that Gemma has a thing for capable, powerful men. Always has. Especially in fiction."

"Why are you telling me this?" He tried for nonchalance and failed miserably.

"No reason." Darby shrugged and grinned. "Just thought you might want to...you know, be prepared."

"Prepared for what?"

She sashayed out of the garage, her giant boyfriend trailing in her wake and leaving Gabe staring after her in confusion and no small amount of alarm. Gemma was interested in men in positions of power and authority—not ex-cons trying to outrun their past. If she knew the truth about him, she'd run in the opposite direction.

He cursed himself for agreeing to another of Darby's schemes. Getting naked in front of Gemma McKendrick was a mistake that could cost him everything he'd worked for.

But even as the warnings flashed through his mind, he couldn't ignore the spark of excitement kindling inside him. He was playing with fire here...

But that had never stopped him before.

The unmistakable scent of Chinese takeout and a faint herbal aroma greeted Gabe as he wearily pushed open the door to Gemma's house. A long day at the auto shop had left him drained, both mentally and physically, but the sight that awaited him in the living room managed to rouse a spark.

Just curiosity, that spark. Nothing else.

Gemma was sprawled on the couch in a tank top and a pair of shorts, hair mussed and glasses askew, her bare legs haphazardly draped over one armrest while her head rested on her palm. The coffee table before her was a chaotic tableau of cartons and cannabis edibles, and a half-eaten egg roll was perched in her teeth like Winston Churchill's cigar.

"I could get into this," Gabe remarked, suppressing a smile as he toed off his boots near the door.

The sight of her did funny things to his chest. He blamed the lingering effects of agreeing to strip for her—for everyone—at Cady's bachelorette party, an impulse decision he already regretted. Sure, he'd done it before, but that was for wealthy women who would often pay more for...well...*more*.

When he was a horny kid, it was all right. As a guy, he didn't carry as much stigma.

But still... There were shadows that lived in that place he didn't need to poke. Shadows that might be unleashed, were he to get too close.

Gemma squinted at him, eyes glassy and rimmed in red, and he wondered just how many gummies she'd consumed. "You're home!" A dreamy smile lit the darkness the evening had painted on her face. "Did you know that unicorns are the national animal of Scotland?"

"No, I did not." Amused in spite of himself, Gabe set down his keys and shrugged out of his leather jacket. "And how did you come by this interesting fact?"

"Research." She waved her phone in a vague gesture, nearly dropping it in the process. "Also, did you know that Scotland has the highest number of redheads per capita? I was thinking I should take a trip. I want to see all the gingers in their natural habitat."

A loud and adorable sniff alerted him to the fact that the red-rimmed eyes might not be THC related. In fact, now he was pretty sure her eyes were puffy.

"You doing okay?" He dropped onto the couch a safe distance away from her.

His gaze snagged on the curve of her hip where her shirt had ridden up, and the long line of her bare leg. Heat simmered in his blood, as unwanted fantasies flickered through his mind.

He needed to not lie to himself. There was no such thing as safe distance from Gemini McKendrick.

"Want some?" She bit off half the little spring roll and handed the other half to him. "I'm so full I might barf, but I can't stop eating."

Heat crept up the back of his neck at her casual offer of intimacy. He'd been less anxious at sex parties. Sharing food was a relationship thing. Politely declining, he snagged a full takeout container from the coffee table and shoveled in as much mu shu pork as he could.

Still, he had to know if she'd been crying.

"Rough day?" he tried again, shoving the food into one cheek.

"Ugh," she groaned, wiping at her already dried eyes with the back of her hand. "It's stupid. Don't worry about it."

"It's not stupid if it hurts," he said, trying to be both cajoling and respectful. "Is your movie sad?"

"Obviously not." She gestured to the dueling pirates on the screen. Some guy kept repeating his name again and again. "This is the best feel-good movie of all time."

"Which you started because something happened today..."

Her next sniff was more pathetic, and her features fell into a brokenhearted pout. "It's Taco Thursday."

He eyed the Chinese takeout with so many questions he dare not ask.

Luckily, the weed made her chatty. "Cady and I always get high and watch movies on Taco Thursday, but they're just not happening lately."

Cady Bloomquist, the proprietor of Nevermore Bookstore—Townsend Harbor's favorite bookshop—and Gemma's favorite person and best friend since forever. It was her bachelorette party for which he would shake his ass...

For better or worse.

"She's too deep in that new relationship smell, huh?" Gabe guessed.

"Not just that—Cady told me that Darby wanted to put on

the bachelorette party, and she was going to let her because, even though I'm the maid of honor, I am so stressed and buried."

Uh oh. Darby was one of the best people on the planet, but sometimes she didn't slow down long enough to test the political landscape, as it were. She'd never step on Gemma's toes on purpose, but her helpfulness could often look (and feel) like a corporate takeover.

Knowing better than to put himself in the way of ladies who were trying not to fight, he wisely kept his own counsel. "That's no good." A safe response.

"Noooouh!" she wailed. "No, it is no good. Because I'd planned the shit out of a wedding shower and completely forgotten about the bachelorette party! She probably knew that, huh? That's why she told me she didn't want one. She knows me better than anyone. She knew I would screw up something and was trying to spare my feelings."

Tears threatened the dams of her eyelids again, and Gabe scooted closer out of sheer masculine panic. "Hey. Hey, that's not it." He reached out to smooth a comforting hand down her shoulder but thought better at the last moment. Her skin was too soft to keep his head, and he had to think fast. "Know what it probably is? Darbs is so new and had such a tough time being accepted by some of the locals, I bet Cady is probably just trying to include her, you know? Darbs mentioned Cady was uncommonly thoughtful and shit."

Gemma swallowed a lump of tears, her eyes shining up at him as she took a rude slurp of a soda. "You think so?"

He shrugged. "Makes sense to me." Now he was talking as if he knew shit about fuck... He should go downstairs, where it was safe. Put actual walls between him and her pretty bare legs begging to be touched.

He'd cleaned up at the huge sink at the shop, but what he needed was a real shower. A perfect excuse to beat feet.

"You're good at this," she said.

"At what?"

His question caused her eyes to widen as if she'd not meant to speak her thoughts aloud.

"Nothing. Want some noodles?"

"Are bears Catholic? Does the pope shit in the woods?"

Her giggle made him feel about ten feet tall, even though he stole the dad joke from an old, four-hundred-pound made man named *Flaco* who was spending a dime in Sing Sing.

"Sometimes, all you need is a distraction," Gabe suggested, his gaze falling on the television screen. "What are we watching?"

She glanced at him and giggled again. "You missed the part about the ROUSs in the fire swamp."

He nodded as if he knew what the fuck that meant. "Sweet. I've known a few Russells I've wanted to set on fire and throw in the swamp after."

A dawning horror stretched across her features. "Rodents of Unusual Size. You know what those are, right?"

He nodded sagely and slurped noodles from his chopsticks. "I had a couple in my apartment back in Dorchester. I named them Hank and Blue, and I think they were a very bonded homosexual rodent couple, and I consider myself and ally, so—"

"*What?*" she screeched, sitting bolt upright on the couch. "Gabriel Kelly, you tell me right now that I didn't allow you to live in my home without having watched *The Princess Bride*. The most cultish of cult classics. I daresay more quoted by high school nerds than *Monty Python and the Holy Grail*."

"Monty who, now?"

Executing a concerning trust fall away from him, she fell onto the couch and began to spasm as if in the throes of a seizure.

Gabe found himself laughing at her antics, enjoying himself like he hadn't in some time. "I'm to understand I've been missing out?" he asked around another bite.

"Damn right you have." She huffed indignantly, her earlier tears momentarily forgotten. "We're starting this over. Right now. Prepare to have your life changed, Gabe Kelly."

"Big claims," he teased, settling back into the couch as the opening credits rolled.

His life had already changed. In the biggest way possible.

He was starting to relax. He was starting to feel... What?

Comfortable. Content.

Like he cared.

What he couldn't tell her was that while he'd spent so much of his childhood in juvie, he had very little nerdy television available to him. Little television at all that wasn't screaming plastic housewives or trash from Jersey. He didn't enjoy cult classics while running B&Es with his brothers. Or dismantling some A-lister's Maserati before they tracked the GPS to the garage.

That was something kids like her who grew up in houses like this got to do.

As they watched the movie together, Gabe couldn't help but feel a sense of camaraderie blossoming between them. Sure, providing emotional support might not be his forte, but for Gemma, it seemed to come easily. Naturally. It could have been the way she preened at the simplest compliment, looking at him like he'd become the human equivalent of mu shu pork.

And as the night wore on, the weight of his own worries and concerns seemed to fade, replaced by the warmth of their shared laughter and the simple pleasure of being in her company.

He couldn't remember the last time he'd enjoyed a simple pleasure. Couldn't remember the last time he'd hung out with a girl. With a girl that wasn't Darby, and she didn't even count.

Most of his relationships were of the pump-'n'-dump variety, his guilt assuaged by the fact that he actively and single-handedly (or mouthedly or bodily) was trying to gain ground on the orgasm disparity.

Muthahfuckah. He'd gone and thought about orgasms in the same room as Gemma's bare legs.

He should go.

Or...he could stay and be a good boy.

Yeah, and maybe Gemma would give up knitting and take up cage fighting.

He looked over to where she munched on a potsticker, eyes glued to the screen. "This is the best part," she claimed after feeling his gaze on her.

She'd said that at least six times, but he did like the two old people with the crazy machine that brought the hero back to life. Kinda reminded him of Vee and Myrtle, though he'd take that opinion to the grave.

"Are you going to kill me if I tell you I dislike Buttercup immensely?" he ventured.

She narrowed suspicious eyes at him and set the food down. Facing him on the couch and stretching her legs out between them, she took up her ocean-blue knitting project as she trained all her gravitas on him. Fingers flying, she didn't look down once.

Uh oh. Rage knitting was a thing?

He wondered if she knew it only took five pounds of pressure to stick one of those things through a jugular.

"Explain yourself," she demanded.

"She's kinda a bi—er, mean. I mean, look at the pirate guy—"

"Westley."

"He's been killing himself for her, and she's not really helping out at all. Like, *I'm* ready to run away with the guy and pledge my undying love. He's a primo badass, and I like Robin Wright in just about everything else ever, but she's too amazing for this bland damsel role."

He'd expected a fangirl's wrath, but instead she just regarded him pensively.

"What?" he asked, wiping his entire face with a napkin in case that was the problem.

"So Westley is your type of guy? But if you hate Buttercup, then...who is your type of lady?"

Alarm bells jangled in his head. *Abort conversation before you just tell her you're beginning to realize it's hot brunette knitters in cat sweaters.*

"I don't really have a type," he said, setting his food down and reaching for the beer she'd grabbed from a fridge in the garage.

"I do," she said around an aggrieved wince. "Narcissistic assholes."

At his frown, she expanded.

"My only long-term relationship was a king baby," she continued, misinterpreting his reaction. "We met in high school and kinda tried to take it into adulthood. He always made everything about him, never cared how I felt. Always wanted me to be this perfect little trophy girlfriend, like some kind of customizable Barbie doll. It was exhausting. I would have done anything for him, and you know what? He didn't go down on me *once* the last year we were together. Said I took too long."

Shit. Fuck. She'd been doing this all night—little inebriated overshares that revved his engine to a low-grade hum of lust.

A woman shouldn't look and smell that good and then let it be known to a guy like him that she was in need of an eager cunning linguist.

"That guy isn't still around, is he?" He was really, *really* trying not to go to jail on the West Coast.

Shaking her head, she asked, "What about you? You're so far away from Boston. You running from a broken heart like Darby was?"

He shook his head, thinking about the asshole who'd abandoned Darby when she was diagnosed with breast cancer in her early twenties. Should have cut that guy's nipples off and fed them to him.

"Ha," Gabe snorted. "My heart is just fine. Most of my romances tend to be brief and intense, like fireworks. Beautiful while they last, but ultimately short-lived and prone to leaving a mess behind. Mostly because I'm not around to help clean the mess up because I told them not to let it get messy in the first place."

He watched her catalogue that gentle warning with confliction tearing his heart apart. He had a lot of regrets, but damned if he'd allow himself to be one of Gemma's. Especially not when she'd opened *her heart* and house to him.

"You deserve someone who appreciates you for who you are, not who they want you to be." He didn't know where that came from, but it was out of his mouth and warming her eyes before he knew what the fuck just happened.

"Thanks, Gabe," she said softly, her eyes meeting his. For a moment, the room seemed to shrink as they stared at one another, the air crackling with unspoken emotion.

She dove back into the safety of *The Princess Bride*. "I'm looking for someone like Westley, I think. There's just something undeniably appealing about someone who knows exactly what they want and will do whatever it takes to get it. Even if it means climbing the Cliffs of Insanity."

Gabe couldn't help but think about how far he was from being an ideal hero. His past was checkered, full of mistakes and bad decisions.

He had sins he still had yet to answer for.

"Sure, he can fight some asshole named Mandy Humperdink or whatever, but I want to see this guy go pirating before I'm all the way sold."

"Pfff!" was her witty rejoinder as she stretched out on the couch, her foot accidentally brushing against Gabe's ribcage.

"Hey!" he yelped, several octaves higher than an anime character as his ticklish nerves engaged every muscle.

A devilish glint entered her eye as she advanced like a lion hunkered in the tall grass.

He shrank away. "Wait, no—"

Gemma launched herself at him, her fingers dancing across his ribs like a pianist playing a particularly tricky concerto. Gabe's laughter burst forth uncontrollably, and he squirmed as he tried to escape her onslaught.

"Mercy!" he gasped between bouts of laughter, attempting to fend off her relentless attack.

"Inconceivable!" Gemma declared, her eyes twinkling with mischief.

"You're evil, you know that?"

"Evil, but effective," she corrected him, gasping as he easily subdued her wrists, suddenly lunged forward, and pinned her beneath him on the couch.

They were both panting now, bodies pressed together, hearts pounding. Gabe's fingers stilled on her ribs where he'd been about to torture her back. Instead, he stared down at her, very aware of how her legs were relaxing open beneath him. How her nipples were hard between the fabric of their shirts.

He lowered his head, drawn to her lips like a magnet.

Her breath caught as he hesitated, a hairsbreadth away from kissing her.

Do it, a voice whispered in his head. *Taste her. Claim her. She wants it. She wants your head between her thighs almost as much as you want it there.*

But her eyes were too wide, her pupils too large and slow to process the gravity of what they both wanted to do.

She was high. Inebriated.

The reminder sent him leaping away and reaching back down to help her to stand.

Upright. They should both be upright. Nothing horizontal happening here!

"I'm gonna go shower," he announced loudly.

She blinked several times, cocking her head as if she couldn't decide how to feel about his declaration.

"Okay," she finally said.

"Okay," he agreed, backing away from her as if her very lovely and obviously braless nipples might be loaded for bear.

"Okay...well... Goodnight." She pointed at the ending credits. "Thanks for keeping me company."

"Okay." Someone call Shakespeare, he was gunning for his job with this fucking poetry over here.

Gathering his things, he didn't look at her again, escaping to the hallway stairs and leaping into the basement.

He'd almost made it to his room when her thin call followed him down the stairs. "Hey, Gabe? The hot water lever is weird down there—just make sure it hits the sweet spot when you turn it off or it'll leak all night."

"Okay," he said, reaching for his toolbox so he could fix the shower. "Okay, no problem!"

But what he was afraid he meant was...

As you wish.

SEVEN

K.U.J.

KNITTING UNDER THE INFLUENCE

THE CRISP AUTUMN AIR NIPPED AT GEMMA'S NOSE AS she hurried down Water Street, pulling her denim jacket tighter around her shivering shoulders. A scattering of auburn leaves fell like confetti as she walked beneath a maple, several droplets from an earlier drizzle pattering down on her from branches rustled by a breeze heavy with wood smoke.

It was the kind of night made for curling up with a good book and a hot beverage.

Not traipsing around town looking like an extra from a Britney Spears video.

Which was, like most other aspects of her current situation, entirely her fault.

Were she not already ten minutes late after changing her outfit for the ten thousandth time, she might have gone back for ten thousand and one.

Gemma quickened her pace, the skirt a good three inches shorter than her norm swishing around her thighs. She wobbled a bit on her heels, cursing herself for choosing fashion over practicality. At least she'd had the sense to wear tights under her skirt.

Not that it stopped her from feeling like every single pedestrian on the street was eyeballing her as they passed.

Why had she thought this was a good idea again?

Oh. Right.

Gabe.

Gabe, whose hooded eyes she'd imagined on her breasts as she tugged on the snug sweater she'd accidentally shrunk in the dryer. Gabe, whose hands she'd imagined sliding beneath the pleated edge of the skirt. Gabe, who'd made her feel flirty, and sensual, and more alive than she had in as long as she could remember.

She huffed a sigh as memories of their evening swam through her mind.

It had felt so easy. So natural.

Until she'd resorted to kindergarten tickle tactics.

She felt a rush of heat beneath her too-short skirt as she remembered what it felt like to have Gabe's dense weight slanted over her, the shocking strength in the rough hands pinning her wrists above her head. His warm breath feathering her cheeks, the softness of his lips as they'd hovered just a hairsbreadth above hers.

If he'd lowered them even an eighth of an inch...

The sidewalk seemed to skate beneath her feet as her knees abruptly softened.

Catching herself mere milliseconds before rolling her ankle, Gemma upended a mental ice bucket on her runaway libido.

Now was *not* the time.

And anyway, her naughty librarian platform oxfords were not *at all* proper swooning footwear.

Adding a hefty bill from the local insta-care to her current financial woes was all she needed. Especially considering that she didn't have medical insurance, despite the many reminders from the helpful healthcare marketplace bots that the open enrollment deadline was looming.

Sucking cold air into her lungs, she tried to push her anxieties aside.

Because that always worked.

Spotting Nevermore's ornate gothic shingle in the distance,

she heaved an exhale of relief. She could at least raid the first-aid kit for some bandages to cushion the blisters already forming on both heels.

She slowed five paces before the door—partly so she wouldn't arrive completely out of breath, partly to remind herself that no matter what else happened, tonight was about Cady. About friendship. About fun.

In theory.

"Hey, guys!" she called out as she entered. "Sorry I'm late. Turns out I have no idea what the maid of honor is supposed to wear to her best friend's bachelorette party."

Whatever reaction she'd been expecting, Gemma hadn't adequately prepared for what she got.

Cady's hand covered her gaping mouth. Darby's eyes widened. Vee's palms sandwiched her cheeks. Had at least one of them covered their eyes, it would have been a remarkable impression of the monkeys miming to see, hear, and speak no evil.

"I look ridiculous, right?" she asked, waiting for what seemed like an unreasonably long time for an answer. "I should go change."

Had they been in season, Gemma was certain crickets would have weighed in.

"I'll go change," she blurted, ready to beat a hasty retreat.

"Don't you dare," Darby said, finally breaking the silence.

"You look..." Cady began.

"Hot," Darby answered when her best friend trailed off.

"Stunning," Vee added.

"It's not too much?" Gemma asked, tugging at the hem of her skirt. "Or not enough? Fabric, that is." She swiveled a pleading look on Cady, whose wide-legged trouser jeans and black graphic t-shirt with the words *This Taco's Off the Menu* constituted by far the most conservative outfit.

"Just enough," Vee chimed in.

But Cady still hadn't said a word.

The silence stretched, and with it, Gemma's anxiety.

Was Cady mad? Disappointed?

Pattern recognition engine that she generally was, the dynamics of their communication had undergone such a tectonic shift since Cady and Fawkes found each other that Gemma no longer trusted her own observations.

"Where the hell is Myrtle, anyway?" Vee asked, perhaps sensing the mounting tension. "She was only five minutes behind me on the way over."

"I can call her," Darby offered.

"Would you?" Vee's lacquered nail was already tip-tapping away on her phone's screen. "I need to confirm our reservation for —" She stopped abruptly. "For the first stop."

First.

Which implied at least a second. If not a third.

Gemma wasn't sure what kind of asshole it made her that the thought only made her tired.

"On it," Darby said. Fishing her phone out of her purse, she lifted it to her ear and wandered toward the back of the bookstore. Vee had opted to stroll down the hall, leaving Gemma and Cady alone.

Gemma couldn't help but wonder if this was no accident.

"So, you ready for this?" Gemma asked. She'd hoped to infuse the question with enough enthusiasm to sound excited but ended up on the wrong side of feverish.

Cady's watery smile didn't quite reach her eyes. "I mean, no. But yeah."

"Is everything okay?" It was a cop-out. A pale substitute for the question Gemma really wanted to ask.

Are we okay?

Cady hugged her arms around her middle. "I just feel really weird about how this party came together."

That makes two of us.

"We didn't really have a chance to talk the other night, and—"

"And you're afraid that I'm torqued that Darby and Myrtle

planned it instead of me?" Gemma finished for her, needing to get this part over as soon as possible.

"I saw your face when you walked in." Cady blinked at her from behind her glasses.

"My face had been pelted with rain after spending almost two hours sliding down my skull out of boredom," Gemma pointed out. "I don't think that's necessarily a fair baseline."

"So you're really okay with it?"

Seeing the plaintive hope written all over her best friend's face, Gemma was powerless to withhold her reprieve.

"Not only am I okay with it," she began, "I'm totally and completely relieved." And to her complete shock, saying these words brought Gemma to the realization that they were true.

Partially, at least.

"You are?"

"Yup. I've been so completely snowed under lately that I couldn't even think about doing a party like this justice. And yet here we are, about to enjoy an evening of dubious entertainment that I didn't have to lift a finger to arrange. It's kind of amazing, actually." A fact she'd only come to realize since fully digesting her talk with Gabe over comfort movies and carb-laden Chinese food.

Cady's blinking eyes narrowed slightly. Not quite suspicion, but a distant uncle. First cousin twice removed.

"I thought maybe..." Cady chewed her lower lip, a dead give-away of her internal barometer. "Your outfit was some kind of... escape plan?"

Gemma knew two things simultaneously. That Cady meant the comment completely without guile, and that knowing this did nothing to lessen the sting.

Judging by how quickly Cady's smile faltered, Gemma hadn't done quite as well as she thought in maintaining a neutral expression.

"Oh no, I didn't mean—" Cady started.

"I know," Gemma interrupted. "I can totally see how you'd think that. I honestly think Uranus must be in retrograde or some shit, because pretty much everything I picked is bad-touching my skin."

Now.

"Do you want go change?" Cady asked. "Because I am in zero hurry to find out what Myrtle and Darby have in store."

A small slick of balm on the acid eating a hole in Gemma's heart.

Before she could respond, the sound of a powerful engine rumbled outside, followed by a honking horn.

Gemma and Cady exchanged puzzled looks before rushing to the window just as a sleek black bus rolled up to the curb, its tinted windows giving nothing away.

The door opened, revealing Myrtle perched in the entrance, a triumphant smile stripping a full decade from her face.

"Surprise!" she shouted, throwing her arms wide. "All aboard for mischief, hijinks, and shenanigans galore."

Seeing Darby and Vee already waiting on the sidewalk, Gemma realized they'd been in on it.

Which raised one very important question.

What other surprises might lay in store?

"HEY!" MYRTLE RAPPED ON THE TINTED PARTITION separating the driver's cubby from the rest of the bus, her bony knuckles sharp despite her rapidly dulling senses. "You think he took off?" she asked, turning to Vee.

"Hold on," Darby said, maneuvering past them and patting around the panel below the window. "Gotcha!"

The smoky glass began to slide with a mechanized whir.

"How'd you do that?" Myrtle asked.

Darby shrugged. "Been in a few tour buses in my day."

"Oh my," Vee said, and all of them craned to see what had caused such a pronounced ripple in her usually unflappable calm.

There, wedged halfway down between the steering wheel and

floorboard, was their driver. Eyes closed, mouth open in a sonorous snore. A small herd of beer cans had accumulated in the passenger seat next to him.

"Well, shit."

Cady appeared in the van's doorway, her cheeks wine-flushed and her miniature decorative veil askew. "What's the matter?" she asked, blue eyes wide with concern.

"Not a thing, poppet." Vee draped a silky arm around Cady's shoulders. "Join me in a champagne on our way to bar number two?"

Darby and Myrtle, who had helpfully body-blocked the open driver's compartment, waited until they heard the pop of the champagne cork before turning back to assess the situation.

"Time for plan B," Darby said, fishing her phone from her purse.

"Who are you calling?" Myrtle asked, peering over Darby's shoulder.

"Ethan," she replied with a smirk.

"The fun police?" Myrtle's mouth puckered as if an invisible drawstring had been pulled. "On a party bus?"

"Do *you* know a more sober human?" Darby shot back.

"Good point," Myrtle muttered.

"Anyway, he— Hey, baby." The shift in Darby's voice from tactical badass to temptress was immediate and impressive. "What? No. I'm fine." A pause, as the low rumble of Ethan's voice crackled over the other end. "We're fine. Everyone's fine. I— What?" Catching Gemma's eye, she gave an affectionately exasperated look as she held up a finger and stepped off the bus.

Ethan's SUV rolled up a mere seven minutes later, followed by Deputy Trent McGarvey, whose hyena grin wasn't contagious when they both stepped out of their car. Together, they hauled the blottoed driver out of the bus and slung him into the back of McGarvey's cruiser.

Spying on the proceedings through the tinted windows, Gemma thought she saw Ethan's boot apply a little more pressure than might be strictly necessary to shove the driver's ass the final few inches to close the door.

Dressed in jeans that Gemma suspected Darby had a hand in selecting and a crisp sky-blue button-up shirt rolled up at the elbows, Ethan appeared in the van's side door.

"Everyone okay in here?" he asked, his voice low but commanding. His gaze swept the cabin like a lighthouse beam, landed on the stripper pole, and ricocheted off to find Darby's face.

You can take the boy out of the sheriff's office...

"All good," Darby said, giving him a saucy little salute.

With a stiff nod, he swung out and closed the door behind him, leaving the van rocking ever so slightly as he levered into the driver's seat.

"You know what I think? I think we all need a shot to get us back in the party mood," Darby announced, approaching the bar. "What'll it be?"

"I know," Myrtle said, vamping with the lime-green feather boa one of the drag queens at the Velvet Vault had looped around her neck. "How about a Wet Pussy?"

At this, the partition slid slowly but conspicuously closed, concealing Ethan Townsend's stone-jawed grimace in the rearview mirror a quarter inch at a time.

The van rolled forward and into their continued revels at cautious, moderate pace.

If only the night had done the same.

Two bars in, and Gemma had run into two separate members of the city council in addition to several of her regular customers, all of whom looked at her like she'd accidentally glued a pitchfork to her face, and she would swear on a stack of Bibles that her skirt and body-hugging sweater were actively shrinking with every passing minute.

And with it, her ability to effectively mask her mounting sensory overwhelm.

The smell of cigarette smoke, beer, and perfume were as thick and heavy on the air as a rain cloud. The sticky sweet-sour earth tones blended into an overwhelming miasma that clung to her hair, her skin, her nose. The music throbbed through her bones like a living organism, and strobing lights felt like tiny needles prodding at her retinas.

Through it all, Gemma forced her smile to stay in place while she sat uncomfortably straight, trying to breathe deeply through her mouth.

Desperately longing for a hot shower and a soft bed, she discovered the unlikeliest of escape hatches.

Letting her eyes fall halfway closed, Gemma allowed herself to wander away from the space behind her eyes, sinking into the memory of sitting next to Gabe on the couch like a tree sinks its roots into the warm, dark earth.

The television screen flickering across their faces. His forearm deliciously brushing hers every now and again as she sensed his solid weight on the cushion beside her like an anchor.

"We're here!" Darby crowed.

They piled out of the van and into—horror of horrors—a karaoke bar.

Which was, in Gemma's personal universe, on level footing with the eighth circle of hell. Stuffed into a corner booth, they sat through ear-bloodying renditions of long-lasting popular songs by Queen, Cher, the Eagles, etc.

"You okay?" Cady asked, her hand covering Gemma's on the booth's tacky table. "You look a little..." She trailed off, probably searching for a word more kind than accurate. "Tired."

"I'm fine," Gemma insisted, forcing a smile. "Promise."

"Here," Darby said, handing her yet another shot. "This one's called Irish Cream Your Panties. Irish cream, espresso, and Kahlua. You'll need it if we're going to keep up with Myrtle and Vee."

Gemma followed her glance to the dance floor, where the sapphic septuagenarians were involved in some kind of dance-off with the members of another bachelorette party.

And holding their own, Gemma had to note.

The song ended and, as moderately lubed women are wont to do, the competition dissolved into aggressively insistent compliments of the kind usually traded in a ladies' room.

No, you're *amazing.*

Edging toward the side of the booth, Gemma was within a breath of making a daring escape back to the van to keep party-averse Ethan company when the first bars of the immediately recognizable intro to Taylor Swift's "Shake It Off" blasted from the speakers.

Cady gasped, flapping her hands in Gemma's direction. "It's our song. We *have* to!"

Unable to resist Cady's infectious enthusiasm, Gemma downed the shot, wincing at the burn that spread through her chest and belly. "Lead the way."

Cady clutched Gemma's hand, and together, they wove their way into the predominantly female crowd.

The infectious beat began to move her body the second she hit the floor, and when Cady pulled her close and spun her around, she laughed for the first time in what felt like a lifetime.

As they danced, Gemma flashed back to the carefree high-school-aged versions of themselves dancing to the same song in her bedroom, laughing until their stomachs hurt and howling along to every lyric with abandon.

What she wouldn't give to feel that again. A time when the future stretched out before them like an open road with nary a speed bump. A time when she couldn't conceive of a mistake the song's simple advice couldn't apply to.

By the time they returned to the bus to aim it toward their third stop of the evening, Gemma's head was spinning. The lights of Townsend Harbor blurred on the dark water despite Ethan piloting the vehicle carefully along Water Street.

Letting the raucous chatter fade into the background, Gemma sank back in her seat. Back into the grounding memory of Gabe. Conjuring her couch, she mined every last detail until she could hear him. Feel him.

Even smell him.

"Psst!" Myrtle hissed, nudging Gemma with a bony elbow. "You're not gonna want to miss this."

Immersed in her sensory Fortress of Solitude, Gemma hadn't even realized that the bus had stopped.

Or that it now had an extra passenger.

An extra passenger dressed in a billowy black pirate shirt, black leather breeches, and boots.

And a black headscarf. And a mask.

Like Westley.

Cady's wide-eyed gaze ping-ponged around the bus's cabin before landing squarely on Darby, who was grinning like the Cheshire Cat.

"Please tell me you didn't do this," Cady asked out of the side of her mouth.

"Do what?" Darby said, innocently batting her eyelashes.

One leather-gloved finger tipped Cady's chin upward, and when he spoke, the bottom dropped out of Gemma's stomach.

"Ready for some swordplay?"

Gabe.

Gemma jumped as a gritty, stripped-down version of the movie's main theme began to thump through the bus's speakers loud enough to double as a defibrillator.

Gabe's hips began to move in a slow, sensual grind. The billowing shirt gaped open to reveal a smooth expanse of pectorals and abdominals that glistened with sweat as he stood with legs planted wide.

Gemma's heart galloped in her chest as warmth spread through her body, settling low and heavy in her abdomen. The sight of all that muscle twisting and flexing under his costume made her breath catch and her knuckles go white from gripping the edge of her seat. She wanted to look away, to escape this sudden onslaught, but she was mesmerized by the electric energy that crackled in the air around him. And though she wasn't even the target of his gyrating seduction, Gemma felt her cheeks begin to flame.

Not that Cady's were any less vibrant. Now that Gabe's gloves and shirt had come off, her best friend had turned a pre-stroke purple.

Perhaps sensing an imminent medical incident, Gabe moved on, arriving in front of Myrtle and Vee.

"Let's see what you've got, young fella," Myrtle said, fishing a sizeable stack of cash from her giant old-lady purse.

Gabe shoved between them on the bench seat, planting his hands on either side of his hips and undulating in a rhythmic wave that probably could have gotten a cactus pregnant.

He let the last roll propel him back to his feet, then his hands snaked down his body to the waistband of his pants. They hovered over his crotch then stroked the general area before gripping handfuls of the leather-like fabric and tearing the pants away with a clean *rrrip* to reveal a G-string that left little to the imagination.

"That's more like it!" Myrtle shouted, bopping along with the song's beat and shaking the cash at Gabe's bulging banana hammock like a geriatric cheerleader. "Oh, hey!" She nudged Vee. "He's got a piercing."

Vee leaned forward, her eyes narrowed, before she shrugged. "Can't make it out."

"I told you not to leave your reading glasses at home," Myrtle said. "Can you hold still a minute?" she called to Gabe over the music. "Vee can't see your piercing with you slinging that thing around like a windsock."

He paused long enough for Myrtle to stuff several bills in the narrow elastic band on his hip. "See?" she said, the tip of knobby-knuckled finger jammed toward his barely covered Johnson. "It's a Prince Albert."

"Well, I'll be," Vee said. "It seems you're right."

Gabe resumed his gyrating, working his way over to Darby.

When he reached her, the van swerved, nearly sending him face-first into the bar. Which was when Gemma realized that at some point during Gabe's performance, Ethan had opened the glass partition and was now watching through slitted eyes.

Gabe's angular jaw flexed below the mask's edge, and he recovered his footing, deliberately planting one cavalier boot on the bench seat next to Darby's thigh. He then commenced with pelvic curls so deep that it was a wonder he didn't mushroom-stamp her forehead when the van took an abrupt corner.

Darby shrieked a laugh that quickly became contagious.

But Gemma sat paralyzed by a bolt of panic, realizing that Gabe had saved her for last.

He stalked toward her like a man about to collect a prize, eyes glittering with mischief behind his mask.

With one hand on the headrest behind her, he leaned down until his mouth grazed her ear.

"If you create a distraction," he said, sending shivers up her spine, "I'll cut the music and pretend I can't get it started again."

"This feels like a trap," she said, trying to focus on anything but the way his muscles rippled with each movement, the pale glow of the bus lights casting shadows that accentuated his tattooed arms.

"Nah. Just a way to end your misery without the others giving you shit."

Gemma blinked up at him as the full meaning of his statement finally sank in.

He'd been watching *her* while he was dancing for the others. He was familiar enough with her body language and facial expressions to know she was uncomfortable.

At this realization, the tension in her body dissipated and she felt a wave of warmth wash over her.

Before her failing reason could talk her out of it, she reached up and grabbed his hips, pulling him down into her lap.

"Pothole!" she shouted, despite the van maintaining a perfectly smooth and sensible pace.

Right on cue, the music cut off to a chorus of *awww*s.

"Thanks," he said quietly before pushing himself off her lap and performing a brief, impressive pantomime at getting it working again. "Sorry, ladies." Gabe shrugged. "Someone was so hot, it must have fried my battery." He glanced over his shoulder and smirked on the side of his mouth only Gemma could see.

Relief washed over her like a cool wave.

"Bravo!" Vee shouted, clapping enthusiastically. "You *must* stay and have a drink with us!"

"My pleasure." Gabe pulled off the headscarf and mask, revealing dark hair slightly mussed and damp. He ran a hand through it, pushing it back from his forehead. "Mind if I use the bathroom to change first?"

"All yours," Darby said, gesturing to the small water closet cubby.

But even with the source of her body's buzzing, electric energy now safely tucked out of sight, Gemma still felt like someone had replaced her circulatory system with an ant colony.

"Actually," she said, pushing herself up from the seat with more force than necessary, "I'm just going to get some air." She smiled apologetically at Cady before making her way to the door. "Be right back."

"You want me to come with?" her best friend asked.

"Nah, I'm just catching my breath."

"Don't blame you!" Myrtle chirped. "You got to put your hands on the merchandise!"

Gemma stepped off the van and onto the sidewalk, taking in deep gulps of night air as she walked past darkened stores toward the waterfront.

Her pulse pounded in her ears as she stumbled onto a nearby dock overlooking Puget Sound. The moon cast a silvery glow on the water, its reflection dancing and shimmering with each gentle wave. With the salty breeze ruffling her hair and the rhythmic lapping of the tide against the shore, Gemma's panic slowly began to ebb.

She had barely caught her breath when the sound of footsteps on the wooden dock made her jump. Turning around, she saw Gabe approaching, his muscular frame silhouetted against the silvery water.

"Hey," he said gently, his Southie accent curling around the word like a comforting blanket.

"Hey," Gemma replied, trying to sound casual despite her racing heart. "Just needed some air."

"Mind if I join you?" he asked.

"Not at all," she mumbled, suddenly very aware of the warmth radiating from his body.

"Nice night."

"It is."

Oh, God. Were they really going to do this? Stand side by side talking about, of all things, the weather?

Conflict averse as she was, Gemma couldn't bear it. Couldn't bear the distance that small talk threatened to create.

"Listen," she began. "I'm really sorry about earlier. I just... didn't grow up in a naked house, and I'm the absolute worst at managing my reactions to these kinds of things, but you were so kind and understanding and you made me feel comfortable even though I acted like an idiot." She paused, feeling the heat rush to her cheeks. "You have this amazing talent, and I just didn't want you to feel like you...like I—"

"You don't need to do that," he interrupted.

"Do what?"

"Apologize. It's okay that you're not into it." He leaned his elbows on the weathered wood railing.

"It's not that," Gemma said.

"Then what is it?"

Feeling his eyes on the side of her face, Gemma turned, and for a tense beat of silence, they held each other's gazes.

With dawning horror, she felt the words rising in her throat with an awful inevitability. Hours of being overwhelmed had left her maskless. Defenseless. Tender and vulnerable as a clam without a shell.

"I'm attracted to you," she said, her voice barely audible above the waves. "Like, a lot. Like, so much that it's basically an obsession at this point, but also you were right, and you scare the shit out of me because you're definitely the most beautiful man I've ever met in my life, and just so...so...*hot*, and I can barely even *look* at you, much less think about actually kissing you. I mean, I totally *do* think about kissing you, but also I can count the number of people I've kissed on one hand and still have fingers left over, so, like, even if the opportunity was there, I probably wouldn't, because you're all experienced and I'm definitely not, and I'm afraid that you'd think I'm bad at it, and that would make we want to die."

The silence that followed her projectile word vomit seemed to stretch farther than the ocean.

"You're right," Gabe said. "I am experienced. Experienced enough to know that how much sex you've had isn't any kind of predictor of how good you are at it. That said..." His fingers were strong but gentle as they molded to the curve of her jaw. "If experience is what you want, I'd be more than willing to help you with that. Anything you want to know, anything you want to try, anything you want do. No strings attached."

Gemma's heartbeat began to appear in odd places. Her eyelids. Her lips. Her belly.

She was under no illusions about what he was offering, but needed one important question answered before she could decide whether to take him up on it.

"Why would you want to do that?" she asked. "I mean, other than convenience. Room, board, and boning. Your basic one-stop-shop kinda deal."

"Because I'm attracted to you too. Like, a lot," he said, borrowing her words. "But there's no scenario where my doing anything about it makes sense for either of us. Other than this."

He wanted her. The knowledge sent a surge of bravery

through her that liberated the answer already forming at the base of her throat. "Yes," she said. "Yes, I would like that very much."

I would like that very much.

Jesus.

A gust of briny air off the water lifted her hair from her sweat-damp neck.

"Close your eyes."

"What?" she asked.

"Close your eyes," he repeated.

Gemma struggled to swallow the lump that had formed in her throat as she studied his face, looking for a hint of playfulness or mockery.

All she saw was an intense earnestness that sent a wave of heat through her body, burning away all hesitation.

Placing both hands down on the old, damp wood, Gemma allowed her lids to fall closed.

The night breeze had grown stronger, and the scent of the sea was wild and clean in her nose as the waves slapped against poles dug deep in the ocean floor.

And then she heard something else: music. Soft but unmistakable, an old folk song on an acoustic guitar that seemed to be coming from farther down the beach.

"Can I move a little closer to you?"

Gemma nodded.

The old boards creaked, and she sensed his exact position by the air's shift around his big, solid body. She felt the warmth near her cheek seconds before rough fingertips brushed away strands whipped into her face by the wind.

"This okay?" he asked softly.

She nodded again, not trusting herself to speak.

"Breathe."

Until his reminder, she hadn't realized that she wasn't. That her lungs had contracted around their oxygen-depleted air like a fist.

No sooner had her lips parted to release it, his were there.

Warm. Soft. Feathering across her mouth.

"Good," he whispered against her lips.

That word again. A key that sprang mysterious locks within her free with a small, definite *click*.

Gemma leaned in, matching their mouths in a moment that arced along her veins like lightning.

Instantly, she was swimming in sensation: the scrape of his stubble against her chin. His hands cradling her face, making her feel delicate in a way she hadn't since her childhood.

But most of all, his mouth.

The firmness of his lips. The way he sucked at her lower one, just hard enough to bring heat to her belly. The warm sweep of his tongue, tracing her top lip, then the bottom, and finally slipping inside to taste her.

She felt her knees weaken, her hands rising to the living steel of his arms for support. And then his hands were sliding down her arms and she was opening wider for him, feeling the rough wood of the railing pressing into her lower back.

Gemma wanted to say his name, to tell him how good he felt.

But before she could, his mouth was gone.

Gemma opened her eyes, finding Gabe's gaze filled with warring hungers. "Good," he panted, his breath ragged as he pulled back. "*So* good."

"Gabe, I—"

The hand cupping her jaw shifted as his fingers pressed to her kiss-swollen lips. "Enough," he said. "Enough for now. You know where I'll be when you're ready for more."

The hand fell away, leaving her cheek feeling cold. Bereft.

"I'mma go take a cold leap in the ocean now. See you at home."

As Gemma watched him go, she couldn't help but feel a strange combination of excitement and uncertainty. She didn't know if she would ever be ready, but about one thing, she was absolutely certain.

She already wanted more.

EIGHT

Suck, squeeze, bang, blow:

THE PROCESS OF COMBUSTION

GABE PACED THE DIMLY LIT BASEMENT, HIS HEART STILL thudding from the electrifying kiss. The anticipation was driving him up the wine-colored accent wall.

Damned if he wasn't acting like a randy teenager waiting to get laid for the first time. Yet here he was, prowling the confines of his basement apartment like a caged beast, unable to keep still.

When had his life become so complicated? One kiss from a woman with eyes the color of summer leaves and a smile that could light up the darkest room, and he was undone. Utterly wrecked. It was pathetic, really. He used to have to gyrate through a full half-hour strip experience.

These ladies barely got a glimpse of the Prince Albert.

Now he wished he could have done the whole pole routine, because at least that workout tuckered him out enough to sleep well.

And kept his ass in "shake your money maker" shape.

Sifting through boxes turned to searching and then to pawing through them like a man possessed. His mind kept drifting to the memory of Gemma's lips pressed against his, soft yet demanding. Her scent lingered on his skin, cinnamon and vanilla with an undertone of womanly musk that made his mouth water.

She was a cozy autumn evening come to life.

With a growl of frustration, Gabe kicked an empty box, sending it skittering across the floor. He should have never offered a "no strings" arrangement. There were always strings, tangled and knotted, just waiting to trip you up when you least expected it.

HE WAS LOST IN THAT THOUGHT WHEN HE HEARD A ginormous truck pull up to the front of the house and Myrtle's squawking demand that Gemma sleep well. "And tell that mechanic to keep his pants on!" she said, cackling at two a.m. "He'll fucking start a riot next time those V muscles are unleashed on the poor, unsuspecting folks in this town. Some of us have pacemakers, you know!"

"Night, Myrtle! Night, Vee! Love you!" Gemma called back.

The front door creaked open, kick-starting Gabe's heartbeat into overdrive, fast enough to power the basement's gently humming mechanical systems.

He froze like a statue as her footsteps paused at the hallway door leading down to the basement, then resumed as she went into the upstairs bathroom and turned on the water.

His fingers tightened around the dusty cardboard box he'd not remembered picking up as disappointment and longing warred inside him.

She'd most likely chosen to *not* continue what they'd started.

With a sigh, Gabe set the box on the Tetris pile and picked up another. Best get used to the ache in his chest where she was concerned. Best not get attached.

His attention was caught by a chaotic array of purple. Actually, *purples*. All the purples on the spectrum. From plum to lavender.

After selecting the storybook from inside the box, Gabe traced the edges of the handmade, silky cover adorned with glittery letters spelling out "My Family." He chuckled as he imagined young Gemma painstakingly gluing each letter in place, never quite getting them straight, but the cuteness lived in the little, off-kilter accents.

Flipping to the first page, he was immediately greeted by an adorably clumsy drawing of the McKendrick family—Gemma, her twin sister Lyra, and their parents.

Her story first warmed his heart, then broke it.

My name is Gemini Cleo McKendrick, and my superpower is that I can feel sounds on my skin and sometimes music makes me feel like I sparkle.

A crayon rendering of a dark-haired girl in a triangle dress and glittery skin melted him all the way.

My sister, Lyra, looks like me, except she's so smart. She remembers everything she reads.

Gabe chuckled at the wonky proportions and scribbled labels, but his amusement turned to empathy as he read about Gemma's experiences as the neurodivergent twin.

My daddy counts numbers for his job. He says I will probably get better at numbers when I learn to pay attention and slow down.

Frowning, he turned the page.

My mommy teaches at my school. I'm not in her class. She says I need to learn to not take so long to finish my work.

A few pages drifted by as she explained her best friends—her cat, Ernie (RIP, probably), and a few other people in her life. He paused at a depiction of a dark-haired man in what appeared to be a long black cassock.

I asked Father Villasenor if God could fix what's wrong with me. He said God already made me just as I should be. I asked him if he could tell everyone else that because they keep asking, "What is wrong with you, Gemma?"

Slamming it closed against the image of Gemma reaching out to a Catholic priest—and the priest reaching back—Gabe shoved the book back into the box and covered it with a few things.

Snooping wasn't among his worst sins, but he probably shouldn't.

Still, he couldn't help but feel a deeper connection with her, knowing they had both struggled to find their place in the world. He couldn't stop himself from finding solace in the shared experience of not quite fitting in.

As the second-to-youngest of the Kelly boys, he'd been predestined to be... Well, whatever the opposite of a teacher's pet was. A little asshole, he guessed. Didn't matter if he was well behaved or not (usually not); he was whipped with the same disdain most other adults had for his entire family. He was labeled a troublemaker before he ever set foot in a classroom. And at home?

Gabe stood, looking for something to do that was not thinking about his home life. Because he'd learned early and often how to look after number one, and that was all he needed to think about that time in his life.

I'm not like them, he'd insisted to everyone.

No one listened.

Even himself.

But Gemma was saying the same. *I'm not like my sister, and that means I'm in the wrong.*

Fuck anyone and everyone for making her feel that way.

As he listened to the creak of floorboards above him and the faint sound of Gemma humming a tune, Gabe couldn't help but feel a connection with her that went beyond their shared struggles.

They'd always been too much for everyone. Or not enough.

It was a shitty thing to know about yourself, sometimes. But at least she had people like Darby and Cady and most of this wicked, wonderful town to let her know she was important.

He wished they'd tell her how perfect she was. She'd like that. She reacted to praise like some women reacted to a caress, and that was just too easy. Too fucking cute.

Sexy, even.

Fuck, he needed to put his mind elsewhere. Like shut it in a steel door or the bottom of the deep freezer. He should brush his teeth and crawl into bed.

Heaving a sigh of resignation, he yanked open his door and nearly had a friggin' heart attack when he uncovered Gemma wearing ridiculous flannel pajamas—with little penguins wearing scarves—that he wanted to peel off with his teeth.

The pajamas, not the penguins.

Her expression told him he'd startled her as well.

"Did I wake you?" Her gaze flicked to the room behind him. "I can...um...come back later if you're busy."

"I thought..." Gabe licked his lips, suddenly, uncharacteristically, nervous. "I mean, I didn't hear you come down, so I assumed..."

"I, um..." She shifted her weight from one foot to the other. "I didn't want to be all nervous and sweaty from the party, so I took a minute."

She'd taken twenty minutes and seventeen seconds—not that he'd noticed.

Well, she was still nervous; that was super obvious. He didn't want this to be scary for her. If it wasn't pure fun, it didn't need to happen.

Swallowing, Gabe watched her face telegraph her conflict with sympathy. "Look. We can just turn in. No expectations, okay? Tonight was harmless fun and doesn't have to—"

"I'm ready," she blurted, falling into her adorable habit of looking at everything but him when she spoke. "I'm ready for more."

Fuck. Yes.

Gabe's entire brain and body shut down and then restarted like a frozen widget just at the thought that he might get to see her naked.

And then he became slightly homicidal at the fact that he'd forgotten to procure some protection first.

Fuck. No!

"Lesson number one," he said, sighing heavily. "Always come prepared, which I'm not."

Gemma stiffened. "Prepared?"

Gabe paused, frowning. "Protection. Birth control." He sighed, scrubbing a hand over his face. "Christ, we almost made a mistake."

"Oh." Gemma flushed and fished a folded piece of paper from her pocket. "Actually, I did come prepared. Sort of." She offered him the paper, which for sure didn't have a condom in it. "I made a list."

Amused curiosity flickered through Gabe as he took it, wondering just what she had to write down at a time like this. Hell, he forgot most of his native English language and how to read her handwriting at the prospect of some mind-bending sex.

Or even some hand stuff.

Gabe raised an eyebrow, skimming the untidy scrawl. "A list?" he asked, his entire body suffused with the kind of heat that couldn't be sated without an ice bath in the Arctic. Fucking A, it was a list. A list that belonged on a porn site.

"I figured if... Well, we might as well have some ground rules." She grimaced, looking like she wanted the floor to swallow her whole. "About the...activities I'm interested in trying. You know, for the aforementioned—uh, education."

Leave it to Gemma to complicate what should be something so simple that all it took was a bit of instinct, the right hormones, and a basic knowledge of how to ring the devil's doorbell.

Luckily, his favorite thing was learning how complicated mechanisms worked.

"Lemme guess," he said. "Green means go ahead, yellow means maybe when I'm ready, and red is absolutely not. And you want me to stick to the green column?"

Gemma worried her lower lip between her teeth. "Is that dumb? That's dumb, huh?"

"Naw, Gemma. That's wicked smart. Hell, I wish every

woman came with ready ground rules." He brushed his knuckles over her cheek, smiling when she leaned into his touch. "But we still need protection. I'll run to the drugstore tomorrow, swear."

She stared at the paper, still yet to meet his eyes. "But, like..." She fidgeted, stilled. Itched at her scalp. "Aren't there things on that list that don't, like... That wouldn't need protection?"

Yeah, the fuck there was, but he wasn't trying to pressure her into anything.

"I'mma tell you something, Gemma," he said, knowing he had to talk without touching her, or he'd be lost. "I know I look how I look, and my past and family are what they are, but...I don't usually sit in the driver's seat when it comes to sex."

"Wha—?" Forgetting herself, she blinked up at him in apparent confusion.

Gabe swallowed hard. In his experience, vulnerability led to pain. But one look at Gemma's open, curious expression told him she wouldn't use this against him. "I started dancing to earn money younger than I should have." Beat stealing cars, and women were easier to please than the cops or criminals. Also, they were infinitely more generous in all ways, and he was a horny little Muthahfuckah. "I started sleeping with women who asked me, sometimes for gifts. Sometimes for money or whatever. That sort of set a precedent, I guess. I don't go asking women for sex; they come to me, so..." He squeezed a muscle tightening at the back of his neck. "I'm not saying this to brag or nothin', but I just want you to know that even though you want a teacher, I'm not in charge. You're the fucking boss of me, got that? It's how I like it."

Her delicate little throat struggled over a swallow, but she managed. "Oh, well, I don't want to tell you what to do..."

Smiling the smile of a shark, he flicked at her list. "You just did."

Gemma's cheeks flushed a delightful shade of pink. "Well, you know... I just want us both to be on the same page," she mumbled, nervously tugging at a loose thread on her flannel pajama pants. "Speaking of, is there anything you don't want me to do to you?"

Gabe stilled. He'd never been asked that before. No one had ever cared to.

Good thing he was an honest man. "Nope. You could dress me up in a pink bunny suit, throw a saddle on my back, and ride me to the reservation—I'd be into it."

Her laugh was both husky and sweet, a combination that threatened to unstitch his resolve to make this night about her. And *only* her.

God, he wanted to press his nose against the softness of her neck and breathe her in until his lungs exploded.

Her hair was rich with the scent of rich autumn spices. Her breath was peppermint and permission as she exhaled against his hovering lips.

His mouth claimed hers, and he crowded her toward the bed. His heart beat like a drum in his chest, and he gasped for air as electric waves of pleasure ignited every inch of his body. He explored the hot recesses of her mouth, enjoying the shy little chase she made with her tongue.

A sexy noise escaped her throat, and Gabe paused in front of the bed, lifting his head to check on her. He admired the way Gemma's dark hair cascaded over her shoulders, framing her delicate face and highlighting the glow beneath. Her eyes sparkled with a mix of anticipation and nerves as he reached for the buttons on her incredibly unsexy nightshirt that was completely doing it for him.

There were things Gabe would always remember, tattooed into his brain like the ink on his body...

And this was a sight that beat them all.

"Y'know," he said, "I've always wondered what kind of treasures were hidden beneath these kindergarten teacher clothes." He leaned in, pressing a soft kiss to her collarbone as he undid each button, taking his time to reveal her skin inch by inch.

Gemma let out a shaky laugh, her breath hitching when he grazed the base of her throat as he parted the folds and dipped his hand against her warm, naked breast. His gaze lingered, drinking her in, while his fingers gently traced the curve of her shoulder.

"A-and?" Gemma asked,

"Absolute perfection," Gabe murmured, his voice deep with sincerity. "Better than I could have imagined."

"Ohh." The word escaped as a sigh, vibrating from her trembling frame.

"Perfect handfuls," he rasped, cupping their weight. He thumbed her nipples, already tight pebbles of sensation. "Damn, you drive me fucking wild. I love your soft skin," he murmured against her throat. "The curve of your waist." He palmed her hips, drawing her close. "These hips were made for holding on to."

A faint blush stained Gemma's cheeks, and her eyes lit with an increasing glow of pleasure. She arched into his touch, wordlessly pleading for more.

By the time he slid her pajama pants down her legs, Gemma was struggling for breath, and a flush spread down her body.

Gabe stared, momentarily struck dumb by the sight of her, all sweet curves and silky skin, made only more stunning by the light smattering of freckles over her shoulders and the soft, trimmed peach fuzz at the juncture of her thighs. He bit his fist as his cheeks stung and his mouth flooded with moisture.

"Every inch of you is unreal," he said, his voice husky with desire while his hands roamed over her body, leaving shivers in their wake. The sight of her flushed and aroused stirred something deep within him, a feeling of connection and desire that he had struggled to find for so long.

"Please," Gemma breathed, arching into his touch, her vulnerability making her all the more beautiful to him.

He wanted to savor her, every inch, every taste. He moved over her body like a painter, mapping out the terrain with his hands before allowing his mouth to follow. He traced paths against her skin with his tongue, whispering sweet nothings of pleasure, feeling the flutter of her heartbeat beneath his hand on the delicate pulse points of her throat, her wrists, her inner thighs.

Her groans of appreciation filled his ears, echoing like church bells on a Pentecost Sunday.

The room was silent except for the sounds of their breathing and the soft pleas she made without apparent thought.

Gabe's heart pounded in his ears. He stretched his big body over hers, stroking her softly, feeling his cock twitching with anticipation.

Keep it in your pants, Kelly. You have enough to contend with.

Gemma gasped, arching up toward him as he slid down between her legs, licking and teasing her in ways that stoked the tenderest fires in his core.

Finally reaching the lovely crease between her belly and hips, he paused for a reverent moment to appreciate the pretty pink flesh of her pussy.

"I'm going to devour you, Gemma McKendrick," he warned.

She might have said words, but all he heard was the green light she gave before he split her with a long, sinuous lick.

He flicked his tongue against her swollen clit as he stroked her thighs with just enough pressure to keep her from slipping away into blissful oblivion too quickly.

Teasing away from the apex of her pleasure, he dipped his mouth into the center as she gasped and writhed beneath him, her slim thighs trembling with effort. He tugged gently with his lips before circling the bud beneath the little ruffle of flesh, increasing the speed as he tasted and teased her most intimate folds. He stroked up and down her inner thighs with his other hand as he teased her until, finally, with one more hard flick of his tongue, Gemma writhed against the sheets, vibrating with pleasure and moaning his name in ecstasy. With a final, gentle suck at her clit, Gabe brought her back to earth using soothing, barely there flicks.

"Lesson two," he breathed against her intimate flesh. "Don't stop until they beg."

He'd thought it would have taken longer, but she only lasted for three more orgasms—well, two if you threaded together the pair that came when he sucked her clit and tickled her G-spot with his rough finger at the same time.

Once she collapsed after that, her limbs damp and trembling, she whispered a plea for mercy.

Only *then* did he gather her up and allow her to curl into the cocoon of his arms.

As he and Gemma lay knitted together, their limbs tangled, his now intensely painful arousal seemed incapable of finding a place to get comfortable and calm the hell down.

"Don't you have some things to teach me about how to pleasure you?" she asked, her jaw cracking on a yawn. "That was the whole point."

No. It wasn't. Especially not now. Now that he knew how she sounded when she came.

"Tomorrow," he whispered, pressing a kiss into her hair. If she touched him now, it'd be over in five seconds. That was not a good lesson for anyone.

"Tomorrow," she said dreamily.

Gabe lay still, tension knotting his muscles as he watched the naked moon shamelessly glow through the floor-to-ceiling windows of the daylight basement.

Never got a view like this in the city.

Never found a girl like her, either.

She would crawl into her own bed any moment now that she'd taken from him what she'd wanted. What he'd been extra willing to give.

Time for her to breeze away and leave him with a cold, lonely bed until—

A gentle snore broke through his thoughts, touching his mouth with a soft smile.

Tomorrow.

For the first time in a long time, Gabe was eager to see what tomorrow was going to look like.

Because it would be the first time in as long as he could remember that a woman trusted him enough to stay the whole night in his bed.

NINE

O.T.N.

ON THE NEEDLES

The first rays of gray morning light pried at Gemma's eyelids, calling her down from strange dreams. From the safety of her cocoon, she began to register a catalog of unfamiliar sensations. A wide, muscular back expanding against hers with deep, quiet exhales. The sole of a large, warm foot pressed against her instep. An ass whose curvature she could recognize blindfolded nestled in the dip at the base of her spine.

Gabe.

Despite it making her feel like a first-class asshole, she couldn't help but compare the experience to waking up next to ex-dude, with whom spooning had been the cuddling equivalent of parallel parking—a too-tight fit that often took so long to negotiate, he usually gave up and opted for more spacious accommodations free of her sensory demands.

Whether Gabe instinctively sought to connect their bodies without suctioning himself to her like a codependent octopus, or sleeping ass to ass was a personal preference, the result was the same: a fit more perfect than boho bookends designed by Our Lady Martha Stewart herself.

With Gabe still asleep, Gemma allowed herself to take in the surroundings, noticing how their night together had transformed the otherwise familiar space. Odd how different everything looked the morning after the most intense orgasms of your life.

Her gaze traveled around the room, taking in the unlikely collage of their combined artifacts. Her handmade pillows next to a neat stack of his automotive magazines. Her bra and panties next to his motorcycle boots. His crumpled jeans next to Lyra's Louboutin heels.

Sucking in a gasp that nearly collapsed a lung, Gemma yanked the covers over her head and squeezed her eyes shut.

Shit, if she could be riding in a party bus with David Bowie one minute and in her parents' basement the next, then maybe, just maybe, the terrible image before might prove to be a mirage. Maybe by the time she pulled the comforter down again, the doorway would be empty and she could go back to lolling resplendently in her postcoital haze.

After counting through a lucky seven Mississippis, she cautiously peeked out from under the cloudlike blanket.

But there Lyra stood, dressed in one of her signature power suits that made her look like she'd stepped off the set of *Law & Order: SVU*. Her posture was stiff and controlled, her bun so tight that it was a wonder her facial muscles could even manage such a withering mix of anger and disappointment.

"Hey," Gemma whispered. Gabe's continued coma was about the only thing she had going for her here.

"*Hey?*" Lyra repeated in a whisper far more sandpapery than Gemma's. "I find the house a total wreck and you in bed with a biker, and all you can say is 'hey?'"

"Good morning?" Gemma tried, carefully maneuvering herself into a seated position so as not to take the full force of her sister's wrath lying down.

Gabe grunted and stirred, and Lyra's icy green gaze lasered onto the tattooed arm that snaked out from beneath the covers to drape over Gemma's middle.

Elegant as origami, the arms of Lyra's tailored blazer folded across her chest.

"I miss a very important meeting, fly all the way from Phil-adelphia on a red eye, reschedule a hearing for one of my most important cases—"

"Why?" Gemma interrupted. Not that she didn't appreciate the precision with which her sister always crafted the catalog of expenditures detailing Gemma's mounting emotional debt, but there was no telling how much longer Gabe's sleep stupor would hold.

Lyra's perfectly lipsticked mouth froze halfway between a grimace and a pout. Her eyes developed a sheen that was quickly blinked away. "I thought you were dead."

Gemma's chest tightened. "Why?"

"I...had a dream."

"I had really weird dreams too, actually."

A fine crease appeared between Lyra's brows. "You did?"

Gemma nodded. "I was in this party van with David Bowie. Like, Thin White Duke David Bowie, not Ziggy Stardust, and—"

"That's not the point!"

Gabe stirred again, rolling over onto his side.

And exposing his bare ass to Lyra in the process.

Her twin's mouth dropped open into a perfect O.

Right? Gemma mouthed, feeling an absurd surge of pleasure and pride. Because somehow, the fact that a man like him would choose to be in bed with a woman like her felt like an accomplish-ment. Like the lucky pebble she could hold up to justify a dive into a dangerously dark pond.

Lyra's nostrils flared on a gusty exhale. "That's not the point. The point is—"

"Fuck yeah, baby." Gabe's voice was a muddy growl that made Gemma's toes curl and her nipples harden against the buttery sheets. "Just like that."

Gemma glanced at Lyra just in time to see a flash of capped teeth release her lower lip.

Apparently, they hadn't yet lost *all* of their biological simi-larities.

"The point is," she began again, but softer, "you weren't answering your phone. Mom and Dad have been worried sick about you, and I wake up in the middle of the night after this terrible nightmare—"

"What time?" Gemma interrupted, the hair on her arms beginning to rise.

"What?"

"What time did you wake up?"

Lyra sniffed, her expression slackening to a look more casual than Gemma knew she felt. "Two o'clock." She shrugged.

And without having a single way to prove it, Gemma *knew*. She knew the way she'd always known things about her sister that Lyra had woken up at exactly two twenty-two.

Gemma wasn't sure when it had started, exactly, Lyra's reaching for logical explanations to minimize every uncanny coincidence they'd experienced. Only that their magical bond seemed to shrink with it, until, like the matching umbilical cords that had once connected them simultaneously to their mother, it had simply dried out and dropped off.

She didn't dare hope that this might be evidence of a possible resurrection, but the fact remained that at two twenty-two a.m.—eleven twenty-two p.m. Pacific—Gemma *had* almost died.

Or, at least, had thought she might.

Gabe Kelly had made her come so hard that, for a moment, Gemma had seen actual stars. A small, circling cosmos where she'd floated briefly before returning to her body.

That she might have inadvertently summoned her twin in the process was a regrettable consequence.

"*Fuuuuck*, Gemma."

At hearing her name growled through Gabe's clenched teeth, Gemma and Lyra both blushed with identical shades of blotchy peach.

"I'm going upstairs." Lyra squared her shoulders as she drew herself up to their full shared height. "We need to talk, and I am *not* having this conversation while some—some...tattooed reprobate has a wet dream in *my* old bed."

Hearing this shouldn't have sent a wave of heat surging through Gemma's middle. Logically, she knew this, and yet the idea of Gabe seducing her in his sleep lit a hot blue pilot light deep in her chest.

"He's not a reprobate," Gemma whispered. "He's a very talented mechanic."

"Congratulations. Get dressed and meet me in the kitchen." Lyra turned on her heel and marched upstairs, obviously no longer bothering to keep quiet now that she didn't intend to be present when Gabe woke up.

And wake he did, his muscles rippling like a big cat's on a powerful stretch that rolled him over onto his back. He blinked hooded eyes at Gemma, his mouth stretching into a sleepy smile. "Morning."

"Morning." She attempted a smile but only managed half of one. Her face was still stiff from shock.

"Hey," Gabe said softly. "What's wrong?"

"Lyra." Gemma chewed the inside of her cheek, worrying the small patch of raised skin. "She's here."

"Shit," Gabe sighed, sitting up and running a hand through his tousled hair.

"Yeah."

His heavy hand landed on her hip though the comforter. "What can I do to help?"

"Hand me my clothes?"

Gabe slid out of bed and tugged on his boxers before gathering Gemma's clothes and turning his back so she could dress. The sun was just beginning to peek through the bedroom curtains, casting long rectangles across the rug. The morning felt like a fever dream, and Lyra and Gabe's presence in the same house only added to the surreal atmosphere.

"Any idea why she's here?" he asked, his back still to her.

Gemma sighed and shook her head. "No, but my guess is that

her fuck-up alarm must have been going off." The words left her mouth before she'd had a chance to really think about their implication, and something inside her clenched when she saw Gabe's shoulders tense. "I didn't mean that like it sounded. It's not you. I mean, it's not what we—"

"You're good." Gabe rose from the edge of the bed, punching his bare legs into a pair of jeans. "It's not like I haven't thought about what your family would think if they knew."

Gemma crossed to him, placing her palm against his bare back. "Please don't do that."

A measure of the tension eased beneath her fingertips.

"I'm not sorry for what we did." Gemma trailed her hand down to his waist. "In fact," she said, stepping to his side, "I'd really like to do more of it."

The dimple flickering at the corner of his lips felt like a pardon. "That can be arranged."

Gemma had taken the coward's way out, and she knew it. Opting to clean up the best she could in the downstairs bathroom, she'd snagged a change of clothing from one of the basement closets she annexed when shopping had become a primary coping mechanism.

She told herself she wasn't so much sneaking out as prioritizing her routine. Finding a way to get to work without a lengthy discussion that could further jeopardize her profits. She'd turned rationalization into an art form.

When she hadn't heard from Lyra two hours later, some small part of her thought—okay, hoped—that maybe, seeing Gemma wasn't in fact dead, she might have decided to hop on the next flight back to Philly.

No such luck.

Gemma was hunkered behind the counter, surrounded by

cardboard file boxes, when the mechanized herd bleated their death-dirge doorbell.

"My God," a male voice said. "It's like a crazy cat lady's craft room threw up in here."

Gemma's hands froze over the box of files like they'd been hit with a stun ray as she recognized the callow, caviar-fed courtroom cadence of one Harrison Lynch.

She suffered a shudder and crossed herself for no reason she could say.

"I don't know," she heard Lyra say. "I kind of like it. In a Matisse meets Grandma Moses sort of way."

"*Like* it?" Harrison asked incredulously. "Upholstering a Chesterfield with faux leather ought to be a prosecutable offense."

Peeking below the waist-high swinging door nearest her cash register, Gemma watched dress shoes that probably cost more than her first four cars stroll toward the display of felted growler coozies she'd designed in conjunction with Ethan's latest microbrew. Detail whore that she was, Gemma couldn't help but notice the extra eighth of an inch of rubber on the shoe's sole. Or how the bottom half of the shoe's wooden heels had been rubbed dull —no doubt by hours spent in offices with deep-pile carpets.

"Beer coozies?" Harrison snorted. "I still can't believe you actually came from this Hallmark hellscape."

Gemma felt a stab of defensive pride on Townsend Harbor's behalf. Whereas Lyra had gotten out so fast she left a cloud of smoke, Gemma had never really wanted to leave—had never pictured herself anywhere but here, despite occasionally bemoaning the lack of delivery food services and non-retiree recreational options.

"It's not so bad," Lyra said, her soles flashing red as she strolled toward the wall of yarn still arranged in a bold rainbow for Pride Month.

Gemma jumped as her phone rang from atop the file box. In her haste to silence it, she managed to both fumble the phone and knock over the neat stack of invoices she'd just finished sorting, sending the papers into an impressive avalanche.

With a heavy heart, she lifted the still-ringing device to find *Mom* glowing on the screen through a brand-new spider web of cracks.

"Fuck," she said under her breath, swiping up the screen to assess the damage. "Fuck, fuck, *fuck*!"

"Gemma? Honey?" Her mother's voice quavered out of the speaker.

Oh, dear Jesus. She'd accidentally *answered* it.

"Mom!" she said, shooting to her feet to find both Lyra and Harrison staring at her. "Hi!"

"Are you all right? I thought I heard—"

"Fine," she said. "Totally fine. I just—um—dropped my phone."

"Oh dear. Is it okay? Your poor father had to fish mine out of Bernini's Fontana del Tritone in Rome last week because I forgot it was in my pocket when I leaned in to make a wish. Luckily, your father found some rice at a local trattoria, and we dried it out. Did you know that he was considered a prodigy?"

"Dad?"

"No, Gianlorenzo Bernini, the sculptor."

Gemma's lips tugged into a smirk despite the stress of her current conditions. She had long suspected Susan McKendrick belonged to the lost generation of middle-aged women who were overlooked in favor of their hyperactive (male) classmates when it came to ADHD diagnoses.

"I didn't," Gemma said. "Did it come true?"

"Did what come true, honey?"

"Your wish."

"Actually, it looks like it might." Hearing the smile in her mother's voice, Gemma felt the lump of ice in her throat melt incrementally. "Is now an okay time to talk?"

"I'm kind of in the middle of something at work, but I could call you back tonight? Or whenever works best with the time difference."

"Tomorrow morning?"

"Okay, Mom. Sounds good."

"Take care, sweetheart."

"You too. Love you, Mom."

Gemma disconnected and set her phone face down on the counter. When she looked up, Lyra was waiting, poised opposite the register while Harrison continued to roam the store, scanning the eclectic displays with an air of superiority.

"Interesting inventory," he commented, picking up a skein of yarn like it was an animal that might pee on him. "But have you thought about diversifying your product offerings?"

Gemma bristled, digging her fingernails into her palms below the counter. "I think they're plenty diverse, thanks."

Harrison gave her a too-white smile. "Let me know if you change your mind. One of my frat brothers from Dartmouth runs a logistics company out of Seattle. I'm sure he'd be happy to run some diagnostics."

"I'll keep that in mind," Gemma said.

Lyra cleared her throat, placing a hand on Harrison's forearm. "Could I have a minute with Gemma?"

"Of course." Harrison bent to place a kiss on Lyra's cheek, his puckered lips making a subtle, dry suction sound that set Gemma's misophonia spinning. He sauntered off, continuing to peruse her store like it was some kind of children's art exhibit.

"You didn't come upstairs," Lyra said tightly.

"I needed to get to work," Gemma said.

Lyra glanced conspicuously around the store, empty save for the three of them, and down to the piles of paper behind the counter separating them.

Gemma crouched to begin sifting it back into a pile. "I'm just catching up on some administrative stuff while foot traffic is slow."

"Would any of that administrative stuff be financial in nature?"

A hot wire of worry woke in Gemma's gut. "Why?"

Her sister took a deep breath. "Dad called me the other day."

"Uh-huh."

"He's thinking of selling of the building."

Gemma felt as if the floor had suddenly shifted beneath her.

All of their lives were so entwined in this building, from their grandpa's old office to the bakery downstairs that had been in their family for generations. And now he was thinking of just getting rid of it?

She could feel all the color draining from her face, and she struggled to keep her breathing even. "What do you mean he's thinking about selling it?" she asked.

Lyra shifted uncomfortably on her shoes. "Mom and Dad are really enjoying traveling, and the upkeep on the property has become more than they want to handle."

Gemma sucked in a sharp breath, fighting back tears that suddenly burned her eyes.

"So, when is this happening?" she asked, her voice barely audible.

Lyra shook her head slowly, looking away as if she was afraid of what Gemma might see if she looked into her eyes. "They haven't made a final decision. Dad was kind of waiting to see how the store does this quarter."

Gemma stared at the counter, speechless and hollow.

"I know you and Harrison aren't exactly close, but he's willing to help take a look at things. See if there isn't maybe a way—"

Anger crawled up Gemma's throat with acid fingers. "You mean *Harrison* knew that Dad wanted to sell the building before I did?"

"He's my fiancé. We talk about things."

And I'm your sister, Gemma wanted to scream. *Doesn't that count for something?*

"He could get started today," Lyra said.

Only then did Gemma understand what her sister was really saying.

This was happening sooner rather than later. Much, much sooner.

"Thanks, but no thanks." She shook her head firmly, her annoyance barely contained. "I'll figure something out."

"Suit yourself." Harrison shrugged, setting the yarn back down and sauntering toward the door, with Lyra following close behind.

"See you at the house," she called over her shoulder before disappearing from sight.

~

GEMMA ZOMBIE-SHUFFLED THROUGH THE REST OF HER day, robotically sliding from task to task despite the brick in her chest.

By the time she locked up for the night, exhaustion had settled into her bones, and she trudged home with heavy steps.

What she encountered when she pushed through the front door did little to improve her mood.

The entire place was spotless.

Gemma blinked in disbelief, her earlier exhaustion momentarily forgotten.

"Lyra, what... Why?" Gemma stammered, her eyes darting around the pristine space.

"I figured I might as well do something productive while I'm here," Lyra said, wrangling the vacuum into the hall closet with a kick.

A quick scan of the surfaces Gemma used most frequently returned nothing but infuriatingly sparkling but bare real estate.

"Thank you, but..." Her voice trailed off as searched for her mail, her notebooks, her file folders. "Where are my things?"

"Can you be a little more specific?" Lyra raised an eyebrow.

"I don't exactly have an itemized list," Gemma protested. "But there are things here I needed. Letters. Bills."

Their argument was interrupted by the sound of a motorcycle engine ripping through the neighborhood's evening quiet.

Gemma's stomach performed an anti-gravity flip.

Gabe.

"Anything paper went into these drawers here," Lyra said, rapping a knuckle against the entryway table's top drawer. "Everything else that looked important, I put in a box in your room."

The anger that had simmered down to irritation over the course of the day began to boil anew. "How would you know what looks important?"

Lyra's hand parked itself on her hip. "You're right. How dare I assume that I have the intellectual capacity to work out the difference between those monthly guilt packets with free mailing labels from the ASPCA as opposed to an electric bill that's *three weeks* overdue?" Yanking open the drawer, she slapped the paper down on the table's surface. "I paid it, by the way."

Before Gemma could reply, the front door swung open and Gabe stepped inside, his face ruddy from the evening chill.

He froze when he saw them. "Hey," he said, nodding toward Lyra. "How's it going?"

Seeing the befuddled expression on her sister's face, Gemma had the sudden and very unwelcome realization that she hadn't exactly shared with Lyra that Gabe was renting the basement.

"Gabe," she said, "this is my sister, Lyra. Lyra, this is Gabe. My, um..."

"Friend," Gabe finished for her, offering his hand to Lyra. "Nice to meet you."

"You too," Lyra said, employing the same firm handshake Gemma had seen her use on everything from co-counsel to cops.

"I'mma hop in the shower, if you don't mind. Got enough axle grease on me to lube an eighteen-wheeler." Offering no further explanation, he strode toward the stairs.

Gemma felt the faintest wisp of victory when her sister's eyes flicked toward Gabe's backside as he walked away.

She wheeled on Gemma the second the door closed behind him.

"He's *living* here?" she asked in a voice that bore a remarkable resemblance to a teakettle.

"Renting," Gemma explained. "He's renting the basement."

Lyra lifted her hands to her temples as if to keep her head from exploding. "But you're *sleeping* with him?"

Gemma opened her mouth to retort but quickly snapped it shut again, realizing there was no possible explanation that would make this make sense to her high-powered, perfect sister.

"Tenant with benefits" was not a thing in her world.

Lyra's phone rang then—one of the standard, perfectly adult default ringtones that came preloaded on her latest-model, screen-protected iPhone—and excused herself to take it.

Gemma made a beeline for her bedroom, where she slung her bags down in front of the closet and gave herself a brief pep talk before returning to the living room.

Lyra had returned and was seated on the love seat with Harrison, who was petting her arm in a way that made Gemma's skin suffer a sympathetic twitch.

He rose when Gemma approached, his arms outstretched as if he were physically holding another argument at bay. "Ladies," he said with a grin that bordered on condescending. "How about I treat everyone to dinner? A chance to relax and enjoy each other's company. You can even bring your...friend."

So, Harrison had been treated to the full download.

"That's so generous of you," Gemma began, "but I don't think he'd be interested."

"Sure he would." Gabe stood at the top of the basement stairs, hair still damp from the shower, shirtless and barefoot in a pair of low-slung jeans.

Gemma felt her heart flutter as she took him in, and a wave of desire coursed through her veins like electricity.

And she wasn't the only one.

Both her sister *and* future brother-in-law experienced a momentary gape before sliding back to a careful neutral.

Which, Gemma suspected, was exactly how Gabe had planned it.

He smiled at them, his eyes glittering with amusement before he perched on the arm of the couch. "I'm always interested in free food."

"How about Sirens?" Gemma suggested. "It used to be our favorite spot, remember, Lyra?"

Lyra nodded. "I haven't been there in ages."

Harrison's nose looked like he'd just caught a whiff of a dirty diaper. "I was thinking we could go to Alchemy instead. That is, unless Gabe wouldn't feel comfortable?"

Gemma clenched her fists, ready to defend him, but Gabe surprised her by forcing out a tight-lipped smile.

"Naw, Harrison, I'm perfectly fine with going to Alchemy. It'll be a nice change of pace from the usual greasy spoon diners."

"Excellent." Harrison clapped his hands together, seemingly oblivious to the tension crackling in the air. "Alchemy it is, then. Shall we say seven?"

"Let me just throw on a shirt," Gabe said.

"Shoes, too," Harrison muttered, not quite under his breath.

"Sounds good," Gemma mumbled, trying to ignore the knot forming in her stomach. She could practically see the gears turning behind Gabe's steely gaze, as though he were calculating just how far he could push Harrison before things got ugly. Or worse, violent.

❧

THE SOFT GOLDEN GLOW OF ALCHEMY'S CHANDELIERS bathed the restaurant in a warm light as Gemma, Lyra, Gabe, and Harrison sat at the cozy corner table. The atmosphere was a far cry from the casual, boisterous vibe of Sirens, but Gemma wasn't immune to its intimate charm. The twinkling candlelight danced across the table, casting playful shadows that seemed to mock her discomfort.

Gemma stared at her wine glass, wondering just how much force would be required to snap the stem. A trip to the insta-care would be far preferable to sitting through another hour of Harrison's passive but incessant commentary about Bazaar Girls.

"Really, Gemma," he said, waving his fork around like a conductor's baton, "you should consider rebranding. I mean, 'Bazaar Girls?' It sounds like just another trinket-pushing digital marketplace."

"Thanks for your input, Harrison," Gemma replied through gritted teeth before taking a very large sip of her wine, "but I'm quite happy with the name."

It had been the one she and Lyra had come up with when putting together their magical manifesting box on their eleventh birthday.

A fact Lyra either didn't remember or didn't feel compelled to point out.

"Besides," Gabe chimed in, leaning back in his chair and crossing his tattooed arms, "it's unique. It catches people's attention."

"That's a fascinating assessment," Harrison said dryly. "I'd love to know more how someone with your—*history* became such an expert in marketing."

"I'm not," Gabe replied, grinning. "But I know a shit-ton about people."

Cutting a slice of steak with surgical precision, Harrison lifted it to his mouth and chewed while they waited what seemed an unreasonably long time for his inevitable retort. "I'm sure that's an asset when it comes to your...*career path*."

"And what's that supposed to mean?" Gabe shot back, his tattooed arms tensing beneath the sleeves of his shirt.

"Guys, please." Gemma pulse had picked up to a brisk trot. "Can we just—"

"I just meant that interpersonal skills must be even more important now that most cars diagnosed and fixed by AI and PCs these days." Harrison leaned back in his chair and crossed his arms. "You basically have to plug your tools in, right?"

"Yeah, I can plug a tool." Gabe's knuckles whitened as he clutched his beer bottle like he was about to shatter it on the edge of the table and stick the jagged edges into Harrison's aorta. "Want me to show you?"

"Please, Gabe," Gemma whispered, her voice competing with the din of the restaurant. "Just let it go."

He hesitated, his jaw working as he considered her plea. Then, without another word, he pushed his chair back and stalked away, leaving Gemma feeling as though she'd been gut-punched.

As she watched him disappear through the restaurant's entrance, she knew with chest-crushing certainty that she'd made a terrible mistake.

TEN

Good Head

WELL-PLACED, THICKER HEAD GASKET

GABE GRIPPED THE TORQUE WRENCH SO HARD HIS knuckles blanched, barely resisting the urge to hurl it across the garage. His chest heaved as he sucked in lungsful of air, rage churning through his veins like molten lead.

To him, anger had always been a living thing, an electrical current thrumming beneath his skin, making his muscles tense and his face flush.

He wanted to punch something. Anything. Walls. Windows. Harrison Lynch's smug, entitled face. Instead, he tried to focus on the engine before him, but found his thoughts and instincts consumed by a familiar darkness.

The Kelly Irish temper, so famously volatile, surged within him like a tidal wave, demanding destruction. He wanted to throw things, to shatter windows and punch walls until they crumbled beneath his fists.

And yet he didn't want to be *that guy*, the one who let his rage dictate his actions. But sometimes, the fire inside him threatened to consume everything in its path. The familiar urge coiled through him, as recognizable as an old friend. As much as he hated that part of himself, it was comfortable.

"Son of a bitch," he muttered, shaking his head in a futile

attempt to dislodge the memories. He stared at Mrs. Schwarzkopf's engine, wondering how to charge for the removal of a squirrel nest on the engine block, willing himself to find solace in the mechanics, in the precise order of parts fitting together just right. It was a struggle, though, when all he could think about was Gemma's hurt expression and the way she'd looked so small and vulnerable after Harrison's cruel words.

Like the motherfucker had slapped her.

With an enraged sound, Gabe hurled the wrench. It ricocheted off a metal workbench in a burst of sparks, landing somewhere in the shadows.

"Shit." He scrubbed a hand over his face, instant regret pooling in his gut. Tool was probably dented to hell now.

Dragging in a ragged breath, he released it slowly. His hands shook as he groped for the rag in his back pocket and mopped the sweat from his brow.

Memories of his childhood home swam in his head: the walls that had resembled Swiss cheese from the constant onslaught of Kelly rage. The mismatched plates because so many had been flung across the kitchen at someone's head.

He didn't want to be that guy anymore. The one who solved problems with his fists. Who left destruction in his wake.

Gabe wanted to build things. Create things. Help people in a way that didn't require violence.

Or sex.

Because all of that energy was directed in one very terrifying direction at the moment.

Gemma.

At the thought of her, he reined in his temper and uncurled his fists. His nails had left half-moon indentations on his palms, but the rage ebbed, leaving behind exhaustion and frustration.

And regret. So much regret.

He shouldn't have lost his temper with Harrison. Shouldn't have left because he felt some type of way. Shouldn't have insulted

Gemma's sister in the process. She didn't deserve to be caught in the crossfire of his temper. No one did.

Especially not Gemma.

Gabe sighed and scrubbed a hand over the back of his neck. This time, the mess she needed cleaning up was of his making. He needed to man the fuck up, he told himself harshly, forcing his fingers to uncurl from their death grip on the OBD scanner as he checked the respectable coupe's computer for the third time to make sure he'd fixed the issue. "You're better than this, you piece of shit."

But was he really? The question gnawed at him, as incessantly as the anger that bubbled beneath his skin. Was he truly any different from his brothers, from the men who had let their rage tear apart their lives and the lives of those around them? Determination hardened within him. He could be better...

And still not take anyone's shit.

There were some things he missed about the Kelly clan. Like how fiercely protective they had been of one another. For example, were he *really* Gemma's boyfriend, Mikey, Johnny, Luke, and Mark would make damn sure Harrison ended up in concrete boots at the bottom of the Mystic River. Then they'd grab a sando and beer and go back to doing more crimes. They were problematic motherfuckers, but despite their frequent brawls, they never hesitated to close ranks when faced with an outside threat. They'd even told his father, Patrick, to let Gabe leave without consequence.

"Let the little boy whore go, Pop." Luke had smacked Gabe in the back of the head. "It's easier to do our jobs without him crying about it like a little bitch."

Gabe hadn't cried since he was nine, but they knew that.

"That little bitch is better with a wrench than you are at jerking your own prick." Patrick Kelly had jabbed a perma-blackened finger at his eldest son. "He stays with the family."

"What family?" Johnny had gritted out, bending his knuckles around a socket wrench. "We're not a family, we're a machine, and that little *fuckah* has always been the grit in the gas. Let him go, Pops. You keep him, he'll end up turning state's evidence, and you know it."

And after his dad had hit Johnny for mouthing off, Gabe rearranged his old man's nose, jumped on his bike, and got the fuck out of Boston.

He had to let that shit go. His old life. The one he'd left on a different coast three thousand miles away.

His family's chop shop was a far cry from this well-maintained place, decorated like a classic car collector's 1950s wet dream. The eponymous Pat Kelly's Cars had been the opposite in every way. Still. It'd been home for twenty-five years. The grease-stained floors, the smell of burned rubber, and the unspoken code of silence that hung heavy in the air all belonged to another world.

Here, in this quaint harbor town, he had customers who genuinely cared about him, and he was beginning to reciprocate that sentiment.

If he brought the Boston Gabriel Kelly here? He'd scare away the entire customer base.

And Gemma.

"Hey, Gabe," came a soft voice that snapped him out of his reverie.

He looked up to see Gemma standing in the doorway. She wore a soft pink cardigan over a white sundress, the demurest outfit he'd ever seen her in. Her hair was pulled back in a braid, not a riot of curls tumbling over her shoulders like usual.

"Hey." He uncurled his fist and wiped his hands on a towel. "Gemma, I—"

"Um, I just wanted to apologize for Harrison's behavior earlier," she began, fiddling nervously with the hem of her skirt. "I never should've let him say those things."

"It's not your responsibility to watch Harrison's mouth." Gabe struggled to keep his voice even as his anger simmered just below the surface, threatening to make a reappearance. "Though someone should. That guy's a grade-A prick, and there's no excuse for what he said, but none of that was your fault."

"I know, but..." She sighed, her eyes downcast. "I just feel awful about it."

"Hey." Gabe stepped closer, lifting her chin gently with his fingers. His heart gave a painful squeeze at the sight of her distress. She shouldn't be the one feeling guilty. Not after the way he'd exploded and torn into her sister's fiancé. "You have nothing to apologize for. I'm the one who should be sorry."

Her gaze, eyes the color of storm clouds, searched his. "You were only defending me. I don't blame you for being angry."

"That's no excuse." He stroked a thumb over the soft skin of her throat, unable to stop himself. "I should have kept my temper in check. I won't have you caught in the crossfire again."

A faint smile curved her lips. "In case you haven't noticed, I have a habit of rushing into the line of fire." Her hands came up to rest on his chest, and the simple touch set his pulse racing. "But I appreciate the sentiment."

Gabe's mouth went dry as her palms glided over his pecs and around to the back of his neck. He was acutely aware of how close they stood, of the floral scent of her perfume and the warmth of her body seeping into his.

"Gemma," he rasped in warning. She couldn't possibly under-stand what she was doing to him. What they would do in the middle of the fucking shop.

"Just kiss me?" Her eyes fluttered shut as she rose on her toes, bringing her mouth a hairsbreadth from his. "I need more of you."

Lust tore through him at her innocent words, this time with claws and teeth.

The tension that had filled the air between them just moments before seemed to have evaporated, replaced by some-thing far more exhilarating and fragile all at once. Something new. Something other than the physical.

Still, when she looked at him with those depthless eyes and parted her lips on a sigh, he was lost.

With a groan, he slanted his mouth over hers and gathered her close. She tasted of wine and woman, an intoxicating blend that went straight to his head. He spanned her waist with his large hands, relishing the feel of her curves as he deepened the kiss.

A sweet moan vibrated in her throat, spurring his desire. She slid her fingers into his hair and held on as if she never meant to let go. As if this was where she meant to stay.

He wanted to drown in her, lose himself completely. When the need for oxygen forced them apart, he rested his forehead against hers, panting.

"Tell me to stop," he rasped, "and I will."

Her fingers tightened in his hair. "Don't you dare."

Triumph and longing warred in his chest as he claimed her mouth again. He couldn't get enough of her, of the softness of her lips and the warmth of her body. The innocence of her surrender only fueled the fire raging inside him.

She was his to devour, and devour her he would.

He bunched her skirt and lifted her onto the workbench, scattering tools and parts. She gasped as her back hit the cold metal, but didn't protest. Instead, she wrapped her legs around his waist and pulled him close.

The position put her mouth at the perfect height, and he took advantage, trailing kisses over her jaw and down the pale column of her throat. Her pulse beat a frantic rhythm against his lips, matching the pounding of his heart.

"Gabe," she whispered, a note of wonder in her voice.

He paused, waiting for her to tell him to stop, but she only tilted her head to give him better access. With a low sound of approval, he slid his hands underneath her clothes, relishing the softness of her skin.

She tensed for a moment but didn't pull away. He gentled his touch, caressing the sensitive skin of her waist and ribs, murmuring praise and encouragement against her throat. Gradually, she relaxed into his touch with a sigh.

Emboldened, he skimmed his hands higher, swallowing hard

when he encountered the lace edge of her bra. She arched into his touch, wordlessly begging for more.

He was happy to oblige.

With deft fingers, he unhooked the front clasp of her bra and eased the straps from her shoulders. The swell of her breasts was flushed and perfect; her nipples tightened in the cool air of the garage.

Reverently, he cupped one soft globe in his palm, testing the weight and feel. She gasped, her eyes fluttering closed. He brushed his thumb over her nipple and was rewarded with a breathy moan.

"You're so beautiful," he said, lowering his head to close his lips over the neglected nipple. She cried out, tightening her fingers in his hair. He suckled gently, teasing with his tongue until she was writhing against him. Only then did he give the other breast the same treatment, savoring her responsive cries. "Fuck, Gemma, you're killing me. How am I supposed to focus on anything else when a body like this exists under those fucking sweaters?"

He was hard enough to pound nails, and the ache only intensified with each sound he drew from her lips. But this was about her pleasure, not his, and he meant to give her as much as she could stand.

Lifting his head, he met her gaze. Her eyes were glazed with desire, lips kiss-swollen, and a becoming flush stained her cheeks.

She was a vision of loveliness, and she was his.

At least for right now.

He was about to fucking blow her mind.

"Wait," she gasped against his lips.

Chaining the snarling pit bull that'd become his libido, he froze. He gritted his teeth. He curled his fists.

But, goddammit, he *waited*.

She leaned back, her legs lowering from around his waist as she looked up at him like someone who was being too naughty and needed permission. "Can I— I mean— What if I—?" She made little fists in his t-shirt as her embarrassment turned her face red enough for a rash.

Gabe wondered if he'd saved that bus of nuns people talked about when karma presented them with a gift they never thought they'd deserve. Releasing her, he leaned his hips on the trunk of poor Mrs. Schwarzkopf's crossover.

"Do what you want, Gemma," he suggested, a wicked grin tugging at his lips. "You have permission to put those soft fucking hands wherever you want."

She swallowed, then scooted off the workbench to stand before him, looking up at him like he was the death of her innocence, and she couldn't wait to get a taste.

And didn't know where to begin.

"Take off my shirt," he suggested, a wicked grin tugging at his lips.

Gemma hesitated for a moment before reaching for the hem of his shirt, her slender fingers trembling slightly as she pulled it up and over his head. She seemed to hold her breath as her gaze roved over his tight torso, taking in the intricate Celtic tattoos that adorned his arms and chest.

"Beautiful," she murmured, ghosting her fingers over the inked designs. "I never realized how much art is etched into your skin."

"They all tell a story," Gabe replied, his voice low and husky. "But right now, all I want is for your hands to trace every fucking line."

Her touch was tentative at first, but as Gabe murmured words of encouragement and praise, Gemma's confidence grew. She explored the contours of his body, tracing the lines of muscle and ink with a curiosity that both thrilled and humbled him.

"Your hands are magic," he told her breathlessly. "One touch and I forget my fucking name."

Flushing with pleasure, she captured her lips between her teeth to hide a secret smile before she leaned close enough to press a shy kiss to his throat. His clavicle. The swell of his pecs.

With a shaky breath, she reached for the closure of his jeans.

He groaned in anticipation as she slowly unzipped his fly, brushing her fingers over the bulge beneath.

"That's it," he said. "Stroke me." She eased his cock free and curled her fingers around the throbbing length. He gritted his teeth against the pleasure, fighting for control. "Just like that," he rasped. "Don't fucking stop. That feels like a miracle."

Emboldened, she began to slide her fingers up his shaft, which rejoiced despite her lack of pressure, until she reached the nub of his cock ring. Gabe closed his eyes, drowning in the sensation, barely resisting the urge to thrust into her grip.

"I want to taste you," she whispered, her breath feathering over his solar plexus as she bent her knees.

His eyes flew open in shock, and her gaze, filled with a mix of determination and vulnerability, met his for a brief moment as she lowered herself to kneel between his slightly parted legs.

Her warm breath ghosted over the sensitive skin of his thighs, sending shivers up his spine and blooming something infinitely tender and possessive in his blood.

"Christ, Gem, you don't have to—" The words died on his lips as she hit her knees and flicked her tongue out, lapping at the bead of moisture on the tip before testing the cold metal he'd jammed through the head on a dare. "Oh, fuck me."

He struggled to suppress a groan as she leaned in, tentatively darting her tongue out to tease the tip of his erection. The sensation was electric, shooting sparks of pleasure through his body. Then she took him into the scorching heat of her mouth, inch by inch, hollowing her cheeks as she sucked him deep. The pleasure was indescribable, magnified by the sight of those cherry lips stretched around his shaft.

Any minute now he was going to wake up having jizzed on her high-thread-count sheets, dick in his hand. Right? This kind of thing just didn't happen outside of nineties porn.

"Jesus, Gemma," he managed to gasp, tangling his fingers in her soft hair. "You're so fucking hot. So. Fucking. Good."

Her movements became more assured as she took him further

into her mouth, swirling her tongue around him in ways that made his thoughts scatter like leaves in the wind. He'd never felt anything like the sensation of her lips wrapped around him, her hands exploring his body with a reverence that left him feeling both worshiped and humbled.

"God, Gemma," he choked out, bucking his hips involuntarily as she worked her magic. "You're going to be the death of me." He was close already; the coil of tension in his belly was wound impossibly tight. "Stop. I'm gonna come," he warned raggedly.

She only redoubled her efforts, gazing up at him with those sea-glass eyes.

The first hot spurt of his release hit the back of her throat, and she made a startled sound but didn't pull away. She swallowed around him, working his tip as he emptied himself into her mouth. As Gabe felt himself hurtle toward oblivion, he knew without a doubt that there was nowhere else in the world he'd rather be than right here. Townsend Harbor. A slave to a pretty, good girl with a wicked, wicked mouth.

When the last shiver had passed, she gently released him and sat back on her heels, her tongue testing her swollen lips.

Chest heaving, he hauled her to her feet and crushed her against him, devouring her mouth in a searing kiss.

"More," she whispered against his mouth. "I want more."

ELEVEN

S.e.X.

STASH ENHANCEMENT EXPERIENCE, SUCH AS: BUYING MORE YARN

Gemma gasped as Gabe pulled her up from her knees and lifted her onto the hood of the cherry-red Kia Sportage he'd been repairing. His callused hands gripped her waist, digging fingers into her flesh with a possessive hunger that woke an answering ache.

Gabe stood before her, heat and desire radiating off his body, his hair falling into his passion-glazed eyes. She felt wet heat gather at her core as he hooked a finger through the waistband of her panties and dragged them down her legs.

Without a word, Gabe dropped to his knees. His mouth covered her, tongue delving deep as he grasped her hips. Gemma cried out at the exquisite sensation, tangling her fingers in his silky hair. He devoured her with single-minded intensity, growling against her sensitive flesh. She could feel the vibration of each sound he made, amplifying the ripples of need moving through her.

She let her head fall back against the hood of the Sportage, lost in the feel of Gabe's mouth and the remarkable sight of his head between her thighs. Her back arched and hips bucked as the first tremors hit, but Gabe didn't relent. She trembled beneath his touch as he slowly stood up, never taking his gaze off hers. Breathless, Gemma slid down to wrap herself around Gabe as he rose to meet her. She could taste her own pleasure on his lips as he kissed her. Could feel his erection straining against his boxers, hot and heavy against her belly.

She reached for his boxers but found her wrist circled in his warm, dry grasp.

"Not yet," he said, voice rough with lust. "I'm not done with you."

A delicious shiver ran down Gemma's spine at the promise in his words. She smiled against his mouth, drunk and dizzy. High at being the source of so monumental a need.

Gemma sighed in protest as Gabe pulled away from her eager lips. "I said, *not yet*," he repeated, eyes dark with hunger as he ran his hands up the inside of her thighs. Gemma whimpered, already aching for more. But Gabe bypassed the juncture of her legs entirely, instead grasping her hips and flipping her over onto her stomach.

A gasp escaped her lips as her breasts were pressed into the cool metal of the hood. Before she could utter another sound, Gabe's hands were on her ass, kneading the flesh with a possessive grip. His hot mouth followed, blazing a trail of kisses over the curve of her buttocks.

"So perfect," he said, nipping at her skin. Gemma moaned as desire clenched low in her belly. "Can't get enough of you."

He dipped his tongue into the cleft just above her ass, eliciting a startled moan from Gemma. Gabe slid his hands around to cup her sex, dipping one thick finger inside her.

"Please," Gemma whimpered, writhing under his touch.

"Please *what*?" Gabe murmured against her heated flesh.

"Please...fuck me."

His hand retreated, leaving her empty as he retrieved a condom from the wallet sitting atop the nearby tool chest. After quickly freeing his erection and sheathing himself, he flipped Gemma onto her back and covered her body with his.

One hand tangled in her hair, he tilted her head to the side as his mouth descended on her throat. The other grasped her hip, angling her to grant him access. The hot head of his cock nudged at her before slipping inside.

Inch by delicious inch.

Gemma's breath caught in her throat at the deliciousness of the sensation. Slow and deliberate, he sank into her with a groan, pausing for a moment when he was seated fully inside.

"Look at me," Gabe said, waiting until Gemma opened her eyes. His gaze seared into hers, his pupils blown wide with lust. "You're fucking *mine*. You know that?"

Gemma shuddered, wrapping her legs around Gabe's waist to draw him deeper still. Claiming him as he had claimed her, she rocked her hips against his, clenching around his length. "Yes."

"Then say it." Gabe's eyes gleamed, and he surged forward, setting a punishing pace.

"I'm yours," Gemma cried out at the pleasure-pain, clinging to his shoulders. His hips branded the insides of her thighs, and the car rocked beneath them, a ship taking her further and further out. Deeper into the waters of the inevitable end building with each thrust.

"Come for me," he growled, angling to hit a spot inside her that made her entire body jerk. Gemma lost herself in a wave that wiped her entire being blank except for the fierce spasms clenching her core around his cock.

Gabe buried his face against her shoulder, dissolving into a guttural shout as he pulsed inside her. Gemma held him close as he trembled through the aftershocks, stroking his sweat-slicked back.

He collapsed onto her chest, breathing heavily. For some time, they lay in comfortable silence until Gabe stirred.

Slowly, he rolled off her and staggered them to the cot, where he reached for the blankets to pull up around their bodies. He tucked her close to his side, wrapping an arm around her waist and sighing contentedly when she cuddled closer.

The cot creaked beneath them as they shifted to find a

comfortable position, but neither of them seemed to mind. They lay in a tangle of limbs for long moments, chests heaving as they struggled to catch their breath. Gemma nuzzled into the crook of Gabe's neck. His arms tightened around her in response, and a low rumble of satisfaction vibrated in his chest as she stretched out on the cot against him with a satisfied hum, muscles pleasantly sore from their exertions.

"Thank you for sticking up for me tonight," she said.

Gabe pressed a kiss to her bare shoulder. "I know what it's like to have siblings who treat you like the kid at the grownups' table. Always with the advice. The criticism."

Gemma winced, chagrined she hadn't considered what a dinner with Lyra and Harrison might bring up for Gabe on a personal level. "You too?"

Gabe nodded.

"Well," she said, lacing their fingers together. "You can always come sit at the fuck-ups' table with me."

Gabe squeezed her hand. "Same goes for you."

Warmth blossomed in her chest at his words, but before she could respond, her phone began to ring.

Gabe reached for her purse and dragged it over. Gemma fished her phone out of the pocket and felt a full-body jolt when she saw Lyra's name flashing across the screen.

She sent it to voicemail, only for it to begin ringing again immediately.

With a sigh, she answered the call. "What is it, Lyra?"

"Mom and Dad," her sister said, panic icy in her tone. "They're on a flight home."

TWELVE

Direct injection

MIXTURE FORMATION SYSTEM FOR INTERNAL COMBUSTION ENGINES

GABE FOUND HIMSELF STARING AT HIS REFLECTION IN the mirror of his shop, feeling like a stranger in his own skin. The crisp button-down shirt Gemma had selected for him was as foreign to him as the idea of sharing brunch with her parents.

How was he—a grown-ass man, by the way—pretending to sneak into the house he'd accidentally secretly rented so Gemma's parents weren't too shocked upon finding out he was a tenant they'd never agreed to?

Blowing out his cheeks, he eyed his cot with longing. Maybe he should just move back here.

But here sucked. Because here wasn't where Gemma lived.

"Too spiky." Gemma licked her flattened fingers and reached up to smooth a stubborn cowlick that always messed with any plans to make his hair look neat.

Even though they were both tense and anxious, the motion did something squiggly to his insides. A little purr escaped his throat, sparking a crinkle of a smile at the corners of her wide, worried eyes.

"Wow, look at you," Lyra said, sauntering through the auto shop door left open to let in the crisp sea air.

"Doesn't he look amazing?" Gemma grasped him by the arm

and whirled them both around to present to Lyra's already skeptical gaze.

"He looks...less like an extra from *Sons of Anarchy*."

"Uh, thanks?" Gabe replied, not sure whether to feel flattered or insulted.

"Although," Lyra continued, her black heels clip-clopping on the concrete floor as she scrutinized him closer, "I suspect that hickey on your neck isn't exactly the accessory they're hoping to find on the new boyfriend." She smirked knowingly at her twin sister. "Almost as dad-impressing as the neck tattoos."

"Yeah, well... Impressing parents hasn't ever been much of a priority," Gabe joked. *Or much of a possibility.*

"Evidently," Lyra said with a wry twist of her un-glossed lips.

"Lyra!" Gemma cried from where she'd been examining her love bite with increasing pallor.

"Hey, I'm just calling it like I see it," Lyra said, rummaging through her purse. "Luckily for your fuckboi here, I've got just the thing." She triumphantly produced a small tube of concealer.

"Seriously?" Gabe asked, raising an eyebrow. He was trying to be cool, but his patience had limits.

"You want to explain to two sixty-year-olds with jet lag what you were doing to my baby sister that turned her into a vampire?" Lyra said, dabbing the concealer onto her fingertip.

Gabe scowled. "No."

"Then hold still."

He winced as Lyra's cold fingers met his warm skin and dabbed away any trace of the damning evidence. Her touch was firm but gentle, a stark contrast to her demeanor.

Gabe gritted his teeth, fighting the infantile urge to swat her hands away.

Yeah...still glad I never had a sister.

"There," Lyra said, snapping the cap back onto the tube. "At least now your neck doesn't look like a tagged freeway overpass."

"Thanks, doc." Sarcasm dripped from Gabe's voice as he thought about the dosh he spent on the Irish torc he'd inked into his neck back when he was nineteen. Fuck her, it still looked good. "Your bedside manner could use some work."

She rolled her eyes. "You want to talk beds? If my parents see those love bites, they'll know you and Gem slept together. And if they know you slept together, they'll feel some type of way about you living in the basement, *capisce*?" She crossed her arms over her chest, staring him down like a Roman general. "It makes you both look irresponsible, and that helps no one."

Gabe felt a largely silent Gemma flinch at his side, and he looked down into her large, open, long-lashed eyes. Had they gotten larger and more dramatic in the last fifteen minutes?

"Someone want to explain to me how me paying Gemma fair rent in a room that isn't used in a house that isn't lived in is irresponsible?" he finally asked. "Like, why can't we just be honest with your parents? Tell them you got a reference from Darby, first, last, and deposit, and I'll sign a lease. No big deal."

Lyra's head kicked to the side as she studied him. Gabe couldn't tell if she was irritated or impressed. Maybe both? This twin thing was going to take a second to get used to.

"You want to spend the next handful of days explaining how my impulsive sister is safe alone in a house with someone who looks and acts like you to a couple of play-it-safe Boomers?"

Gabe opened his mouth, then closed it again. She had a point. An asshole point. But still a point.

"Lyra, you need to be nice," Gemma said, an incredibly foreign thread of steel strengthening her sweet voice. "You and Harrison both."

Lyra's eyebrows lifted as she turned her intense regard on her twin. After a second, her expression softened in increments as she reframed something in her brain.

"'Kay." She turned on her heel and stomped toward the door.

Gabe's boots remained locked to the floor. What the fuck was he doing? How did he let anyone make him think this would be a good idea? And why? Why would he put himself through this kind of torture? Open himself up to the judgment of people who would automatically think they were better than him?

He started as cool, slim fingers threaded through his, and Gemma pressed her temple to his shoulder in a sweet gesture of affection. "You don't have to go through all this," she said hesitantly. "I mean, if I'm—if *it's*—too much trouble, we can forget the whole thing."

Oh. That was why.

She was why.

She was becoming a lot of his whys, and he needed to check that real quick.

"Come on." He summoned a smile. "Let's do this. It'll be fine."

～

GABE FOLLOWED GEMMA AND LYRA THROUGH AN eerily tidy house into the kitchen, his heart pounding loud in his chest. The aroma of freshly brewed coffee and sizzling bacon filled the air, but his nerves left him with very little appetite. He had never been good at first impressions for obvious reasons. Never much cared about that sort of thing before.

"Mom, Dad," Gemma began, her voice wavering only slightly as she moved into the kitchen to enfold her parents in a welcoming hug. "This is Gabe."

Her mother looked up from the stove, a warm smile spreading across an elven face her two girls had inherited from her. "Oh, you must be the young man who's renting our basement that we heard about from Harrison and not our own daughters." The censuring gaze she slid to her girls contained more mischief than irritation, but also carried that unspoken promise of a later discussion. Damn, even nice parents did that, huh? "I'm Susan, and this is Gemma's father Tom. So nice to meet you."

At least that part felt genuine.

"Likewise," Gabe replied, forcing a polite smile as he shook hands with both of her parents. They seemed friendly and relaxed enough, but he could feel the weight of their scrutiny like the sword of Damocles.

"Please, Gabe, have a seat." Gemma's father gestured toward an empty chair at the granite table. His hair shone thick and dark as his daughters', though his features were wider and less striking then the McKendrick women.

As Gabe sat down, he gave a curt nod to Harrison across the table. One that could have been a greeting or a threat.

No one seemed to notice.

"Your accent is remarkable," Susan said shyly, ladling a cheesy scramble of some kind on a plate that Lyra set in front of him while Gemma retrieved utensils and her father filled the appropriate number of coffee cups. It was like a ballet he'd never been to. Riveting and kinda weird. He'd been paying such close attention that he missed Susan's question.

"What now?" he asked when Gemma squeezed his shoulder gently.

"She was asking where you're from," Tom said, handing him a mug. "Though I'd recognize a Boston accent anywhere."

Oh fuck. Did he have Boston ties? Would he know of the Kellys? Was the world really that small?

"Dad was stationed with the coast guard there for several months," Gemma explained.

"Thought I wanted to be a meteorologist." Tom chuckled with a self-effacing grin. "I didn't last long. Some people are just meant to be indoors-y."

Gabe couldn't relate, but he chuckled at Gemma's dad's dry sense of humor. So far, not bad. So long as he didn't say something to fuck things up.

"Took over Jim's Auto, did you?" Tom continued over a testing sip of hot coffee. "Jim Conter's old place?"

Gabe nodded. "It's a primo space, and this town had a mighty need for a master mechanic."

"I've always wondered," Harrison cut into the conversation,

making Gabe want to cut into his arteries, "just what separates a regular old mechanic from a 'master' mechanic?" He used goddamn air quotes.

God Gabe hated this motherfucker.

"Means I have the extra training and certification to identify several kinds of massive tools and use them to fix very obvious problems."

Gemma, who'd taken her place next to him, reached out and clasped his hand, draining him of tension immediately.

Harrison didn't matter. A wolf didn't concern himself with the bleating of sheep.

"Not that I wanted to bring up any problems right away..." Tom used the awkward silence to segue into whatever conversation Gemma dreaded, as Gabe could feel every one of her soft limbs turn to iron. "Gemma, we came back to attend Cady's wedding, but after that, we need to talk about Bazaar Girls."

"I know," Gemma said into her mug, her enthusiasm deflating like a punctured balloon. "Things really have been getting better, but I just need a few more quarters and maybe one more tourist season like this one before—"

Harrison cleared his throat, drawing everyone's attention. "If I may," he began, his voice dripping with condescension. "Tom, have you considered that perhaps putting up the building for sale would be better in this market? The interest rates are tilting toward a seller's market in the commercial sector, and with the pandemic having driven people from the inner cities—"

"Excuse me?" Gemma bristled, her grip on Gabe's hand tightening.

"It'd be good for you, Gem," Harrison continued, unfazed by her reaction.

Gabe wanted to murder him for using a nickname. Did he know her like that?

"In your mid-twenties with nothing more than your high school diploma. Without that business around your neck, you could finally have the chance to go to college, maybe even meet a guy who would support you." Harrison lifted a meaningful brow at Gabe. "Creative types like Gemma often need that kind of grounding to thrive."

Gabe clenched his jaw, resisting the urge to tell Harrison exactly where he could shove his unsolicited opinion. Instead, he focused on the comforting weight of Gemma's hand in his, trying to convey his support without overstepping his boundaries.

"Thanks for your input, Harrison," Gemma replied through gritted teeth, clearly struggling to hold on to her composure. "But I don't want to go to college. I want to run Bazaar Girls. And trust me, I know small businesses struggle a little before they take off, and I'm going to make it work. In fact, Gabe is going to—"

"Your determination is admirable, sweetheart," her father said, though his eyes held a hint of skepticism as he patted her arm. "We can talk about this later."

Rage boiled in Gabe's veins. But he swallowed it down, remembering this was all for Gemma's benefit. He wanted to tell her parents to back off. Couldn't they see how hard she was trying? How talented she was? How much she needed them to encourage her?

How much it would mean if they did?

He glanced at Gemma, at cheeks flushed with frustration as she dug into her breakfast.

They weren't building anything here. He wasn't her boyfriend...but he knew he'd do anything to help her prove everyone wrong, even if it meant lying to these good people who obviously loved her (and fucking Harrison).

Even if that made him a bad guy.

Breakfast was probably the most normal meal he'd ever eaten. And it felt stupid weird. Cooked by a mom who'd cooked a million breakfasts just like it. Cleared away by a dutiful father who cleaned up so his wife could take a turn to chill at the table.

Was this what normal looked like?

His phone chimed in his pocket, and he would have ignored it, but that sound notified him that the security camera at the shop had been triggered. Thumbing open the video, he frowned to see a perfect helmet of blue-gray hair atop a patiently waiting Vee Prescott.

"Excuse me, folks," Gabe said as he rose from the table, his tone carefully neutral. "I've got to head to the shop. Duty calls."

"Of course, dear," Susan replied, her voice betraying genuine regret. "Thank you for joining us for breakfast. Hope to see you again soon."

"Pleasure," Gabe offered with a tight smile. He looked at Gemma, whose eyes were stormy. "I'll call you later?" he said, leaning down to drop a quick kiss on her forehead.

Harrison made a disapproving sound in his throat, but Gabe ignored him. He had to get out of there before he did something he'd regret.

"It was a pleasure meeting you," Harrison said smugly, as if they'd not already shared an almost-violent moment.

Much as he should have, Gabe couldn't bring himself to reply, so, without another word, he strode from the kitchen.

As he stepped out of the McKendrick house, the crisp morning air was a balm against the lingering tension from breakfast. Slinging his leg over his bike, Gabe couldn't help but replay the scene in his mind, feeling the sting of Harrison's words and his own powerlessness to defend Gemma.

Not his job. So why did he want to do it?

As he pulled up to the garage, he saw a familiar blue sedan parked out front. Vee was sitting on the front steps, knitting something pink and lacy.

"Morning, love," she said brightly, accepting his help to stand on her rickety joints from the low stoop. "Myrtle has informed me the voltage regulator has given up the ghost again. I was hoping you might take a look at it for me if I left it?"

Gabe smiled, and some of the tension eased from his shoulders. Vee had a way of making everything seem right with the world.

"Course," he said, parking his bike. "Why don't you come on in, and I'll get you sorted?"

She beamed, gathering up her knitting. "You're a gem, you are."

Yeah, he was a friggin' piece of coal trying to be a diamond.

Gabe shook his head, leading her into the garage. At least here, he was on solid ground. Here, he could fix things. Here, he was in control.

He slid open the heavy metal door and flicked on the lights, illuminating the organized chaos within. His domain.

"You look like you're dressed for a funeral, not fixing cars."

Gabe glanced down at his button-up shirt and slacks, suddenly conscious of how out of place they were for his job. "Yeah, well, I had an unexpected family breakfast to attend this morning."

Vee raised an eyebrow, eyes twinkling with mischief. "Oh? And did you wear your conservative attire over that sexy little G-string number you wore on the party bus? Or is that tucked away for special occasions?"

"Ha, very funny," Gabe retorted, feeling the corners of his mouth lift in a reluctant grin. Naughty jokes were always funnier from proper British beauties in their seventies who owned small-town sex shops. "The G-string is safely retired, I promise."

"Good," she replied, her tone shifting to one of gentle concern. "I just worry about you getting those nice clothes all dirty. Feel free to change at your leisure." She gave him a saucy wink.

"Don't you have a wife?" he shot back.

"I do indeed. The best wife in the entire world. That categorically means I must admire the male pulchritude on my own time."

"You're one classy broad, Vee," Gabe said sincerely, touched by her affection. "But I think I'll go grab my coveralls." *In case I get a boner thinking about what Gemma and I did here.*

As he retrieved the protective gear from a locker, Gabe couldn't help but feel a warmth envelop him, like a comforting embrace from an understanding mother he never had. He quickly pulled on the coveralls, then turned his attention back to Vee as she pulled her wheezing Jaguar into the service bay.

She took her knitting project and shut the driver's door. "So, you met Tom and Susan today—that's often a harrowing ordeal."

"Nah," Gabe said as he lifted her hood to look for anything glaringly obvious. Like a squirrel nest. "It's only harrowing if there are high stakes. None of that here."

Vee raised a skeptical eyebrow, settling onto a stool near the service counter.

"It's nothing, all right?" he said gruffly. "Just a favor for a friend."

Vee sighed. "You can't lie to save your life, love." She stood, crossing to him and squeezing his arm. "It's permissible to take a run at Gemma, you know. Even if it scares you."

He snorted, shrugging off her knobbly hand. "I don't scare easily."

"Mmhmm." In her circumspect way, she returned to her perch, and knitting needles clicked together as pink yarn spilled from her lap. "So how was breakfast with the parents?"

Gabe shrugged, leaning against the car's open hood. "Her dad's intense. But we talked some shop."

"I was not surprised to learn he enjoys a good pegging now and again," she said wryly.

He snorted. "I can't know that, Vee, damn." He connected the scanner to Vee's car and looked over the diagnostic report.

"Tell me, Gabe," she began, folding her arms across her chest. "What brought you all the way to our quaint little town? Not Darby, as I initially would have assumed."

He hesitated, suspicious of Vee's motives, but something about her gentle demeanor made it difficult for him to keep his guard up. It was as if a warm English fog had settled around them, softening the edges of their conversation.

"Let's just say I needed a fresh start," he finally admitted, not looking up. "Boston wasn't the right place for me anymore."

"Ah, yes." Vee nodded sagely. "Sometimes we must leave behind what we know to find what we need."

Friggin' Confucius Churchill over here.

Gabe couldn't help but wonder how different his life would have been if he'd grown up with a mother like Vee—someone who offered wisdom and understanding instead of the memories of brake lights and burned rubber.

"Enough about me," he said, trying to redirect the conversation. "You and Myrtle must have a fun story."

Vee's eyes twinkled mischievously. "You mean, what's a proper English lady doing in a place like this, running a sex shop like Vee's Lady Garden?"

"Something like that." He chuckled, intrigued by her candor.

"When Myrtle and I first met, our families were less than thrilled. Our backgrounds couldn't have been more different: she was from an...agricultural family, while I hailed from the bustling streets of the West End of London."

"Really?" Gabe asked.

"Indeed," she continued. "We faced all sorts of obstacles, from disapproving relatives to gossiping neighbors. But we stuck together, and look at us now. We've built a life together, and we're happier than ever."

Gabe grunted a response, unsure of what to say to that.

"Life has a funny way, doesn't it?" Vee mused, her gaze distant. "And sometimes, it takes a bit of chaos before everything falls into place."

Chaos. It was a word Gemma used. It was the thing about her he liked the most. To a man like him, people were predictable. They could always be counted upon to look after their own self-interests.

Not Gemma, though. She looked after other people, sometimes to the detriment of her own needs.

"There's the problem." Gabe grabbed on to the salvation of something to do. "Voltage is shot. Tell Myrtle she was right."

"Well, no surprise there." Vee peered up from her knitting, her brow furrowing. "The car's older than Gemma, poor thing."

Gabe's mouth twitched. "I can replace it today, have you back on the road this afternoon."

"You're a lifesaver," she said warmly. She set aside her knitting and looked at him with eyes full of understanding. "How are you, really? Is there anything you need?"

Gabe looked away, feeling a lump forming in his throat. He busied himself gathering new tools. No one had asked him that in... Well, maybe ever.

"I'm good. I'll call you when your car is ready." She should leave. He wasn't feeling well. Or maybe he was *feeling*...and that was FUBAR. Either way, the old woman saw too much and said what she thought.

"Really?" Vee moved closer. "You're not going to tell me what is grinding your molars to dust?"

Gabe sighed, realizing that she wasn't leaving until he opened up. "I mean... I'm kinda in a weird situation right now."

"Go on," she said, leaning against the hood of her car.

"See, Gemma didn't tell her parents I was renting the basement, and they didn't tell her that they were coming into town for Cady's wedding, so Lyra and Gemma cooked up this plan where I'd pretend to be Gemma's boyfriend. But it feels wrong, you know? I mean, I care about her and all, but there's no universe out there where a muthafuck—er—a guy like me ends up with a girl like her."

Vee smiled. "I see—you think you're not good enough."

Heat rose on the back of Gabe's neck, but he didn't like the simple answer to that question. "I'm an ex-con with more baggage than Logan Airport. Gemma doesn't need that in her life."

"Maybe you should let Gemma decide what she does and doesn't need." Vee squeezed his arm again. "You're a good man, Gabe Kelly. If Gemma can't see that, she's not half as bright as I thought."

He huffed a laugh and shook his head. "You don't get it."

"I do, actually. Myrtle's family was horrified when we got together. Thought I was too wild, and she was too proper, if you'd believe it. But love is love, and it makes its own way." She patted his cheek. "Chin up. What's meant to be will find a way, you'll see."

Unwilling to pop the old lady's romantic bubble, he just smiled.

"Well, I'm glad we've crossed paths now," Vee said with a cryptic grin. "And remember, dear—you're never too old to learn from someone who's been around the block a few times, if you catch my drift."

"Thanks, Vee," Gabe said, genuinely touched by her warmth. As he set to work on her car, he couldn't help but think how different life might've been for him and his siblings if they'd had someone like Vee guiding them along the way. Someone to gentle their angst. To kiss their scrapes.

Gabe wanted to believe her, to let the warmth blooming in his chest take root and grow. But the shadows of his past loomed, cold and unforgiving.

She sighed, recognizing the dismissal for what it was, but let him go without further argument.

Gabe dove into the familiar task, letting the clatter and grind of wrenches and bolts drown out the longing in his heart. Gemma's world might be bright, but he would always remain in the dark.

No matter what Vee said, some stains just didn't wash clean.

THIRTEEN

Lifeline

A LINE OF THREAD, YARN, FLOSS, ETC. THAT IS
RUN THROUGH THE ACTIVE STITCHES AND
USED AS A BACKUP POINT.

GEMMA APPROACHED THE BRIDAL SHOP, HER STOMACH feeling like a cold, tight ball behind her ribcage. The storefront was a confection of lace and tulle, with the delicate mannequins in the large picture window wearing gowns that seemed to defy gravity. Taking a deep breath, she pushed open the door, stepping into a veritable cloud of satin, chiffon, and enough sequins to blind passersby.

Before she could bolt, Cady rushed forward and enveloped her in a hug. "You made it!"

Gemma sighed in relief and returned the hug.

The shop owner glided over, a vision in a beige suit with billowing palazzo pants. "Welcome to Happily Ever After bridal boutique, where forever begins," she said in a melodic voice. "I'm Marguerite. How can I help you today?"

"Cady Bloomquist. Final fitting for the wedding gown." Cady beamed.

"Of course you are!" Marguerite turned her megawatt smile on Gemma. "And you, dear? Sister, cousin...or perhaps another blushing bride-to-be?"

"Maid of honor, actually. Gemma McKendrick."

"Lovely! And is there a special someone in your life, Gemma?" Marguerite asked with a sly wink.

"Just my best friend," Gemma replied evasively, already feeling the weight of the proprietor's expectations.

"Isn't that lovely?" The woman sighed. "Right this way."

Marguerite guided Gemma and Cady to the back of the shop, where a fitting area was tucked away in an alcove. The walls were draped with shimmering cream-colored satin giving off a soft glow that cast everything with a dreamy ambience. A selection of mannequins stood at attention in the corner, each holding up a different dress for inspection. Along one wall was an array of accessories—glittering tiaras, pearl-encrusted jewelry boxes, and beaded sashes—all designed to add personal touches to the perfect wedding ensemble. At the center of it all was a small platform where the bride could examine herself from all angles, scrutinizing any disastrous gaps or puckers.

"Would either of you like any champagne to celebrate this momentous occasion?" Marguerite asked.

"Yes," Gemma and Cady answered enthusiastically in unison.

With that, Marguerite snapped her fingers, summoning an assistant who dutifully handed out flutes of bubbly liquid.

"Thank you!" Gemma grabbed the glass a little too enthusiastically and took a large gulp, willing the champagne to soothe her frayed nerves.

Between her parents' ambush arrival and their meeting with Gabe, her insides felt like bowstring drawn tight enough to snap.

"If you'll excuse us for just a moment, I'll go get our bride ready." Marguerite gave Gemma a beatific smile and whisked Cady away in an aggressively rose-scented cloud.

As soon as they were gone, Gemma allowed herself to sink to a velvet settee, her carefully contrived expression of excitement wilting as she took another nose-tickling sip of champagne. Maybe the sea of satin and lace might muffle the reality looming large in her periphery.

Her momentary respite vanished when her phone buzzed with a text from her father.

Got a minute to chat later?

Chat. Her father's deceptively casual term for an impending one-way communication/lecture.

Shoot!! At a fitting with Cady, and then I need to help with some decorations for the reception, she typed, carefully avoiding any mention of her shop. *Check in with you later?*

Three dots appeared. Disappeared. Reappeared.

Gemma turned the phone facedown on the velvet. She couldn't do this. Not during Cady's fitting.

Surrounded by the fitting area's many mirrors, Gemma couldn't help but feel scrutinized by the multiple versions of herself staring back. The soft lighting did nothing to ease her discomfort as she fidgeted with her hand-knit sweater vest, a reminder of her crafting skills that seemed so insignificant amid the grandeur of the bridal boutique.

Her thoughts drifted to Gabe's recent meeting with her parents, which had gone surprisingly well. She found herself wondering if his tattoos and Southie accent had charmed them or simply left them too bewildered to object. Who'd have thought they'd take to an ex-con former stripper/escort mechanic like ducks to water?

"You the maid of honor for the Bloomquist-Fawkes party?" A flat, toneless voice snapped her out of her reverie.

"Yeah," Gemma said hesitantly.

"Someone forgot to mark the hem on your dress. I need you to try it on so I can pin it."

"Really?" The idea of wrestling herself into the shapewear necessary for the body-hugging satin shift made Gemma's skin itch. "Couldn't I just hold it up to my body or something?"

"Sure." The wildly enthusiastic seamstress's thin lips flattened into a disapproving line. "If you want it dragging through the mud every time you go to pick up your bride's train."

Gemma sighed, reluctantly setting her champagne aside. "Fine."

In a curtained stall far less luxurious than the bridal area, she slipped out of her clothes, stifling a gasp as she caught a glimpse of herself in the full-length mirror.

Little bruises and scrapes dotted her skin, evidence of her sweaty, urgent clash with Gabe in the auto shop. A little thrill sizzled through Gemma as she ran her fingers over them, imagining them on her skin beneath the gown. A secret road map of their shared passion.

She could almost feel his hands on her body, sending sparks of pleasure through every nerve ending as he—

"You dressed yet?" The seamstress's grating voice sawed straight through her fantasy. "I got a lot of dresses to get through this afternoon."

"Just another minute." Gemma snatched the hanger and quickly wriggled into the tight-fitting satin gown, feeling like a sausage being stuffed into its casing as she shimmed it up her body. "I'll need a little help zipping up," she told the seamstress, holding the back closed.

"Wouldn't have picked a square neckline with shoulders like these," the silver-haired woman said, giving the zipper an aggressive tug.

"We thought it would distract from the hump on my back," Gemma muttered. Gathering the excess fabric, she shuffled toward the mirrored platform in her socked feet.

And stopped dead in her tracks.

There was Cady, standing at the center of the platform in her wedding gown—a romantic confection of creamy layers of chiffon and antique lace. The kind of gown you could absolutely imagine the heroine of a gothic novel wearing as she ran in slow motion through the corridors of a windswept castle. With the sides of her long blonde hair pinned up and the rest cascading down her back, she looked like an ethereal creature torn from the pages of *Wuthering Heights*, or perhaps a lost Brontë sister.

Gemma's throat tightened as she blinked back tears and her heart swelled with the tender ache of love and pride.

Cady glanced up, grinning as she caught Gemma's eye in the mirror. "Are you crying?"

"Shut up." Gemma sniffled, swiping at her traitorous eyes with a trembling hand. "It's just... You look so beautiful, and I'm so happy for you."

"*Gemma.*" Cady's eyes shimmered with unshed tears of her own as she stepped down from her platform, wrapping her friend in a tight hug. "You've seen this dress before."

"I know," Gemma said, blinking rapidly. "But it's just, like, so real now. The wedding. You. Fawkes. I can't believe you're really doing it."

"I know, right?" Cady honked a half laugh/half sob. "Remember when we used to stay up till three doing those stupid retro MASH games?"

"Oh my God." Gemma giggled. "Remember how you always tried to get it to land on *mansion* for the house and *Ethan* for your husband?"

"And here I am getting married at Townsend Mansion, but to a totally different guy." Cady pulled back, swiping a mascara smudge from beneath one eye. "So much for teenage predictions."

"I mean, I don't think fucking Nostradamus could have predicted Fawkes," Gemma muttered half-jokingly.

Cady's expression shifted from playful to serious. "I know things have changed since I met Fawkes but—" Her throat tightened, momentarily choking off the words. "I couldn't do any of this without you. I couldn't do *life* without you. You know that right?"

Gemma snorted. "I've been exactly zero help through this process, and I know it. I'm the literal worst." Somehow, admitting this made the brick lodged in Gemma's chest feel thirty-seven percent smaller.

Cady shook her head emphatically. "No, *I'm* the literal worst.

Here you are, going through all these things, and I'm all disgustingly obsessed with a goddamn *man*."

"I mean," Gemma said through now-stuffy sinuses, "he *is* a pretty amazing man." She couldn't deny the catalog of hero shit her best friend's husband did on a daily basis—from healing his own scarred psyche to single-handedly helping forge Cady's dreams.

"He really is, isn't he?" Cady said, her smile softening around the edges. "My point is, I just need you to know that no matter what happens with me and Fox, you and me? We're non-negotiable. I could literally lose anything else in my life, but not you. Not. You."

A fierce pulse of love seemed to surge through their clasped hands and straight into Gemma's swollen heart.

She pulled her friend in for a sternum-crushing hug. "If the future doesn't involve us being cranky old bitches who shit their pants together at bingo, I don't want it."

Cady laughed into Gemma's hair. "You better fucking believe it."

They released each other. Gemma swiped tissues from the box provided and handed a wad to Cady.

"Ugh, is it too late to elope?" Cady said, dabbing at her cheeks. "These feels are going to be the death of me."

"You and me both," Gemma said.

Side by side on the raised platform, they turned to face the mirror.

"Now," Cady said, having recovered her composure. "Catch me up."

And as the seamstress and boutique owner bustled around them, pinning and tucking fabric with all the enthusiasm of reality TV wedding planners, Gemma did.

First about her father's ultimatum, Lyra and Harrison's arrival, her parents' unexpected return for their second honeymoon, and then, finally, about Gabe.

They were well into their second glasses of champagne by

then, and Gemma's cheeks felt equipped with their own internal furnaces as she spoke.

"Okay," Cady said, hands buried in her dress's billowing skirt. "This is just un-fucking-acceptable."

Gemma's stomach tightened. "How so?"

"You had sex with Gabe Kelly, and I'm just *now* getting the details?"

Relief flooded through her as they slid back onto familiar territory. "My ending the post-ex-dude drought isn't exactly at the top of your priority list at present."

Cady kicked her train out in an impressively stroppy *harrumph*. "After I get back from the honeymoon, we are *so* putting Taco Thursday Couch and Kush nights back on the schedule."

"Yes, ma'am." Gemma saluted. She'd dearly missed their ritual of watching trashy TV while eating delivery food and getting high. "I'm one hundred percent on board."

Turning to the side, Cady reached into her bra to rearrange her impressive rack in the gown's sweetheart neckline. "I'm thinking a martini and a rom-com marathon at my place. We can ogle Colin Firth in a wet shirt, and you can tell me about all the amazing sex you've had while I'm gone."

Gemma felt the vise around her chest tighten again. "I'm not exactly sure there will be much to report. Gabe and I have more of a short-term arrangement."

And why, in that moment, did this revelation make Gemma feel like her chest was scooped hollow?

In a beat that surprised Gemma to her very core, Cady held her gaze. "You never know."

Gemma forced herself to roll her shoulders back. "Next topic. So how do we want to handle this whole rehearsal dinner debacle?"

Cady grinned, her eyes twinkling with mischief. "What debacle? It's just a couple extra seats at the table."

"Seats occupied *by my parents*. Who are under the impression that Gabe and I are in a committed relationship, and will need to stay under that impression until they fuck off back to Brussels. It might get...awkward."

"You want to talk awkward?" The cathedral-length veil lifted from Cady's shoulders as she turned to Gemma. "This morning over cream of wheat, Fawkes's mom was explaining to my mom how, on the ranch, she uses her mouth to pull out the testicles when she has to castrate calves solo. To which my mom replied she'd take a bull's balls over prison toilet hooch any day."

"Okay, you win," Gemma said, feeling the weight of her worries lighten just a bit. "You're sure you really don't mind?"

"First of all," Cady began, her tone firm yet gentle, "I highly doubt your parents would want to cause a scene at my rehearsal dinner, especially seeing as they were like my second family growing up. Second, we'll have Vee and Myrtle on standby, ready to swoop in with a well-timed distraction if things start to head south."

"They're pretty excellent in that respect," Gemma conceded.

"Exactly." Cady nodded. "And worst-case scenario? We can always suggest a spontaneous game of charades. I've yet to meet anyone who can stay angry while acting out ridiculous phrases."

"All right, ladies!" Marguerite said, clapping her hands together. "I believe we have everything we need. Let's get you changed so we can make the final touches."

"Do you think Gemma could help me?" Cady asked, heading the overzealous attendant off. "Just for practice," she added when Marguerite's smile slipped from its moorings. "Since she'll need to do it the day of."

"Of course," Marguerite said.

Gemma and Cady both took up their glasses, and after a lengthy tour of the dress's various hidden hooks and hoops, Marguerite finally left them alone in the bridal changing suite.

"So," Cady began after Gemma had gently worked the last of the delicate fabric free from the elaborate buttons. "How was it?"

"Not too bad," Gemma said. "I can't promise it won't take me a few tries to find the loopy thing, but—"

"Not the dress." Cady nudged her. "The sex."

"I have no words." Gemma sighed.

"Well, make some up, because I am *dying*," Cady said.

Gemma swallowed hard, focusing on unlacing Cady's corset while she searched for an appropriate metaphor. "So, like, you remember my first car?"

"That Volkswagen Beetle with the hole in the floorboard that would always leak on your shoes whenever it rained, which was always?"

"Exactly," Gemma said. "And you remember how I kept a box of Ziploc bags in the car so I could just put one over my shoe to keep my sock from getting wet when I had to shift gears?"

Cady shuddered. "How could I forget?"

"Well, sex with Gabe is kind of like going from the Bug to a Bugatti. Kind of like you don't even realize how bad you had it or what you've let yourself get used to until all of a sudden you're in this brand-new leather interior with all these lights and knobs and buttons, and you hit a turbo switch and all of a sudden you're breaking land speed records and rewriting the laws of physics and you're not even sure if what you're doing is legal but you don't really care because it feels so damn good."

Cady stepped braced herself against Gemma's shoulder as she carefully stepped free of the puddle of fabric. "Holy shit."

"Yeah."

"Holy shit," Cady repeated.

"Yeah," Gemma said again.

"And this is a short-term arrangement *why*?"

The question was a dart aimed at the balloon of Gemma's sex-hazed high.

Because he's told me every possible way that we have no future.

Gemma summoned a shrug and lifted Cady's dress toward the padded hanger with *Mrs. Fawkes* spelled out in loopy rose gold wire between the sides.

"I'll do that!" Marguerite called, her hand sprouting through a crack in the curtain like a fleshy flower.

Cady and Gemma exchanged a look and suppressed a shared snicker.

After handing out the dress, Gemma turned her back so Cady could help her unzip.

Behind the lenses of her glasses, Cady's eyes widened.

Oops.

Gemma had forgotten about the roughly Kia logo-shaped bruise on the back of her thigh.

"It sort of started on the hood of this Kia," Gemma offered.

"And here I thought you were reaching for car metaphors out of nostalgia," Cady teased.

"The only thing I'll be reaching for out of nostalgia will be more of this," Gemma said, lifting her glass.

Cady followed suit. "Did your dad every figure out Lyra was the one who stole the bottle of Dom in his study?"

"Please," Gemma answered before draining the last of her glass. "Lyra could straight up confess and Dad would assume it was a noble act of self-sacrifice on my behalf to take the rap." A vivid image of them all seated around a table at the rehearsal dinner drifted into her mind, and with it, a fresh wave of pit-dampening anxiety.

Gemma idly wondered what the odds were that they would all get through this wedding without their plan exploding disastrously in all their faces.

For once, she didn't have to follow in her father's mathematical footsteps to know they weren't good.

FOURTEEN

Stiff Chassis

PROVIDES CONTROL, KEEPS ALL FOUR WHEELS ON THE GROUND

GABE TUGGED AT HIS COLLAR. THE STARCHED WHITE fabric chafed against his neck. He felt like an imposter in the one black suit he owned. The one he'd bought for court appearances back before he'd gotten a few extra prison muscles.

Guess it wasn't a lucky suit.

It fit kinda tight, but he was lucky enough the style seemed to tend in that direction these days. At least he didn't look *too* out of place amidst the manicured lawns and ivy-covered brick of the sprawling Townsend estate.

Damned if he didn't feel like he'd driven through a tree tunnel and landed in Narnia or some shit. Or at least Downton Abbey.

Caryn Townsend, the silver-streaked beauty at Ethan's other elbow, had the kind of money his father Patrick Kelly had only ever dreamed about. Aspired to.

Hurt people for.

Gabe broke that thought beneath his boot heel. Nothing about his past belonged in this enchanted place. No cinder blocks. No blackout curtains. No doors lined with every lock ever made. No machine parts or city mist that stank of humans and bad deeds.

Pretty good security and surveillance system, though. He'd

have to do some acrobatics to get into the garage and see what was going on there.

Gabe shoved the thought aside, reminding himself that wasn't something he noticed anymore.

The sun hung low over the horizon, casting the rehearsal dinner in hues of gold and rose. Candlelight flickered across the long farm table set up on the lawn, surrounded by Roman Fawkes and Cady Bloomquist's closest friends and family for the night-before-wedding-rehearsal dinner.

It was out of a movie. The prettiest place Gabe had ever been.

And still he wanted nothing to do with all this wedding bullshit in his own life. What a wicked lot of work and stress for something that rarely lasted and was *never* happy.

He looked across at Tom and Susan McKendrick as she licked her finger and smoothed down an unruly eyebrow of her husband's. Tom caught her hand and kissed the finger she'd licked with as much mischief a CPA in his fifties could muster.

Well. *Almost* never happy.

Gabe's eyes landed on Gemma. Her dark hair was lambent with an astonishing auburn under-glow in the sunset as she chatted with her twin. He still couldn't believe he was here as her date, about to spend an entire weekend playing boyfriend to the most captivating woman he'd ever met.

He really thought he'd hate this more.

She could make you happy.

Yeah, he agreed. *But what would I make her?*

Gemma was already happy. Sure, her life wasn't perfect, but it was good and, compared to what he'd had, fucking idyllic.

He was probably the worst thing she'd ever done, and he was committed to not being the biggest regret she ever had.

She turned to him, her dark curls cascading down her back, her eyes sparkling with joy and welcome as she patted the empty chair between her and Myrtle.

A place she'd kept for him.

Taking it, he remembered to smooth down his violet tie, courtesy of Marguerite's boutique making FAWKES AND CADY wedding paraphernalia.

Small towns. He'd never get used to it.

To Gemma's left, Lyra sat frowning at something Harrison whispered in her ear.

The ever-stylish Vee perched elegantly next to Myrtle, who kept jabbing Gabe with sharp elbows whenever someone said something that could be taken in the worst possible way. Vee's silver hair had been dyed lavender for tomorrow's event, setting off her regal, elegant features, while Myrtle's unruly mane of multi-streaked hair framed her round, rosy-cheeked face. Their laughter rang out across the table as they shared an inside joke, providing the perfect comic relief amid the light atmosphere.

Gabe was unaccountably glad when Darby and Ethan breezed in late, Darby taking the blame for a last-minute hair emergency.

She looked like a pink-haired Bettie Page with an extra poufy poodle skirt and her very obviously braless tits jostling a lacy camisole situation that was begging for a sweater or shawl or something.

Somehow, she made it look classy, so far be it from Gabe to question the Fashion Gods. Still, he didn't look below her neck. It would be like checking out your older sister's nipples.

Gross.

Ethan seemed both pleased and perturbed by said bosomy freedom, so *that* was fun to watch. Gabe knew the ex-cop wanted to stamp PROPERTY OF ETHAN TOWNSEND on Darb's every curve and then hide them behind corduroy. If he didn't treat Darby like she was some ancient sex and coffee goddess he'd pledged his eternal boring existence to, they'd have a problem.

But so far, so good.

"Would you look at that centerpiece!" The empty chair diagonal to Gabe was claimed by the one person he'd been pretending didn't exist: Father Aiden O'Malley. The man was actually *from* Ireland, which was hopefully the only reason he'd been invited. People loved to hear the Irish talk. Which was why Gabe's grandpa, Eoghan Kelly, had so many consecutive young, pretty wives even though he was a stone-cold monster.

Well, Gabe wasn't about to be fooled.

"Gemma, your creativity is a gift to us all." The priest flashed a wide white smile that lit his ginger complexion from the inside out. Man, if the dude didn't have a beard, he'd look like he still might need to finish puberty.

Don't fucking talk to her, demanded the voice in Gabe's head. The one he worked very carefully not to hand the microphone to.

Instead, he drained his champagne and wondered who talked fancy people into serving this shit to their guests. It went with nothing and made everyone blow circumspect burps into their napkins.

As the laughter around the table subsided, Gabe couldn't help but feel a tinge of unease. Father O'Malley picked up the bottle chilling at his elbow and refilled Susan and Lyra's champagne flutes before offering it to Gabe with a wordless tilt toward the rim of his glass.

Gabe had to swallow convulsively as he avoided looking at the dog collar. He couldn't glimpse one without choking on the faint smell of incense. Without feeling the rough fabric of an old cassock, and the cold, hard floor of the confessional box. Yup. All of it came rushing back, sending a shiver down his spine.

"More wine, Gabe?" Father O'Malley asked, his eyes crinkling with a warm smile.

"Nah," Gabe replied tersely, tightening his fingers around the stem of his glass. He watched, jaw clenching in silent protest, as the priest moved on to top off Gemma's glass.

"The little papier-mâché flowers mixed in with the knitted and real ones are a stroke of genius," Father O'Malley continued, apparently sporting a hard-on for Gemma's crafts that Gabe didn't appreciate even a little. "I'll have to commission a scarf for these Pacific Northwest winters I keep hearing about."

How about a noose?

"What did you say?" The priest's serene smile hadn't melted

one inch, though Gabe nearly shit a brick when he realized he'd accidentally muttered his inner thoughts to the table.

"Nothing. Sorry."

Gemma's fingers slid into his, but it didn't feel like censure. It felt like a habit.

A habit they'd never had the time to build. She was good at this, he realized. Pretending. She wore so many masks each day, and the girlfriend one was just too believable sometimes.

He could almost believe she adored him.

Gabe clenched and unclenched his jaw as he tried to breathe deeply and enjoy himself. It wasn't that he struggled to fit in with Gemma's family and friends. He was doing fine, and they'd really embraced Darby within their ranks, which boded well for him. With Vee and Myrtle holding court as the unofficial matriarchs of the table, it was destined to be an inclusive one.

Still... His muscles tensed beneath the fabric of his shirt, and an almost imperceptible tic developed at the corner of his eye. Where it was once inviting, the laughter and friendly banter around him now only seemed to amplify his sense of isolation.

That and the fact that Father O'Malley had that famous Irish gift of gab and wouldn't stop being charming as fuck.

"Hey," Gemma whispered, touching Gabe's arm gently as she made sure none of the soup course remained on her lips by dabbing them with her napkin. "You okay?"

"Uh, yeah," he muttered, forcing a weak smile.

"You're kind of quiet. Is it the food?" The concern in her eyes melted the iciest rage in the darkest places.

And he hated it. Because he needed that rage. It kept him safe.

"Don't worry, babe," he said, nudging her nose with his in an unplanned gesture of affection. "Just got a bit warm all of a sudden."

"You can take off your jacket if you'd like," Tom suggested kindly, his brow creased with concern. "You do look a bit pale."

"Thanks, but I'm good," Gabe insisted, checking Gemma's

dad for feeling some type of way over his physical proximity with his daughter.

Gabe *was* uncomfortably warm for a guy who didn't really like to wear much, and his tattoos would be painfully obvious because his concession to a jacket had been leaving off an undershirt.

The Irish didn't like layers in the heat.

It wasn't that he was ashamed of his art—he loved it—but he was still making first-ish impressions here. Shit like that mattered.

He cast a glance down the table at Fawkes, a famously scruffy kinda guy. The man wore a simple olive sweater pushed up to his elbows. Several blue tats flexed and shifted on his forearms, and no one seemed to notice.

Still. He got those in the military... People were cooler about that kind of thing.

Maybe Gabe just didn't want to take off any clothes or reveal any skin in front of—

"You sure you feel okay?" Myrtle asked, after he'd not even noticed her most recent jab. Someone had said the number sixty-nine, he thought, but he wasn't paying close enough attention.

"Just a long day at work. This food is fixing it, though." He summoned a smile he hoped didn't show too many of his teeth and unclenched his jaw to see if he could taste the lobster bisque yet.

"Okay." She accepted his lie and moved on to the next thing. "So, Father, I happen to know that the bride and groom aren't Catholic," Myrtle mentioned like the itty-bitty bull in the China shop that she was. "You still cool with marrying them? It won't even be in a church."

It was well known that Fawkes's PTSD kept him from the confines of walls as often as possible.

Father O'Malley gave a good-natured shrug and thanked the cater-waiter who took his soup bowl. "God is everywhere, Miss Myrtle, and I'm happy to bless any union as well matched as Cady and Roman's."

"What about theirs?" Gabe dipped his head toward Myrtle and Vee.

Aiden O'Malley's gaze finally sharpened, and his eyes skittered to the two married women. A direct abomination, according to his religion. "I believe love is love, Mr. Kelly."

A safe answer, Gabe thought, making room for the plate of wild mushroom risotto. "Tell that to your pope."

"Gabe, would you pass the rolls, please?" Gemma's mother's gentle, cultured tones were a courteous nudge in a safer direction.

Gabe blinked at the expectant faces turned his way, his hands frozen in place. She was cutting the tension he'd created with a butter knife.

He needed to pull his shit together.

Finally his brain caught up, and he passed the rolls, making sure his movements were gentle and unconcerned.

As she thanked him, he snagged a roll from the basket and tore into it, and the familiar comfort of food momentarily steadied his frayed nerves.

"So, Kelly." Harrison leaned around Lyra with a smirk. "How does a man of your...big Boston background...end up in a charming little nowhere town like Townsend Harbor?"

"It's Gabe," he reminded the douchewaffle who already knew what his fucking name was. "Kelly's my last name."

"My mistake. Kelly is a well-known last name from back where I come from," Harrison remarked, lustily sawing at his fillet.

Gabe's jaw clenched, turning the roll to sawdust in his mouth. Did Harrison know? He was from further up the New England map, where all the scrotum-swinging Wall Street yuppies lived.

Still. They got the news. News his family had made a few times.

"What brought you to the West Coast, Mr. Kelly?" Father O'Malley asked blithely.

"It's Gabe," he said *again* without looking at the man. "I came out here to visit my friend Darby, and learned Townsend

Harbor needed a master mechanic. I thought, why the fu—er why not?"

"'Master' means he took extra classes," Harrison explained to their end of the table.

Gabe wondered if he could do those air quotes with broken fingers. Man, someone needed to talk to the McKendrick women about their questionable taste in men.

"He's the best mechanic this town has seen." Gemma beamed at the table, squeezing his knee. "*And* he's a fabulous dancer."

"Yeah, he is!" Myrtle crowed, inviting half the table (the female half that'd seen just about everything he had to offer) to indulge in wicked little giggles.

If Gabe had to look at Gemma's dad, he might just pass the fuck out.

"You *are* warm," Gemma noted, wiping at a drop of sweat running from his temple with her napkin. "Here." Ignoring his feeble protests, and before he could figure out what had happened, she'd peeled the suit jacket down his shoulders and draped it on the back of his chair.

He had to admit, it was better now that he could feel the breeze through the thin shirt.

Reminding himself he'd once mouthed off to Bobby "the Butcher" Callahan and lived to talk about it helped him to gather enough nutsack to look Gemma's parents in the eyes.

They *were* noticing his tats beneath the thin cotton of his shirt, but they didn't seem distressed by them. In fact, Tom turned to the priest and said, "Gemma met Gabe when he answered her call for a tow truck. She said he's a handy guy to have around, and if anyone needs a fixer, it's Gemma."

Father O'Malley's eyes lit up. "Well, that's a bit of serendipity, isn't it?"

"Luckiest call I ever made." Gemma's glossed lips split into an angelic smile, and Gabe's insides liquified.

This isn't real.

"Well, with a name like Gabriel Kelly, it's sure as certain you were born with a bit o' the Irish luck." O'Malley winked, and Gabe swallowed bile. "It must be wonderful finding love in such an unexpected place."

Gemma blanched. "Oh, we're not—"

"Yeah, real lovely," Gabe said tightly. "Gemma gets a ton of flack from those around her, but I think she's the best person in the world. She's perfect. I can think of nothing about her that needs fixing."

Unsettled by the fact that he meant every word, he flicked a glance at her parents, Lyra, and Harrison, all of whom appeared a little stunned.

"Are you two planning to tie the knot, then?" the priest asked around an oblivious bite of his risotto.

Gemma's entire family froze in unison, and Gabe realized Vee and Myrtle were being uncharacteristically quiet.

Fuck. Fuck. Fuck. Fuck.

"I'm not Catholic," he announced, apropos of exactly nothing.

O'Malley's ginger brow lifted. "I saw the ghost of a tattoo beneath your white shirt that suggests otherwise."

The fuck was this asshole doing looking so close at his skin? Was he some kind of pervert?

"Hey, Darbs?" Gabe's temper was starting to outrun his brain, which meant his mouth was about to follow, if the intensity of his accent was anything to go by.

Which it was.

The barista looked over from the other side of the long table where she'd been talking to Caryn Townsend, her boyfriend's mother. A woman who, by all accounts, had been a "Karen" of the highest order until recently.

"Yo, bebe Gabes," she chirped back, using the nickname she'd come up with when he hadn't hit his seventeen-year-old grown spurt yet.

Gabe never looked away from Father O'Malley as he asked, "What's that church you made us all join so we could help women get abortions in Texas?"

"The Temple of Satan?" She snorted a laugh. "Texas has some religious laws they must apply to all churches, much to the legislature's dismay."

"The Temple of Satan." Gabe tapped the air as if he'd been perusing a menu. "That's about the extent of my religious leanings, father. I tend to avoid institutions who protect child molesters over women and queers, no offense."

Welp. He'd said that out loud at the dinner table.

With his face.

"I don't think you're supposed to use that word," Gemma whispered, her eyes wide, confused, and gathering moisture.

Her fingers became claws on his knee, and, with a sinking sense of inevitable pain, he knew he'd shit and fallen in it. It was bound to happen sooner or later, and Gabe would be mother fucked if he could stuff the darkness rising from his chest to his tongue back down. Not for anyone.

Not even for her.

Some wounds were too deep. Some damage too chaotic.

"It's okay!" Myrtle chimed in. "I'm queer as a three-dollar bill. And strange, too. Can't say I don't have the same question about your church, father. And I'm an old lady, so I can mean offense if I wanna."

Gabe allowed his shoulder blades to relax into the back of his chair.

Thank God—or whoever—for badass old hippie ladies.

He and Father O'Malley had almost the same color eyes. And neither of them blinked for longer than was healthy, probably, as the air around them crackled with tension.

Gabe let the priest see his demon, the one that was always lurking beneath the surface, ready to do something dangerous. His entire body was coiled iron. Cold. Hard. Impenetrable.

Say something. I dare you.

Gabe knew he'd not said a word out loud, because every part

of him was locked down to fight a very particular sort of tremble that often started in his bones.

To his astonishment, a strange glint streaked through the suddenly somber vicar. A spark of understanding followed by a deflating breath and a slight curl to his shoulders.

He knew what the fuck was up now. He. *Knew.*

O'Malley examined him in a different way than before. The man seemed to understand that Gabe was a tempest caged in human form, and one wrong move could unleash the storm. He broke eye contact first, took in the tattoos above his collar. The visible skin pinkened by rage. The arms bulging over Gabe's chest.

The priest *knew* who lurked in the shadows with the little boy Gabe used to be.

And it sure the fuck wasn't God. Just a man in a black cassock.

"Gabe?" Gemma's gentle whisper preceded both her hands winding with one of his, her palms clutching, damp, and freezing.

Fuck. That was his fault. He was doing that to her in real time.

He relaxed his neck muscles enough to look down at her.

"I don't know if this is great wedding dinner conversation," she whispered.

Son of a bitch. She was on the edge of tears, clearly panicking.

Suddenly aware of a blanket of silence, Gabe looked down the table, where necks were turned his direction in curiosity.

"Yeah. Right. Sorry." His throat had closed too far to say anything else. His breath sawed in and out of his chest like he'd run a triathlon before dinner. He wanted to say more. He wanted to say it so fucking bad. All of it. He wanted to scream it at everyone. Vomit his pain onto the pretty tablecloths and watch them streak with the filth that would never wash off. The same shit that tainted his entire fucking soul.

There wasn't enough bleach in the entire goddamn world.

He needed to leave. Now. Run. Get out and not look back.

Roman Fawkes snapped his fingers, pulling all attention to him.

Which wasn't hard—the guy was built like a Mack truck had had sex with sasquatch and squirted out a decent-looking dude. He was the only man at the table Gabe truly knew he should be afraid of. A silent, scary ex-soldier who moved though the world like he *wished a motherfucker would.*

Gabe was the motherfucker who probably wouldn't.

He glanced from Fawkes's shark-dark eyes to Cady's green gaze of concern and back.

"We good?" Fawkes asked him tersely.

Though they weren't the exact same animal, Fawkes and Gabe were able to engage in a language that wolves and lions had been using amongst themselves since the dawn of time.

Fawkes: Don't distress my queen before her wedding or we will have a problem.

Gabe: I didn't mean to show my claws and teeth on your turf. I will retract them.

It wasn't submission. Just concession.

"We're good," Fawkes said, his features softening in a way that filled Gabe with shame.

Licking on the heels of that shame came a rush of disgust. At himself. At everything. His teeth clenched against bile rising in his throat.

Everyone needed to look away. He was too naked. Too wound up. The walls were closing in, but there were no walls.

Dropping Gemma's hands, he stood abruptly, and his chair screeched against the stone floor as if he'd just laid rubber on the asphalt. "Excuse me."

Without waiting for a response, he stalked to the pool house in front of which they'd all parked. He made it to the nearest bathroom just in time to lose the contents of his stomach in the toilet.

Braced against the bowl, chest heaving, he could hear Father

O'Leary's smug voice in his head, assuring Gabe his suffering was God's will. He squeezed his eyes shut against the memories clawing at the edges of his mind, trying to break through. His body convulsed again, and he retched up whatever was left after the food was gone.

A soft knock rattled the bathroom door. "Gabe?" Gemma's concerned voice filtered through the wood.

Gabe rocked back to a crouch, wiping a trembling hand over his mouth. He looked toward the door as he struggled to breathe through an acid bath in his esophagus.

A body-length mirror had been affixed to the door, and the reflection staring back at Gabe was a stranger, pale, haunted eyes peering out of a face damp with cold sweat.

He could *feel* her standing there. He always seemed to be able to feel when she was around. When she was in the house. When she was awake or asleep.

His body just knew where her body was.

And wanted to be there, too.

Biting his cheek hard enough to taste blood stemmed the threat of frustrated emotion. He'd been enough of a little bitch today.

He was sorry now that he'd purged a little.

Just... So fucking sorry.

Sorry he was a freak. He didn't belong out there. With those people.

With her.

Another gentle knock. "Gabe... Are you okay?"

He swallowed hard, steeling himself.

Steel. It was cold. Strong. Hard. Heavy.

"I'm fine," he said gruffly.

"Gabe, what happened? What can I do?"

"I said *I'm fine*," he insisted, before softening his voice as much as his tight throat would allow as he ripped at his hair and tried to keep it together. "I'm just sick, I think. Sorry if I was an asshole." It sounded thin, even to him.

Something shifted against the door. Her hand, maybe? "Do you... Should I take you home?"

Home? What the fuck was that? Gemma had a home. A family. She had the love and concern of everyone in this town. And still she deserved more.

More than a broken fuckboi with more issues than intelligence.

"Go back to your family, Gemma," he begged. Though...there was enough gravel in his voice by now, it sounded more like a command.

"Um...okay." Her hurt reached through the solid oak and ripped the rest of his heart out of his chest. "If that's what you want."

What he wanted was to yank the door open and bury his face in her hair. He wanted to remind himself there was softness in this world. That there were people like her, who handed their hearts to whatever monster reached out in need of it.

If he saw her now, there was no telling what might happen. He was a live grenade right now. He could detonate in any and every conceivable way.

She didn't deserve that. Nor did anyone else.

Besides, he needed to go pack his shit and leave before Gemma's old man very understandably kicked him out.

"Just go," he groaned.

Only because he knew she already had.

When Gabe gathered himself off the floor, he splashed cold water on his face and scrubbed a hand over the back of his neck. The ache behind his eyes had blossomed into one hell of a headache.

Shit. He didn't know what to do. What would a good man do in this situation? Having not known many, he realized he had no idea what the next right thing would be. Any one of the Kellys would saunter back in and start some shit.

Should he leave? Was he more of an asshole if he bounced or stayed?

He should probably go out there and apologize... It was the last thing he *wanted* to do, so probably what he *should* do. Especially to Gemma.

Besides, this was a real tidy way to "break up." She now had a public excuse why this wouldn't work out.

His guts clenched again as he washed his hands and rinsed his mouth out with some travel mouthwash he found under the sink. Rich people's staff thought of everything.

His feet wouldn't move now. Because he didn't want to break up with Gemma.

She's not your girlfriend... Especially not after tonight.

Feeling like he was about to face a very well-deserved firing squad, he yanked open the door and marched into the fragrant evening.

To find that no one even noted his approach.

They were all laser-focused on Ethan Townsend's mother squaring off with another woman in a similar dress. If he remembered his introductions, the woman sat on the city council with Gemma. Janet? Judy? Jane?

"I don't know why you're so upset, Caryn," the woman was saying with treacle-sweet ironic bitchiness. "It's not the *same* dress, just similar. I mean, you should be flattered that I loved it so much, I wanted one of my own."

"Really?" Caryn's sneer uncovered wicked teeth, sharpened on the bones of her basic-bitch enemies. "You loved my dress?"

"Of course."

"Did you love it enough to fuck it like you did my late husband?"

Any other night, Gabe would have happily stuck around for the ensuing bloodbath. Instead, he turned his back on the pandemonium, crawled on his bike, and left.

FIFTEEN

All-knitter

A KNITTING MARATHON THAT RESULTS IN SLEEP LOST OR KNITTING ALL NIGHT.

GABE STORMED AROUND THE BASEMENT, SHOVING clothes into a duffel bag.

Worthless. Useless. A fucking dirtbag.

The words circled in his head like starving vultures. He'd shown his true colors tonight. And those colors were black and blue.

Time to get the fuck out of this house. Out of the bed he and Gemma had shared for a couple nights of bliss he had never even dared to dream of.

God, how could he have been so stupid? Guess you could take the kid out of the Kelly family, but not the Kelly temper out of the kid.

Just when things were feeling...

Feeling what? Hopeful? incredible?

Real.

That was where he'd gone off the fucking rails. Gabe had always been a great liar... Turned out he could fool himself over just about anyone.

The door creaked open behind him. "Gabe?"

He whirled around, heart pounding.

"I was worried when I didn't find you that you'd gotten really si—" Gemma hovered in the doorway staring at his bag, hazel eyes luminous with tears. "Wait. You're leaving?"

Gabe crossed his arms to keep from reaching out and dragging her into his chest. "Yeah, well. I'm a grown-ass man, Gemma. I can't cower in your parents' basement and pretend not to be the ex-con with charges that would make poor Susan clutch her pearls."

"But..." Gemma blinked. "Mom only wears prayer beads."

Gabe scrubbed at his forehead.

"It doesn't matter," she said quickly. "Sorry, my brain just spits stuff out like that sometimes. Look, Gabe, I want to talk about what happened back there."

"No, you don't," Gabe snarled.

Her teeth clacked shut, and he wanted to punch himself in the dick. It would be perfect to make her afraid of him on top of all his other crimes.

"Listen, Gemma, I'm not built like those people out there." He gestured at the entire world outside this room. "I can't sit by while Harrison's smug face is in need of rearranging. I can't keep my mouth shut while your parents shit on your dreams, because their concern looks too much like fear." He dragged both hands through his hair. "I won't smile and make nice with a priest who probably spent his life covering up for monsters like the one who—"

He bit off the rest of the sentence, chest heaving as he struggled for breath. Gemma stared at him, eyes wide and glassy with tears.

"Anyway. This was a bad idea. I knew it from the first, and damned if you aren't tempting enough to talk me off the edge of the cliff. But this?" He gestured between them with his tattooed fingers. "This was dead before *we* were even born."

Gabe shifted uncomfortably, trying to find a way around her that wouldn't bring their bodies into contact. He could feel the weight of her gaze, and it was both infuriating and intoxicating. He didn't want her pity, but he couldn't deny how even the sensation of her looking at him felt better than just about anything ever.

"Look." Gemma took a brave step forward, taking a deep breath. "I know you're angry."

"I'm not mad at you, Gemma," he said. "I'm an angry man, but not at *you*."

"I know," she said, grasping his arm and stunning him into stillness. "But I also saw something in you tonight, Gabe."

"A violent Southie piece of trash?"

"No," she insisted. "Something real and raw and vulnerable. Something I don't think you even know exists."

"Stop right there," Gabe sneered, the bitterness in his voice betraying his inner turmoil. "This isn't that story, Gemma. I'm not someone who needs saving from himself, or anyone else, okay? I look out for myself. In fact, I'm the only person I care about, okay? I'm just a selfish motherfucker who likes to corrupt nice girls like you... So...mission fucking accomplished. Can I leave now?"

There. Maybe she'd be disgusted enough to stop looking at him like that.

Instead, she stepped inside and shut the door behind her with a soft click. "I don't want you to run from me, Gabe. I don't want you to run from this. Not when—" She caught herself and visibly pivoted. "What I'm saying is, I don't want to save you." She caught his face between her hands, and her gaze burned into his. "I'm not scared of you, Gabriel Kelly. I'm not trying to change you or pity you or even push you into anything. I just... I want to know you. I don't want you to go."

Her words sliced through his defenses, threatening to illuminate where his shadows lived.

"If you knew me, you'd regret those words." He gently removed her hands, steeling himself against the heartbreak in her eyes. "Let me go, Gemma."

He meant she needed to move so he could leave.

Naw. He meant it in every way he could.

Gemma's chin trembled, but her gaze remained steady on his. "You once told me everyone deserves a chance at happiness. Maybe a second or third chance. Why don't you believe that about yourself?"

Gabe turned away, unable to bear the compassion in her eyes. "Because the things I've done..." His throat closed around the words. "There's no coming back from them. I came here so I couldn't hurt anyone. To keep to myself. Anything else isn't going to work."

"You don't know that." Gemma touched his arm, radiating warmth through the sleeve of his shirt.

"Shows how much you know." He quirked a halfhearted smile at her, but it just seemed to make her more likely to cry.

"Please, Gemma," he begged, splitting open the cracks in his heart to reveal the dark and rotted places inside. "Just let me leave. Not for my sake... For yours."

"No." Gemma hadn't so much said the word as felt it dragged from the deepest recesses of her being. No wonder people were always telling her she needed to use it more often. She watched it transform Gabe's face from resolute to astonished.

"No?" he repeated.

"I'm not letting you go," she said quietly. "Not until you tell me what this is really about." Gemma's heart thumped with the effort of holding her ground, pretending like inside, she wasn't quaking like an aspen.

Gabe's eyes flicked up, then away as he resumed shoving things in his duffel bag. "I already told you."

Employing the open posture she might when approaching a feral cat, Gemma took a step closer to him. "What you told me was a bunch of recycled rhetoric that I'm pretty sure you've been handing to anyone who expressed even remote interest in your wellbeing from the time you could talk."

Gabe zipped his bag and straightened. "Your family—"

"Screw my family!" She dragged a hand through her hair. "This is about the priest, isn't it? What he said at the rehearsal dinner." She stepped closer and grasped his arm. "Gabe, talk to me."

A muscle in his cheek jumped. "Leave it."

"I *can't*." The sudden fierceness of her voice startled them both. "I can't," she repeated, softer.

"Why the fuck not?"

Gemma took a deep breath and met his gaze. "Because I care about you."

The silence that followed was so thick that it seemed to press on her skin like a physical weight. All the times Gabe had put up walls between them, all the times she'd been too scared to let him in —it had all led to this moment. She couldn't bring herself to look away, feeling exposed and vulnerable as she waited for his response.

"You care about everyone, Gemma." His voice was gruff. "That's part of the problem."

"Not like this." Her throat worked over a difficult swallow. "Not like you."

His nostrils flared as he turned away from her, bunching his hands into fists at his sides.

"Please." Gemma placed a careful hand on his elbow. "*Please.* Let me be here for you. Like you've been for me."

Gabe's eyes shuttered, but not before she glimpsed the deep well of pain lurking beneath.

All at once, she knew.

The priest.

Gabe's questions. Accusations. All the things he'd said.

And the one thing he hadn't.

"Oh, Gabe." His name came out as a strangled groan as the full weight of her newfound knowledge rained down on her like hot tar.

For a long moment they stood there, his arm still fastened in her grip, the air between them charged with uncertainty. Then his shoulders slumped and she knew she'd won.

Victory, however, felt hollow.

With a ragged sigh, he sagged against the wall. Avoiding her gaze, he began to speak. "When I was a kid, we went to St. Augustine's sometimes. There was a priest there..." He trailed off, jaw clenching. "Younger guy. Had the 'cool priest' act nailed. Always ending classes early. Letting us swear when the bishop wasn't around."

Already, Gemma's palms had gone clammy, and the delicious dinner gathered in a heavy clot beneath her sternum.

"He invites me to be an altar boy. Says I have potential, unlike the other boys, who were mostly goof-offs and assholes." Gabe shrugged. "Show me a twelve-year-old boy who isn't."

Gemma nodded, afraid to speak lest the interruption pull him out of the narrative.

"I hadn't taken my first communion yet, but he said he'd teach me private classes, get me caught up."

Gemma's heart twisted. Oh God. She didn't want to believe— but the pain etched into Gabe's face told her all she needed to know. She reached for his hand and found it clammy, absent its usual warmth.

"What he taught me is just how easy it is for a man like him to get away with whatever the fuck he wants."

Revulsion and fury rose in equal measure. *That son of a bitch.* "Did you tell anyone?"

Gabe shrugged. "My brothers."

"They didn't believe you?"

"Oh, they believed me. Fuck, they'd even warned me, told me to steer clear of him, but I thought they were just giving me shit. Trying to ruin my chance at actually doing something good for once."

His bitter laugh made the hairs lift on Gemma's arms.

"Gabe." She softened her tone with effort. "I'm so sorry."

He shrugged, but his nonchalance rang hollow. "Like I said, ancient history. Got over it a long time ago."

"You don't just 'get over' something like that."

"Yeah?" Gabe looked up, gaze hard and challenging. "Watch me."

"I have." She lifted her chin. "And what I see is a man who's been carrying a hurt boy's burden for way too long."

His eyes widened even as his lips flattened into a line. "Horseshit. What happened *happened*, and no amount of bitching about it is gonna change that."

"You could reach out to the local diocese. Press charges—"

"And what's that gonna solve?" he asked. "What's the point of dragging it up now? The fucker died years ago. It doesn't matter."

Gemma grasped his hands, clutching them tight. "What was done to you *matters*. Your pain matters. *You* matter, Gabe. You deserve to feel angry, hurt, betrayed—"

"I don't want to *feel*!" Gabe wheeled on her, his eyes smoldering like banked coals. "I spent years outrunning this shit every way possible because I knew if I stopped for one second, I'd fucking drown." His features contorted in a tortured grimace. "But then I come here, and I meet you, and you say you want to know me, but how the fuck am I supposed to do that, Gemma? How the fuck am I supposed to open up when every time I do, this river of dark, ugly shit comes flooding out of me?"

Gabe's face crumpled, and the anguished sound that tore from his chest threatened to rend her heart.

Gemma pulled him against her, and for a long moment Gabe stood rigid in her arms. Then a shudder went through him and he sank to his knees, clinging to her middle like a drowning man as his ribcage shook with silent sobs. Imperfect anchor that she was, Gemma felt something solidify within her.

"You hold on to me," she whispered, stroking his hair. "You hold on to me, and I hold on to you until all the rivers run out."

And he did.

They did.

Hot tears slid down Gemma's cheeks, and she did nothing to stop them—hoping, irrationally, hers could be added to the balance owed for the years he'd carried this alone. He stayed there with his powerful arms circling her waist and his ear against her heart until the storm had eased.

"Come here." Gemma guided him to his feet and tugged him toward the bed, where she lay back and held her arms open to him.

Gabe buried his face in her neck, inhaling deeply. It was a small gesture, but the intimacy of it sent a shiver down Gemma's spine.

Mistaking her reaction for discomfort, he pulled back, his eyes dark with emotion. "Sorry," he said roughly. "That was—uh—wicked weird."

Gemma shook her head. "Don't you dare apologize. You have nothing to be sorry for."

For a long moment Gabe just gazed at her, eyes shining with wonder and awe.

"You're so light, Gemma McKendrick," he said softly, stroking her cheekbone with the rough pad of his thumb. "Such a shiny goddamn soul that I can barely look at you sometimes."

Gemma shifted closer, wrapping her arms around him until she felt his body begin to relax, his breathing deepen. The closeness between them seemed to break down the walls he'd built up around himself, and he spoke again, his voice barely a whisper. "I've never told anyone the whole story before."

"Never?" Gemma asked.

"Never."

"Thank you for trusting me," she murmured, tracing patterns on his arm.

The weight of their shared vulnerability seemed to pull them closer, charging the space between them with an electric current neither could ignore. Their eyes met, and it was as if they were seeing each other for the first time—raw, open, and real.

She leaned in and kissed him then, and as Gabe's mouth

moved hungrily against hers, she could feel the edges of his pain worn smooth by the clash. He slid his hands under her shirt, splaying fingers across her stomach.

Gemma arched into him, craving the heat of his skin against hers. Letting their bodies finish the conversation their tears had begun.

Gabe's tongue stroked against hers, waking within her a hunger that left Gemma feeling dizzy. Ravenous. Reckless.

A place within herself she rarely had permission to plumb. Like her impatience. And aspirations. And appetites. Her hot-wired mind's relentless engines churning out a thousand cravings all at once. Starved for dopamine. For sensation. For stimulation.

And always, always being denied. Delayed. Deferred.

Until now.

Until him.

Until this man who could match her on every point. Give as much as she could take. More, if she wanted it.

And dear God, did she want it.

With a throaty demand that caught even her off guard, she rolled over to straddle Gabe's lean hips.

His eyes grew heavy-lidded, and his hands settled on her waist as she yanked at his belt, zipper, and buttons until she could feel him already hard beneath the soft fabric of his boxer briefs. Gabe let out a low groan as she molded her palm to him and leaned down to nip at his lower lip. Deciding to test a hypothesis she'd formed after seeing how ticklish he was, she lightly scraped her teeth along his jaw until she reached his ear.

Flicking her tongue along the lobe, she was rewarded with a full-body shudder and a raw cry that made her instantly, mercilessly wet.

A fact she communicated by grabbing Gabe's hand and under the skirt of her cocktail dress.

No time for lists. No need, when she intended to take exactly what she wanted, exactly how she wanted it. For once.

Gabe's eyes were wide as he slipped his fingers beneath her

panties and ran them along the slippery seam of her sex. "Jesus, Gemma," he groaned, echoing her thoughts exactly.

She sat up abruptly and yanked her dress over her head with more enthusiasm than skill before reaching down to pop the clasp of her bra.

Gabe made a noise somewhere between a growl and a whimper as he cupped one in his hand, sucking hard on her nipple before sliding his finger inside her and circling her clit with his thumb.

Gemma's back arched and she came hard and fast in a quick succession of pulses that wrung her ragged. "You have something?" she asked, her voice smoky with anticipation.

Gabe's other hand slid up to cradle her back as he reached for the nightstand drawer and came back with a foil packet.

She peeled his shirt off as he sheathed himself, lifting her hips just enough for him to thumb his jeans down his hips and pull her panties to the side before she sank on him to the hilt.

Gabe's rippling abdominals flexed as he sat up, bringing them face to face. It was shockingly intimate to look him in the eye while he moved inside her, his hips angling and undulating, his piercing an occasional grazing pressure in places that made sparks pinwheel to Gemma's middle.

All the while, she watched his face carefully, knowing by some unnamable instinct that she could draw from him not only passion and pleasure, but the darkness that made her heart skip and her breath catch.

His anger. His sadness. His pain.

She imagined them flowing from him to her through the place where their bodies fused, filling her heart as he filled her body, both being changed in the process.

They fell into a rhythm that made Gabe's fingers dig into her hips as he trembled, his face flushed and his eyes sparking with flecks of gold as he met her gaze.

Gemma could feel the moment building inside her, shaking the walls of her control. Tightening around her like a fist. A hand she didn't know how to release. "Gabe," she whimpered, rolling her hips against his on a collision course with oblivion.

"Take us there, baby. Take us both."

So she did.

Gabe let out a roar as he surged deep and held her tight, and a cascade of sensation rolled out beneath them like the tide. His hands shook as they tangled in her hair, and his breath came in ragged grunts.

And then, with a gasp that felt like surrender, Gemma let go. Let go of control and fear and all the things she thought she had to prove.

The power of it sent jolts through her body until Gabe's grip on her waist was all that kept her from flying away.

They fell back on the bed together in a sweaty heap.

Gabe's breath slowed, then deepened.

Gemma pushed a damp lock of hair from his sweat-kissed forehead and knew she'd bought with her body the peace that smoothed his features in sleep.

She wasn't sure how long she'd wanted to comfort him this way, only that having him here, like this, felt so damn good.

Like maybe the best thing she'd done in a really long time.

And as they gave themselves over to pleasure, they found something far more precious in the temporary home of each other's bodies.

They found solace.

SIXTEEN

T.O.A.D.

TRASHED OBJECT ABANDONED IN DISGUST

Gabe leaned over the open hood of the '67 Mustang, inhaling the familiar smells of motor oil and gasoline. As he tightened a bolt, his mind wandered to Gemma.

Her smile. Her thoughtfulness. The way she scrunched her nose when she was deep in concentration.

Her perfect ass.

This whole time he'd assumed he'd followed his dick in her direction...

And then?

And then, while he was revisiting the sight of her riding his body into the sunset...he sometimes found himself thinking about mundane domestic moments—kissing her goodbye in the morning, cooking dinner together in the evening, picking up after the casualties of her burgeoning creativity.

Things he never thought he'd have or want.

But with Gemma, he was starting to imagine a real future together rather than just playing the part of fake boyfriend. Waking up tangled in her long, wild hair. Following her around the house just to watch that gorgeous ass sway in her chaste skirts.

He could get used to all that shit.

He *wanted* to.

"How's she running?"

A voice interrupted his daydream. Gabe looked up to see a short but striking Black man leaning in the open doorway, police badge glinting in the sun.

"Purring like a kitten," Gabe said cautiously, making sure to keep the car between him and the cop. If he had to, he could bolt out the back and jump the six-foot wall before the guy pulled his weapon.

"'67 'Stang, huh?" The man ran an appreciative hand along the gleaming chassis. "My dad had one just like it when I was a kid. Spent every weekend tuning her up together in the garage. Brings back good memories."

Gabe just nodded, hoping the deputy would state his business and move along.

As if plucking it from his head, the man said, "I'm looking for Gabriel—er—Cat-haul Patrick Kelly?"

It was *Cathal*, but no one expected an American to be able to say it.

"Who's asking?" Gabe replied warily.

"Deputy McGarvey," the man said, adjusting his shades. "I've got a court summons for you from"—he looked down at the envelope—"Massachusetts?"

"Great," Gabe said as he took a step forward while wiping his hand on the towel from his back pocket.

"Sorry to be the bearer of bad news," Deputy McGarvey said. "Just doing my job."

"Don't worry 'bout it." Not at all wanting the cop to sense the spike in his stress hormones, Gabe reached out and took the envelope, trying to end the interaction as quickly as possible.

Had to admit, if McGarvey wasn't wearing a uniform, they might've chatted for a bit. The man clearly knew his cars.

"Well, I'll let you get back to it," McGarvey said, pulling a form from somewhere. His ass, probably. "Just need you to sign for this."

While Gabe scrawled his signature hastily, the deputy cast an appreciative glance around the shop before patting the Mustang on the ass and ambling back to his cruiser.

Gabe ripped open the packet. His eyes widened in disbelief as he scanned the summons, heart sinking.

Identity theft? Credit card fraud?

In his name?

It didn't make any sense.

He'd done some shit in his life, but he'd never lowered himself to white-collar crime. Also, he'd kept his nose clean since getting out of prison, determined to leave that life behind. The only person who would have access to his personal information was...

"Dammit, Mikey," he muttered. It was *him*. He knew it. His younger brother had always been jealous of the way their father treated Gabe and had been a snide little fucker about him leaving.

Mikey didn't know old Pat Kelly's debatable soft spot for his second-to-last son had been born of a very Catholic guilt complex. Also, Mikey was a dumbass who'd gotten into public trouble more than once trying to emulate his big brothers' criminal activities, bringing the cops to their door.

But Gabe had no idea Mikey's resentment ran this deep. Clearly, he was trying to sabotage the fresh start Gabe had made for himself in Townsend Harbor.

To call him back to the fold? Or to send him back to prison?

Crumpling the summons angrily, Gabe cursed again. This changed everything. The life he was starting to build here, the sense of belonging, the possibility of a real future together... It would all go up in smoke if the extent of his criminal past came to light. Rich people didn't tend to hand their cars and cash to violent thieves.

On top of that—on top of everything—there was no way he could let an innocent like Gemma get dragged into the ugly mess his family had created. She deserved so much better than that. Better than his record that would keep them from ever renting anything. From his inked skin that would always need to be explained to the "nice" people in her life.

From his now apparently *ruined* credit.

He released his rage on a string of words that would have had old Deputy McGarvey drawing his weapon and kicked a dent in his new shoulder-high industrial tool storage tower.

Fucking thing was on wheels, so it just retreated over there. Unsatisfying.

Pain lanced through Gabe's chest as a realization hit his solar plexus like a sledgehammer.

It was over.

All of this? This fucking fantasy life? It wasn't safe anymore. He was an asshole for trying to have it in the first fucking place.

The old Gabe would have grabbed a tire iron and gone to work on shattering everything that made the Mustang beautiful before abandoning it all to hell.

But...he just couldn't. Mr. Tanaka loved that car. Gabe had found that out after a long and uncomfortably oversharing conversation about how Tanaka had raced his best friend to ask out the woman who'd become his wife in that car fifty-two years ago.

The man had lost his virginity in the back seat. It was kinda sweet.

And gross that Gabe knew that.

He caressed the flawless paint, wishing he could own something with a good memory attached to it.

It wasn't fair. For once in his goddamn life, he was trying to do the right thing. Could no one just let him have this? He was actively trying to be a good man.

Trying. So. God. Damn. Hard.

Gabe's hands curled into fists as he struggled to accept what he had to do. He had no choice—he'd have to leave Townsend Harbor. Disappear before Gemma's reputation could be tarnished by his sordid history. It was the only way he could protect her, even if it meant giving up the one person who made him feel whole.

Leaving Gemma would destroy him. But he knew it would be far more selfish to stay.

Gabe pictured her smiling face, those warm honey eyes that saw the good in him when no one else did. Losing that connection, that unwavering belief in him... It would leave an unfillable hole in his heart.

But her future, her happiness, had to come first. Gemma deserved to live her dream without being dragged down by his past mistakes.

Gabe swallowed hard against the ache in his throat. He had to do this last thing for her, to protect the life she'd built here.

Even if it killed him to walk away.

A GUST OF WIND SENT FALLEN LEAVES SWIRLING outside Bazaar Girls as Gemma clutched her Dirty Earl as if it were a life raft. She felt a burst of gratitude that she'd had the foresight to stop at brownies earlier for the dirty chai latte. The shop had been a complete and total madhouse, and after her and Gabe's exertions, exhaustion gnawed at the corners of her threadbare consciousness.

"Thank you, come again!" she called after a customer, her voice tinged with disbelief. Gemma couldn't help but marvel at the steady stream of patrons that flowed through her shop like tributaries merging into a river. Was this what success looked like? She could hardly remember the last time she'd felt so alive, so in control of her own destiny...

So completely, utterly, and deliciously fucked.

In the good way.

A flush rose on her cheeks as she recalled his strong, tattooed arms wrapped around her, his stubble grazing her skin...

"Ahem." A woman who looked to be in her late nineties or early triple digits huffed, giving her basket a nudge.

"That'll be forty-two fifty," Gemma said, bundling an impressive assortment of crocheting hooks. The woman clipped open her handbag and began stacking quarters, and Gemma's stomach tightened as another clump of patrons pushed through the door.

Exactly what in the shit was going on here?

"Welcome to Bazaar Girls!" she called.

While it lasts, her supremely unhelpful brain added.

Reeling backward in her memory, Gemma wrapped Gabe's voice around her much like the blanket they'd been under when they had their talk after Cady's rehearsal dinner almost a week ago.

After fully analyzing what a fucker Harrison Lynch was—how did the man manage to scrape his fork on his teeth *every single time* he took a bite—they agreed the best way to get back at him would be to snatch Bazaar Girls from his manicured grip.

Which meant proving to her father that Gemma had built enough of a business worth saving. Which meant reaching out to Gabe's "financial consultant"—i.e., his brother Mark. The kind of enterprising, entrepreneurial spirit capable of creative number crunching.

"Guy's an artist," Gabe had said. "The Houdini of hedge funds."

"But I don't have a hedge fund," Gemma had protested. "And didn't he die during one of his own tricks?"

"Only because some brat had punched him in the stomach," Gabe said. "Bad example. Point is, there all these laws on the books to help rich fucks hold on to their money. Mark knows 'em all. And then some. If he can't get your numbers in the black, we're just going to have to try something else."

"Like what?"

"Like never you mind," Gabe had said.

Was that it? Were all these customers part of the "never you mind?" Did that mean Mark hadn't found diddly?

The deliciously spicy chai turned to acid in Gemma's stomach. She nudged the cardboard cup aside and glanced down at her phone for approximately the ten thousandth time.

Nothing.

"I'll take these."

Gemma glanced up to find a woman with a ballet bun and thick-framed glasses holding a sheaf of Knotty Knitting Patterns Gemma had begun to sell recently at Darby's urging.

"Of course," she said. "That will be seventeen dollars even."

The woman handed over her card, but before Gemma could finish swiping it, her phone pinged from the counter. A regular old chime this time.

Thanks, Gabe.

From: M. Kelly

Subject: Financials

Gemma's pulse quickened and sweat instantly beaded on her upper lip.

What if it was bad news? What if everything she'd worked so hard for was about suck her down like shit-flavored quicksand?

"Here's your receipt." The thin slip of paper trembled slightly as Gemma held it out. "Have a great day!"

"Thanks—love your store!" the woman replied, leaving Gemma alone with her dread.

Her finger hovered over the email icon as if it might bite her. Her heart pounded a dull throb in her ears, drowning out the ambient buzz of the store.

"Okay, I'm looking," she announced to no one in particular. "I'm looking. I'm going to look."

Her finger remained stubbornly stationary.

Relax, baby. I got you.

Only, it sounded like *got-chew* the way Gabe said it.

And somehow the memory of that sound and its attendant sensations acted like a battery. A power source from which she could draw the will to move forward.

She pressed.

She read.

She read again.

The words swam before her eyes, refusing to coalesce into anything remotely comprehensible.

But then they did.

Mark's findings stated that Bazaar Girls had been profitable not only last quarter, but the one before that as well. That her tendency to avoid unpleasant tasks and the innate mortal terror of spreadsheets made her a lackluster bookkeeper was no shock to Gemma.

That the multitude of mistakes she almost certainly made might have artificially skewed the results to the negative hadn't occurred to her for even a second.

Because for as long as she could remember, Gemma had just operated on the assumption that, however bad she thought she was doing, in reality, it was probably worse.

That she didn't deserve the small sliver of self-deceptive daylight she allowed herself, but that she could be forgiven for preserving her own sanity.

And here was Gabe's brother telling her that she was actually doing...*better* than she thought?

Despite her best efforts to remain stoic, Gemma felt a grin of IQ-reducing breadth spread across her face.

"Is everything all right?" yet another patron she didn't recognize asked from the other side of the counter.

"Yep, just peachy," Gemma babbled while her mind floated somewhere in the ether. "Anything I can help you with?"

"You can try."

As the customer rattled off her request, Gemma darted her eyes back to the screen, skimming the email with growing impatience.

Another throat was aggressively cleared in her direction.

"Let me just sprint to the back and see what I can do," Gemma said, only having half heard the request. "I'll be right back."

As she hastily gathered the parts of the order that her short-term memory had managed to hold on to, she glanced back at the email on her screen.

She could scarcely feel the ground beneath her feet.

Gemma marched down her stepladder and out to the front of the shop, where she handed the items to her waiting customer and rang up the purchase.

She floated on a cloud of optimism and caffeine, basking in the heady vision of presenting this information to her father when the day was through.

At least, that had been the plan.

"Hello there, Gemma." The syrupy voice of Harrison Lynch oozed into her daydream, yanking her back to earth with a jolt. "Busy day?"

"Yes," she replied, gritting her teeth. "What do you want, Harrison?"

He stepped aside to reveal the woman beside him. "You've met Elizabeth Billings, the proprietress of Star-Crossed?"

Gemma took in the vision of flowing skirts and jangling bracelets. Elizabeth's silver hair was twisted into an elaborate braid adorned with beads, and her eyes sparkled with bright curiosity.

Gemma snorted. "Of course I've met her." She might have said this a hair defensively, considering she'd never actually made an effort to initiate a conversation beyond "good morning" or "have a good one" despite the fact that Elizabeth owned the neo-hippie new-age shop next door.

"It's lovely to finally see the inside of your place," Elizabeth replied, her voice melodic as wind chimes. "The energy is so...vibrant."

"Isn't it just delightful?" Harrison cooed like an obsequious pigeon. "I'm sure you can see the potential for the kind of expansion we discussed. With this additional space, you could expand Star-Crossed into an all-encompassing emporium of spiritual enlightenment. Think about it: yoga classes, meditation workshops, maybe even a vegan café."

"Expansion?" Gemma's mind raced, trying to decipher the full depth of his fuckery. "And, uh, how exactly would that work?"

"No need for you to worry about the practical details," Harrison said smugly, waving a dismissive hand. "Elizabeth and I can talk about that offline."

"Or we can talk about it now," Gemma said, her blood simmering beneath her skin. "Because I have this crazy idea that I ought to have a say in the fate of my own business."

"You mean your father's business," Harrison pointed out coolly.

Gemma's nostrils flared, taking in the scents of patchouli and lavender as Harrison leaned closer to Elizabeth. She watched with growing irritation as he attempted to massage her ego like a skilled puppeteer manipulating his marionettes.

"Just think of the synergies between the businesses. The Bazaar Girls brand would be perfect for the imports you were describing. It's a match made in metaphysical heaven."

"Hold it right the fuck up." Gemma's voice cut through the air like a guillotine, causing both Harrison and Elizabeth to startle. Her heart thudded in her chest as she widened her stance, subconsciously mimicking the posture she'd seen Gabe slide into in the handful of situations where he'd been threatened. Lifting her chin and straightening her spine, she came out from behind the cash register/fabric cutting desk and squared off with her sister's fiancé.

It felt odd...and a little thrilling.

She hadn't been this close to an outright confrontation since Nikki Windham had stuck patches to the Velcro fastenings of Cady's back brace on their field trip to the Wild Waves their junior year.

"I'd appreciate if you didn't show *my* store to prospective clients without prior notice *and* consent."

Harrison winked as if they'd shared an inside joke. "I'm simply helping your father explore his future options."

"Bazaar Girls isn't an 'option' you get to haggle over."

Gemma's voice rose, drawing the attention of several customers. She refused to let the slimy lawyer intimidate her. "This place means everything to me, and you might as well know now that I'm not going anywhere without a fight."

Harrison stared at her for a moment, opening and closing his mouth like an apoplectic carp.

But it was Elizabeth who spoke. "Perhaps we should discuss this another time," she said gently but firmly. "I'm hosting a full-moon cleansing circle, and I have to be very careful about exposing myself to conflict." Turning to Gemma, she placed warm fingers bedecked with chunky silver rings on her forearm. "You're very welcome to join us. If there's any negative energy you need help cleansing." The look she flicked at Harrison was entirely absent of any love and/or light.

Burn.

"I'd love that," Gemma said.

Harrison straightened his tie and turned to Elizabeth, his oily smile returning in full force. "I apologize for any confusion. But I'll get this straightened out and be in touch by EOD on Friday. Should I reach out via cell or—"

"These things have their own timing." Elizabeth gave him a deceptively mellow smile. "If it's meant to be, it will unfold in the universe's timing."

Gemma enjoyed a lingering surge of satisfaction.

Apparently, being filled with love and light still left plenty of room for a truly impressive passive-aggressive streak.

Elizabeth drifted toward the door, wispy skirts trailing behind her, and Gemma rounded on Harrison, her fists clenched.

"Get out of my store, Harrison," she demanded with a steely determination she'd never felt before.

His grin widened into a shark's predatory smile. "Oh, Gemma," he said in tone that made her want to punch him right in his stupid, smug face. "I'm so sorry for the confusion, but you don't seem to understand that this *isn't* your store. I'm here on your father's behalf."

"Funny, my father never mentioned to *me* that he'd already decided to sell."

He leaned in close enough for Gemma to smell his expensive aftershave and suit starch. "Perhaps he thought you couldn't handle the news, given your recent...instability."

Gemma took a deep breath and locked eyes with him, unyielding.

"Listen up, you weasel-faced, lying snake," she spat, jabbing an accusatory finger in his direction. "I have no idea what my father or sister see in you, but deep down we both know that you don't deserve to even kiss the ground Lyra walks on, much less become a part of our family."

Harrison flinched at the verbal assault but quickly composed himself.

"Really, Gemma?" he drawled, rolling his eyes. "That's a bit dramatic. Even for you."

"You want dramatic?" Her body trembled with adrenaline, and she could feel her heart pounding in her chest like a war drum. "I may not be able to force you out of my sister's life, but I sure as hell can force you out of my store. Because I'll cause a real scene right here and now."

"Enough, Gemma!" a familiar voice snapped from behind her.

The blood drained from Gemma's face as she whirled around to see Lyra standing there, her arms crossed, and her eyes narrowed in disapproval.

"Lyra, I—" she stammered, but her sister cut her off with a dismissive wave of her hand.

"Save it," Lyra said coldly. "I heard everything."

"Lyra, please, just—"

"You know what? No. Just...no," Lyra replied, her gaze flicking between Gemma and Harrison. "This man comes all the way from New York purely to help me pull your ass out of the fire, and this is how you respond?"

Gemma's jaw dropped as a mixture of hurt and disbelief

washed over her. She searched her sister's face for any sign of understanding or concern but found only indifference.

"How can you defend him?" she whispered, her voice cracking with emotion. "When all this time, he's been a manipulative, condescending—"

"*Enough!*" Lyra snapped. "I don't want to hear another word about it."

Gemma's face prickled with the sting of a thousand needles. All the fire that had fueled her just moments ago flickered out, leaving her feeling utterly lost and alone.

"I've tried." Lyra's voice was tight as she pinched the bridge of her nose. "I really have. I mean, Jesus. I've compromised months of work I put in on one of the most important cases of my career, postponed my own happiness, even *lied* to our parents, all to try to spare you from dealing with the fallout of your mistakes."

Gemma recoiled under the crushing weight of Lyra's disapproval, feeling it descend on her with suffocating force. Every breath had been wrested from the iron fist crushing her lungs.

The barest crescents of quicksilver gathered in Lyra's lower lids.

"Maybe it's time you learned to handle things yourself."

Gemma blinked rapidly, refusing to give Harrison the satisfaction of seeing her cry.

"Wow," she said, forcing a shaky laugh. "You must have graduated magna cum laude from the School of Tough Love. Thanks for the pep talk."

"Sometimes tough love is the only way to get through to you," Lyra retorted, her voice dripping with frustration.

"Or maybe, just maybe, it's code for 'I don't care enough to try anything else.'" The bitterness in Gemma's voice surprised even her, but she couldn't help it.

"Look, Gemma." Lyra sighed, rubbing her temples. "I love you, but I can't keep doing this. You need to figure this out on your own."

"That's literally all I've been doing forever." Gemma bit back the swell of emotion in her throat and took a deep breath to steady herself. "I figured out how to function in school even though I never understood why I had to struggle so much more than other people just to do the most basic tasks. I figured out what I had via TikTok, of all things, and then figured out how to get an official diagnosis. I figured out how to accept that I would always be the disappointing one despite it breaking my goddamn heart every time you got a smile, and I got a sigh. But the one thing I can't figure out is how to pretend that I'm happy you're with a man who doesn't see a tenth of who you really are."

A flicker of understanding crossed Lyra's face before it burned off like coastal fog. "I'm sorry you've struggled with this, Gemma. I really am. I know it's made things harder for you, and I wish to God it didn't. But you need to recognize that it's also made things harder for me." Red climbed her slim neck like the mercury in a thermometer. "Having a name for your problem may make the chaos it creates easier for you to accept, but it sure as hell doesn't make the consequences any less difficult for the people who love you, and it doesn't make it any easier for me to pick up the slack."

"You think I don't know that? You think I don't spend every day of my ridiculous, inconvenient life wishing I never have to see the look that's on your face right now? You don't think I wish that *I* could be hero child for once, or make our parents proud?"

The elegantly tapered shoulders of Lyra's beautifully cut suit sagged. A tiny gesture of comprehension that Gemma grabbed with both hands.

"Will you do one thing for me?" Gemma asked.

"You mean *another* thing?" her sister snapped, and though Gemma could see the flash of contrition that often followed one of her infamously sharp-tongued salvos, Lyra didn't apologize.

"Go home and open our time capsule box. Read what you wrote down when we were eleven and ask yourself if there's any part of the life that girl dreamed about that you still want."

Lyra's face remained a determined blank.

She didn't remember.

Or didn't *want* to.

They stared at each other, while poison from a decades-old wound infected the air between them.

Just then, Gemma's phone buzzed on the counter, drawing both their eyes to Gabe's name lit up on the screen.

"Right," Lyra replied acidly. "Because your judgment has always been so impeccable."

Without another word, Lyra grabbed her purse and stalked out of Bazaar Girls, her heels clacking against the concrete floor. Harrison followed shortly after, giving Gemma a smug smile on the way out.

When both figures had disappeared from sight, Gemma hurried behind the curtain separating her stockroom. There, she surrendered to the cold, empty sensation yawning open inside her.

When she pressed her forehead against the cool glass window, the first tears came.

Years of masking driven by an inexplicably messy brand of perfectionism had made her adept at living in the last minute— panicking all the way down to the wire, only to execute an uncanny last-minute play that saved the day, the relationship, whatever.

And for the first time in her life, Gemma wasn't sure if that was enough.

SEVENTEEN

Banged in the Plower

HOSE ISSUE CAUSES WEAK AIRFLOW TO PASSENGER CABIN

LIKE MOST PEOPLE NOT IN THEM, GABE FUCKING HATED weddings.

This one, though, was especially painful. Mostly because he would have been enjoying himself if he weren't so miserable.

As Gemma's plus-one, he was seated way too forward in the audience, but thoughtfully placed next to Darby.

"WTF was with you the other night?" she'd asked before his ass had hit the seat. "I texted you."

No one else seemed to remember his whole outburst, which was fine with him. Gabe didn't want to say why he couldn't come to the phone.

"You want to talk about it?" she offered, putting a hand on his shoulder.

Not today.

Probably not ever.

"I'm okay, Darbs."

Now she really looked worried. "Gabe. Tell me what is up," she ordered him, nudging him with her shoulder. "C'mon, fess up. Baristas are kind of like priests, except I can fuck who I want. Also, I can gossip about you later."

"You're nothing like a fucking priest, Darby," he said—the nicest compliment he could think of.

"Hokaaaay," she said, putting up her "don't shoot me" arms. "Christ, I forgot you Irishmen get cranky if you're left in the sun too long."

Not in the fucking mood for her ribbing, he snapped, "Darbs. *Stahp*. Could you just, like...fuck off a little bit?"

Ethan surged to his feet. "Excuse you?"

Darby threw her hand out to stop Ethan's advancing torso before he'd even finished deciding to come at Gabe. "It's okay—he can say that to me."

"The hell he can."

"*Fuck* isn't a bad word to the Irish." Darby's graceful neck twisted like an owl's as she looked back and up at her man. "He was being polite. Come sit by me, love."

Ethan sat. But he didn't look happy about it.

That was going to be his life with Darbs. Gabe hoped he was up for it.

He did his best to relax into the wedding. Or at least disappear into it. Autumn sun filtered through the lush canopy above, dappling the guests in shades of gold and green. The sweet scent of sun-ripe apples wafted through the air, and he couldn't help but feel a sense of awe. The picturesque scene was made all the more enchanting by the bride and groom exchanging heartfelt vows beneath a canopy of blossoming boughs.

Gemma stood at the altar in a chiffon dress, her hair swept up in artful curls. She looked like a wood nymph from one of the fairytale paintings Cady had in the fantasy section of Nevermore Bookstore.

But prettier.

He remained transfixed on her, taking in every detail of her maid of honor gown that accentuated her curves and highlighted the warmth of her skin. The setting sun cast a halo around her tousled hair topped with a crown of flowers, making her appear like an earth goddess descended from the heavens just to torment him with her allure.

Or some sappy horseshit like that.

Gabe blinked, trying to focus on the wedding instead of Gemma's slender neck and the way the fabric clung to her hips.

Fawkes's voice echoed over the gathering, earnest and full of emotion. "Cady, the moment I heard your voice...I knew everything would be different..."

Gabe fought the need to clear his throat. He'd felt that way about Gemma from the first. Apparently, there was an emptiness he hadn't known was there until she filled it.

Fawkes slid a ring onto Cady's finger. "You are my best friend, the one person I know I can count on. You're the love of my life, the start of my day, the final thought before I go to sleep..." The big man had to pause for a second, and even Gabe almost stopped breathing.

The raw vulnerability in Fawkes's voice struck a chord somewhere deep in his guts. Gabe found himself unexpectedly relating to the man's unwavering intensity about his woman. Unsettling thoughts began to surface, as he realized that his feelings for Gemma were being identified in real time.

At her best friend's fucking wedding.

And yet he knew the path before him led away from her, not toward.

"You're my world," Fawkes finished with *mostly* dry eyes.

Gabe's chest tightened as an evening breeze lifted Gemma's heavy hair off her shoulders.

The thought of leaving her behind tore him to shreds inside.

He was aware that his feelings of intense devotion for Gemma would bring him nothing but pain. But he was determined to savor this one blissful day and allow himself to indulge in fantasies a little while longer.

"By the power vested in me, I now pronounce you husband and wife," Father O'Malley declared. "You may kiss the bride."

As Fawkes dipped Cady into a passionate embrace and a kiss

only just this end of proper, Gabe couldn't tear his eyes away from Gemma. Her cheeks flushed with emotion, and her eyes sparkled like stars as she watched her best friend's happiness unfold.

Then she found him in the crowd, and their eyes locked.

The crowd erupted in applause, but he couldn't seem to join in.

Because he was watching the death of a dream he was never allowed to have.

∼

A PAVILION HAD BEEN SET UP BY A LANDSCAPED fountain, and as soon as the wedding party tromped toward the gardens for pictures, what remained of the guests beat feet for the open bar provided by Raven Creek Brewery, Ethan's fledgling new business.

Gabe lingered near the edge of the reception, nursing a glass of Irish whiskey to calm his nerves. His gaze tracked Gemma as she posed and posed. Fixed Cady's dress. Posed some more. Tripped on her own shoe and laughed with everyone when Fawkes caught her by the elbows and saved her from a nosedive.

That should be me. I should be holding her in those pictures. Standing with her. By her. Behind her. Being shuffled around by a bossy gay photographer, letting her shine while I block out the sun.

He chased the thought away with a huge gulp of single malt and then ordered a double.

Glancing over the crowd, he looked for a glowing pink head just so he could find someone familiar.

Friggin' Dudley Do-Right was behind the bar dealing with the initial rush, pulling pints, opening bottles of wine, and flashing his Superman smile above his—no fuckin' lie—dimpled chin.

Fuck, Darbs, way to sell out.

Maybe her Ken doll was packing heat under those khakis?

Didn't matter. Gabe didn't want to know.

The unseasonable early-autumn heat warred with his whiskey-warmed and Nordic-by-way-of-Irish blood, sending him sauntering toward the shade of an oak the size of the John Hancock building.

Before he could stake his claim to the tree on the outskirts of the gathering, a tall blonde woman lurched into the shade and leaned against the trunk three times her size to mess with her shoe.

Wait... Gabe paused. Wasn't that the mother of the bride?

He looked over his shoulder toward the garden, noting that pictures were all about the groom's family now. Cool, well, he'd pick a different tree to loiter under until Gemma was done.

Glancing back toward Cady's mom, he found himself staring into her gray-green eyes rimmed with the red of proud tears and maybe a little extra.

"Hey there, handsome," she said in a voice created by years of smoking and other terrible decisions. "Sorry about this..." She fished deeper against the heel of her shoe. "Fucking aerating this rich bitch's lawn over here isn't good for Payless pumps." Giving up, she yanked her shoes off with a sigh before saying, very unapologetically, "Apologies for my mouth."

"Not a fucking problem, ma'am. I'm from South Boston." In spite of himself, Gabe chuckled and cocked his head as he assessed the...everything about her.

Cady's mom had been in prison. Recently or frequently, he couldn't tell. He just knew. It was the way most former prisoners had about them.

Overstated courtesy. The shamelessness of having to shit in the open and living on a barter system for survival. Awareness of people's space and not to fucking be in it without permission. Unwillingness to put their back to a room full of people. A walk that was deceptively loose-limbed but tight in the chest and shoulders. Head on a constant swivel looking for a sucker punch. Eyes darting to escape routes and avoiding people who looked like narcs, snitches, and undercover cops, which—Gabe looked around—was everyone here but them, basically.

Gabe decided he didn't need to find another tree. This one was great.

"Uh. Congratulations to your daughter," he said, remembering his manners.

"My daughtah?" she teased, enjoying his accent. "Well, aren't you an adorable little hoodlum? Come stand by Momma, honey —I know that cute butt doesn't belong in slacks any more than my corns belong in heels."

Relaxing a little—okay, a lot—Gabe parallel-parked his "cute butt" by her and didn't even mind when she stole his tumbler and took in a gigantic, appreciative sniff, eyes rolling back like she'd done a line.

"Sober," she explained as she handed it back and stood shoulder to shoulder with him. "Damn, this town has way too many sexy people in it for its size," she lamented dramatically.

"Must be the farmers' market." He shrugged. "Everyone eats so many greens and seafood out here in the PNW, and what else is there to do but hike in paradise and kayak on a calm ocean?"

"Sure wasn't that way when I was *the trouble* passing through, or I might not have left. Which one of these girls do you belong to?" Her forehead wrinkled. "Or pretty boys—we're not supposed to assume anymore."

The trouble. If that wasn't accurate as fuck...

Gabe rewarded her with his most devilish Irish smile. "What makes you think I belong to anyone?"

"You kidding me? That smile's too dangerous to be let out of the house without permission." She cackled. "You were my fella, I'd chain you up in the basement."

"I just moved out of a basement, actually," he said, feeling his heart shriveling beneath his good nature. If only someone could chain him back to the bed...

He felt a presence before Myrtle sidled up next to him, her fingers wrapped around an incredibly pink drink that matched the boutonniere in her buttonhole. "Quite the shindig, no?" He glanced over to find the fertilizer maven already reaching out to

Cady's mom for an enthusiastic handshake. "We haven't been properly introduced. I'm Myrtle."

"Sheila."

"Gabe." He shook her hand next, a wry grin tugging at his mouth. "You're lucky to meet Myrtle—she and Vee are practically celebrities in this town."

"Infamous is more like it." Myrtle jabbed him in the ribs, as she seemed to love to do. "This the cool kids' tree?"

More like the hanging tree...

Vee arrived with a stein the size of all of Germany and a lovely new foam mustache. "To the Fawkeses!"

Gabe let Sheila take his whisky again so she could clink it with the other—er—older ladies before she indulged in another sniff and handed it back.

This woman liked to play with fire. He'd been the fire women like her paid for sometimes. He had a soft spot.

"To my baby girl," she said, her smile tighter and tougher than it should be.

They lapsed into a comfortable silence, observing the revelry around them. It felt good to have a place to stand, people to be next to, in a place like this. Ones who didn't need to constantly talk about their happy-people problems.

Problems he wished he had.

After a moment, Myrtle said, "Gemma sure looks pretty, eh? All that hair." At Cady's mom's inquiring look, she clarified, "He's Gemma's plus-one."

"Oh!" Sheila's eyes lit in such a way that Gabe could see her daughter lurking in them...with at least twenty fewer rough years. "That girl of yours is something special," she said with obvious warmth. "She takes care of my Cady when...when I can't." She swallowed three times, so Gabe looked away to give her a second to compose herself.

He followed her gaze to Gemma, catching her eye across the room. His heart swelled at the sight of her smile. "Yeah, she is something."

She was everything.

"Hold on to her. She's as lovely and loyal as they come."

Her words struck deep. Loyalty. Another thing extra important to criminals.

Criminals like him.

The only way he could let her go was because he couldn't face the way she'd eventually hate him if he held on to her.

Vee—who'd licked the foam from her lips—patted his arm, drawing him from his thoughts. "You look like a man with a lot on his mind."

"Nah." He sighed, scrubbing a hand over his jaw and wishing for another drink even as he drained the last of his.

"Are you sure?" Myrtle chirped. "Because the other night you were acting crazier than a straitjacket full of amphetamines and clown pubes."

Gabe almost shot expensive whiskey out his nose and was grateful for three pairs of old-lady hands clapping him on the back as he cleared it out of his lungs.

Looking up through watering eyes, he panicked to see that Gemma was almost upon them, trailing Lyra, Darby and...ugh... fucking Harrison.

Gabe already wanted to punch the guy, and he hadn't opened his mouth yet.

With a smile that told him she was still a little shy about the other night, Gemma slid against his side and clicked in like the missing piece to his puzzle. "Hi," she whispered.

"Hi," he said, breathing her in.

How many breaths did he have left with her?

How would he breathe again without her?

"You must have liked those bagpipes while they walked down the aisle, huh?" Harrison said to him. "Didn't think Cady's hubby was Irish."

"Bagpipes are Scottish, just like the last name Fawkes." Well... Kinda. Gabe didn't have time to address the complicated dynamics of the Scots-Irish to someone who had to take his shoes off to count to twenty. He turned to Darby. "Where's your Jolly Blond Giant?"

"Still at the bar." She sighed as she gazed back over the lawn and through the crowd to where the band was conducting a sound check. "I think he's just trying to avoid me making him dance."

"I'll save a dance for you," Gabe offered. "We'll have to show them how it's done."

"Keep your pants on this time," Harrison joked, inordinately pleased when the blue-hairs cackled like a trio of pervy witches.

Gabe didn't. Nor did Gemma.

The rest hadn't been around Harrison enough to hate everything that came out of his stupid mouth. Gabe preferred the feel of veneers cracking to real teeth... Did less damage to the knuckles.

Maybe someday he'd get to test Harrison's.

"You could teach me how to dance," Gemma said shyly. "I'm not good at it, but I follow directions well."

Yeah she fuckin' did. And then some.

"Dude, leave some of the females for the rest of us," Harrison said, his smile a little too bright in his evenly bronzed—if somewhat ochre-tinted—features. This guy must use a certain former president's color-blind spray tan people.

"You're standing right next to your fiancée." Lyra scuzzed him so dirty, even Gabe winced.

"I'm sorry, did you just call us *females*?" Darby stepped closer to Harrison, displaying that look in her eye that even cowed his father, sometimes.

When Darby went full-blown feminist, she was like a shark who smelled blood in the water. Hell, she'd taken a few chunks out of his own hide when schooling him in how to treat, worship, and revere women.

Lest she scratch his balls off with her wicked-sharp nails.

Harrison shrugged, unaware of what he was in for. "Yeah,

that's what *you* all are, isn't it? Or did one of you choose to be non-binary since last night?"

"Choose?" Vee echoed. "I beg your pardon, son. Did you say *choose*? As in you believe it's a choice?"

"He sure the fuck did," Darby answered, taking off her metaphorical gloves.

Selfishly, Gabe wanted to step in and throw his weight—or fists—around, but Darbs had a gun for a mouth and a bullet with Harrison's name on it. Instead, he instinctively tucked Gemma closer so she was out of the blood-spatter radius.

"I'm sorry." To his surprise, Darby turned to Lyra with a disgusted sneer. "Sorry you brought the dry broccoli."

Lyra's brows pointed up as her skin tightened over her skull and she folded lean, mean arms over her bony chest. "What did you say to me?"

"The bro-cco-li," Darby said louder and slower, as if she were talking to a particularly dense child. "You know, it's always the last vegetable left on the tray because no one wanted it there, and even ranch dressing won't make it edible."

Vee's gasp was all the sound for a full *one Mississippi*, until Myrtle took a loud sip of her drink. "Someone had to say it," she murmured, tossing an apparently unwanted pimento over her shoulder.

Harrison's ears turned a satisfying shade of purple.

"That's uncalled for," Lyra hissed, though she was staring holes into Darby's clavicle rather than her eyes.

Harrison pouted at Darby. "We're in public. You should calm down."

Oh no he didn't.

Again, Darby refused to grace the motherfucker with her attention, addressing Lyra in her cultured, clipped tones stolen from the trust fund that raised her. "I don't have the time or patience to properly *ignore* your problematic asswaffle of a boyfriend, Lyra—could you take him over there and ignore him for all of us?"

"Muzzle him, too," Gemma grumbled.

Gabe almost dropped all the way dead—would have, if doing so wouldn't have squished Gemma into the loamy ground that tried to swallow Sheila's heels.

Before he could figure out whether to laugh, die, or propose, Gemma caught his hand and stepped out. "Cady and Fawkes are finished with pictures. We have to be the first ones to dance when they invite people to the floor."

Allowing himself to be dragged along, Gabe said, "I thought you didn't know how."

The protest wasn't real, but he thought it made him seem more like a man who wasn't planning on abandoning her later.

"We'll just rock back and forth." She shrugged. "I've been doing that since middle school. "And don't you even think about showing up the bride and groom. Fawkes is a terrible dancer, but it's their day."

No surprise there. The groom fucking wrestled with bears and shit—who had time to learn the waltz?

"I would never."

He totally would. But not today.

He didn't feel like dancing.

They passed Tom and Susan, who each smiled their way but didn't break off from their group of... He was going to say middle-aged accountants? Teachers? Whoever they were, they looked like they golfed on purpose.

Luckily, the McKendricks seemed to have forgiven him...

Or Gemma had smoothed things over.

Trying not to think about what that conversation looked like, he decided to just savor this.

A last dance.

He would get to hold her one more time. He would get to indulge in her stolen glances, shared smiles, and every brush of her fingertips against his skin. He felt tight and needy. Craving the warmth of her body pressed close to him, and the sweet smell of her perfume mingled with the fragrant evening.

If this was to be their last night together, he would drink it like a relapsing addict.

Because there was nothing more intoxicating than Gemma's particular flavor. And he could travel the world over and never find anything like this. Like her.

"Isn't this beautiful?" she asked, eyes shining with unshed tears as she watched Fawkes and Cady—both of whom were fatherless—take the first dance. "They are so perfect for each other."

"Yeah," he said huskily. "They've got something...rare."

Something I could have given you if I was born under the right star. If loving you wouldn't ruin your whole fucking life.

Tonight, he wouldn't take his eyes from her. He'd memorized the curve of her smile, the softness of her touch, and the way her eyes sparkled in the moonlight. But he needed more.

Enough memory to last the rest of the years he'd live without her.

EIGHTEEN

Knit-picking

THE DREADED & TIME CONSUMING WEAVING IN THE ENDS OF YARN WHEN A PROJECT IS FINISHED.

GABE'S HAND CLOSED AROUND GEMMA'S AS HE LED HER out onto the dance floor beneath branches lit up by constellations of twinkling fairy lights overhead. A cool evening breeze sifted over her flushed cheeks, finally evaporating the perma-sweat she'd worked up seeing after Cady. And although Gabe had attentively taken care of her while she'd been tits-deep in maid of honor duties, Gemma felt every muscle in her body ache with fatigue.

"Ugh," she groaned, wincing as she shifted her weight from one sore foot to another. "These shoes are gorgeous, but I'm pretty sure the designer was secretly a sadist."

Gabe raised an eyebrow, concern etched on his rugged face. "I could rub them, if you want."

A curl of heat unfurled low in her belly at the thought of those strong, callused hands on her arches, working out the tension. She leaned in, brushing her lips over the sensitive shell of his ear. "Sir, you can rub anything you want, anytime you want."

His grip tightened briefly on her hip, then loosened. That fleeting flash of heat in his gaze cooled into something more guarded.

The flicker of alarm she'd felt on several occasions throughout the day flared back to vibrant life.

It wasn't necessarily that Gabe had been *quiet*. Quite the opposite.

She'd watch him hold his own with everyone from the white-shirted waitstaff to the wedding planner, putting everyone at ease with his particular brand of self-deprecating humor and easy East Coast banter.

Everyone but her.

Even now, in his arms, she couldn't shake the lingering feeling that something was...off.

Gemma burrowed further into him, needing his warm, solid body to wall off her spectacularly unhelpful thoughts.

"Have you ever noticed how passive-aggressive this song is?" she mused aloud, glancing up at Gabe with a wry smile as the familiar strains of "It Had to Be You" floated over them. "Like, 'with all your faults, I love you still.' What the hell is that about?"

"Maybe," Gabe conceded, his voice low and brooding. "I personally always thought it was refreshing. Like reassuring someone that they don't have to be perfect to be loved."

"Admitting your *own* faults is refreshing." Gemma toyed with the velvety, close-cropped hair at Gabe's nape. "Burying vague hints about someone else's in the middle of a love song is a dick move."

Speaking these words, she couldn't help but wonder if one of her own faults was responsible for Gabe's retreat. Turned out, a wedding was just about the perfect high-pressure scenario to send each and every one of them screaming to the surface.

Had she been too demanding? Too bossy? Too needy? Probably all of the above, and then some.

"Thanks for everything today, by the way," she said. "I couldn't have done it without you."

"Yeah, you could."

"Well, maybe. But I would have been ninety-six percent more miserable."

She felt his mouth lift in a smile as they danced cheek to cheek. "That's a very specific number."

"Oh!" she said, drawing back so she could look him in the eye. "Speaking of numbers, Mark was amazing."

"Was I right or was I right?"

"You were right," she said. "I mean, I have no idea what kind of wizardry was involved in producing those numbers, but I'm about it."

"The kind that's likely to pass a standard audit." Gabe's brows lowered in a gaze that was as sexy as it was crafty. "What did your dad have to say about them?"

"I haven't exactly had a chance to talk to him about them yet."

She hadn't exactly had the chance to talk to her dad about a lot of things. The true origins of her relationship—if she could call it that—being one of them.

"He has any questions, Mark would be happy to go over them in person."

Gemma wasn't sure if it was the accent or his personal history that made everything sound like it might be a euphemism, but she found it intensely endearing.

"Duly noted," she said, winding her arms about his neck.

Gabe's hand slid from her hip to her lower back in response.

Better.

But still...

Gemma closed her eyes, trying to focus on the subtle but solid beat of Gabe's heart as it reverberated through her body. "Are you okay?" she asked.

"Yeah," he said. "Why?"

Gemma pulled back to look up at him. "Because you've been about as chatty as a mime convention today, and frankly, I'm starting to get worried."

"Sorry," he replied, offering a halfhearted smile. "Guess all this wedding stuff kinda weirds me out."

"Anything specific?" she asked.

"Not really." Gabe pulled her closer as the song drew to a

close, but it felt like some kind of consolation prize. Like even as their bodies pressed together, an invisible chasm was widening between them.

"Whatever happens," she whispered, resting her head on his shoulder, "I'm glad I get to dance with you."

"Me too," he murmured, his breath warm against her hair. And for a moment—just a fleeting, fragile moment—Gemma allowed herself to believe that everything would be okay.

The song came to an end, and they disentangled themselves.

For no reason she could think of, Gemma made the monumental mistake of establishing eye contact with her parents. Her mom smiled and lifted her hand in a little wave.

"We're being summoned," she said with a sigh. "Do you mind if we go say hello to my parents? I promise to invent an emergency if it goes on longer than five minutes."

"Not at all."

Gabe laced his fingers with Gemma's as they made their way over to the side of the dance floor where her mom and dad were chatting animatedly with Cady's mom.

"Hey, there," Gemma greeted them, trying to sound casual.

"Sweetheart, you look lovely," her mother gushed, enveloping her in the familiar scent of jasmine and orange blossoms as she leaned in to plant a peck on Gemma's cheek.

"Thanks, Mom," she replied. "But the corset in this thing is slowly crushing my ribcage."

"Tell me about it," Cady's mom grumbled, pressing her hand to her lower back. "If hadn't ditched my waist trainer after all those pictures, I'd have stabbed someone with my shrimp fork. And this damn thing," she said, fussing with the sparkling beige shawl she'd been wrestling like it was a paralytic python, "I promised Cady I'd keep it on, but it's driving me batshit."

"I thought all bets were off once the bride and groom left the premises," Gabe said. "Isn't that how it usually goes?"

"Easy for you to say," Sheila muttered. "You look like all your tattoos are post-prison."

"Prison?"

Ice water spilled down Gemma's spine at the sound of Harrison's scotch-slurred voice behind them. His smoky, high-octane breath fumed Gemma's neck as he sidled up to them, claiming a place in the circle.

"You've been to prison?"

Gabe's jaw tightened, and Gemma could feel the tension radiating from him in dark, heavy pulses. She silently willed the verbal ball to drop, but Harrison chased it with dogged determination.

"It's nothing to be ashamed of," he said, his voice dripping with insincerity. "In fact, I'm sure everyone would *love* to hear your story."

"Yes," Gabe said through gritted teeth, locking gazes with Harrison. "Yes, I've been to prison."

The admission hung heavy in the air, casting a shadow over the festive atmosphere at the Townsend Mansion.

"See?" Harrison said, clapping Gabe on the back with a slap that made Gemma wince. "Wasn't that cathartic?"

Her thoughts raced as she struggled to find a way to defuse the situation. This conversation was taking the express train to Nowhere Good in short order.

"Anyone tried the cake yet?" she asked. "Because the pumpkin maple streusel layer is supposed to be insane."

"Do we get to ask what you were in for?" Harrison's chin elevated a notch.

"Harrison." Lyra's hand landed on the forearm connected to the hand clutching a sweating glass of amber liquid. "This is hardly the place."

He shrugged her off. "I'm just making conversation. And anyway, I'm sure your parents would like to know what kind of man their daughter has been sharing a roof with in their absence."

The blood drained from Gemma's face in a prickling rush.

"Sharing a roof with?" her father repeated. He'd gone pale beneath the blue-gray stubble beginning to shadow his jaw.

"Tom," her mother said. "Don't you think this is a discussion that would be better had tomorrow morning when we're all well rested and—"

"It was my idea," Gemma blurted. She and Gabe locked gazes. "I offered to rent the basement to Gabe because I thought it would help me get financially caught up before the deadline."

Her mother's freckled brow pinched at the center. "Deadline?"

"The deadline," Gemma repeated, more than happy to have someone else carry this information with her. "I had until the end of the third quarter to prove that Bazaar Girls was profitable."

Her mother's mouth dropped open as she turned to face Gemma's father. "You gave our daughter a deadline?"

He sighed and sheepishly looked at his shoes. "I thought it would motivate her. Get the engine running," he said, flicking a glance at Gabe, for whom Gemma was certain he'd chosen the metaphor.

"And did it?" Until that point, everyone seemed to have forgotten Sheila was there. Now all she was missing was popcorn and a box of Raisinets.

"Yes," Gemma said. "It did. And thanks to Gabe, I have the numbers to prove it."

"As touching as that is," Harrison interjected, "I still don't understand exactly how Gabe fits into this cozy picture. Are you...*together*, or aren't you?"

Gemma looked to Gabe. Not to seek an answer, but to give one.

"When Gabe first moved in," she began, addressing her parents rather than Harrison, "it was purely a business arrangement. But then you guys came home all of a sudden and we—*I*—lied. We pretended to be in a relationship so you wouldn't find out that he was living there because I was behind enough financially that I needed to rent the basement out to catch up."

Her parents stared at her, their expressions a mixture of confusion, hurt, and disbelief.

"But the truth is," she continued, afraid her nerve would fail her before her voice did, "I would be lucky to be *together* with Gabe. And whatever else comes of this, whatever you think of me or decide to do with the building, I'll never regret what we did. Because even just pretending to be with him has been the most real happiness I've felt in longer than I can remember."

Gemma swallowed against the painful lump in her throat as a tense frown carver deeper into Gabe's stony jaw.

"Gemma, I just don't understand why you would do something like that," her father said, his voice betraying his pain. "I know you used to tell fibs when you were younger, but I thought you'd grown out of that."

"I have," she insisted. "Mostly. It's just—" Gemma shook her head, willing the jumbled words in her mind to fall into some kind of order. "I *hate* letting you down, and every time I do, it gets that much harder to try anything at all. When you're constantly trying to live up to all these expectations, it gets so exhausting, and this was just easier. For me."

And the Academy Award does not *go to...*

"Sweetheart, it's not about our expectations," her mother said quietly, wringing her hands.

"It's about what you're capable of, Gemma," her father finished softly.

"You mean, what I *should* be capable of," Gemma said, her words sharpened by the hurt and frustration that had been building up inside her for years.

Her parents exchanged guarded looks, clearly uncomfortable with where this conversation was going.

"Sweetheart, that's not true," her mother protested, but the lack of conviction in her voice only fueled Gemma's anger.

"Isn't it? You never acknowledge how hard I've worked to build my business, or how much my neurodivergence affects every aspect of my life. I'm constantly trying to prove myself to you, but it's never enough. *I'm* never enough. Because I'm never going to be Lyra."

"Well, that's for damn sure," Harrison muttered. "In a way, it's kind of like she used up all the aptitude allotted and you —" his wet lips slanted in an ugly grin "— got what was left."

Gemma hadn't even fully registered the anger and humiliation when Gabe launched himself at Harrison with a guttural snarl. There was a sickening crunch as knuckles met nose and Harrison crumpled to the ground in a heap.

"Hey!" Ethan rushed over with Deputy McGarvey hot on his heels, both men moving to separate Gabe from the now prostrate Harrison, whose nose was leaking scarlet.

"Let go of me!" he spluttered indignantly from his position on the ground, glaring up at Gabe. "Arrest this man!"

"Sure thing, buddy," Deputy McGarvey replied with a dismissive eye roll.

"We'll get right on that," Ethan added.

As Gemma stared at Gabe, at his chest heaving with rage, she felt a shiver of fear race down her spine. The man she thought she knew so well had slipped through her fingers like sand, and she was left grappling with the sharp-edged reality of his violent past.

"Are you okay?" Lyra asked quietly.

"Fine," Gemma choked out, forcing herself to look away from Gabe. She focused instead on the lights twinkling above them, trying to steady her racing heart. "Just...didn't see that coming."

"Neither did Harrison," Lyra quipped, amusement peeking through the worry in her eyes.

Gemma managed a weak smile, but her thoughts were a tangled knot of fear and uncertainty. In that moment, she realized just how little she knew about the man who had become such an integral part of her life. And as Gabe stood there, fists clenched and fury burning in his eyes, she couldn't help but question everything she thought she understood about him—and herself.

"Come on, my guy," McGarvey said, reaching down to help Harrison up. "Let's get you to a bathroom."

Harrison slapped the deputy's hand away. "I'm more than capable of standing on my own."

Ethan and McGarvey traded a look. "You heard the man,"

Ethan said. Then, turning to Gabe, "Do I have any reason to assume that your continued presence here will be a problem?"

Gabe's jaw flexed. "No."

"Good." Ethan reached into the pocket of his pristinely creased khakis and came back with one of the small purple packets of tissues branded with Cady and Fawkes's wedding logo. After he tossed it at Harrison, he and McGarvey turned and sauntered back toward the beer tent.

Gemma's father cleared his throat. "I think we're going to go see about that cake," he said, glancing from Harrison to Lyra, to Gabe, to Gemma.

"I'll come with you," Lyra said.

"Hey," Harrison whined. "Aren't you going to help me?"

"I'm sure you're more than capable," Lyra said icily before turning back to Gemma. "Will you be all right?"

Gemma nodded. "Save me a piece."

"Will do." Their eyes met, and Lyra startled Gemma to the very core by wrapping her in the kind of bear hug they'd only ever exchanged as kids. After releasing her just as suddenly, she picked her way over the ludicrously green lawn to catch up with their parents.

Harrison's features contorted with disgust as he glared after her then kicked a lounge chair before he stalked toward the parking lot.

An eternity passed before Gabe finally spoke, his voice low and ragged, an apology burning in his eyes long before it found its way to his lips. "I'm sorry," he said. "I'm so sorry."

Gemma's throat constricted as she took in the remorse in his expression.

She wanted to reach out to him, to tell him that everything would be okay, but for once, her overdeveloped imagination and underdeveloped commitment to reality refused to cooperate.

The music receded into the distance and the world seemed to spin with dizzying speed, leaving Gemma lightheaded. Desperate for something solid to hold on to.

But knowing it couldn't be him. Knowing if she went to him now, he would still do what he'd already decided.

She could see it in his eyes, the way his face contorted with a mixture of regret and longing.

His heart was breaking.

And so was hers.

It was like a physical force between them, an invisible tether that threatened to drag her to him if she dared get too close. So instead, Gemma did the only thing she could think of to help him.

She stayed. She stayed, so he could go.

In the ambient party lights, his red-rimmed eyes fastened on hers, speaking the words his mouth couldn't.

"I should go get cleaned up." *I'm leaving.*

Gemma answered him in kind, her heart speaking when words failed. "Okay." *I know.*

"See you in a bit?" *I miss you already.*

"I'll be here." *Please don't go.*

With a heavy heart, she watched him turn and walk away, and his silhouette blurred through her tears.

In the distance, she could hear the sound of waves crashing against the rocky cliff that Townsend Mansion loomed over.

The sound seemed to grow louder as Gemma watched Gabe's retreating figure fade into darkness until all that was left was a faint outline against an inky-black backdrop, his pain radiating like a beacon in the night.

NINETEEN

Master/Slave Cylinder

THE DEVICE THAT CONVERTS PRESSURE FROM A DRIVER'S FOOT INTO HYDRAULIC PRESSURE

THAT NIGHT, GABE FINALLY ALLOWED HIMSELF TO REV the engine of his motorcycle, and the throaty roar echoed through the tree tunnel as he left Gemma—Townsend Harbor—behind. The evening air was crisp and cool, invigorating him as he sped down the twisting road. The scent of pine and damp earth filled his nostrils as he approached Highway 101 and Brewbies— Darby's quirky Airstream coffee shop.

She'd closed for the evening, but the little porch area was bathed in the soft glow of strung fairy lights that shimmered like a thousand stars against the dark canvas of the night sky. Fireflies flitted lazily through the air, their gentle bioluminescence casting a warm, ethereal light on the trailer that had been lovingly transformed into a cozy haven for caffeine addicts.

"Heya, kiddo!" Darby greeted him with that familiar grin, her eyes twinkling mischievously as she watered her outdoor planters with a colorful old watering can. "You know, I think your arrival might be responsible for at least half the downed tree lines, because *holy balls your bike is loud.*"

"Can't help it if she has a mind of her own," he replied with a slight smirk as he toed the kickstand and parked. "I know better than to tell a woman to quiet down when she roars."

Banter helped him pretend like his heart wasn't a lead weight in his stomach now.

"Are motorcycles women, too?"

He nodded. "Just like ships, storms, and God."

"True," she said, taking a step back to lean against the counter. "So, what brings you out at this hour? A late-night caffeine fix before a midnight ride?"

"Actually, I've got some news." Gabe shifted uncomfortably, mentally rehearsing the words he needed to say as he pulled a packed envelope from his deep jacket pocket and handed it to her. "I've earned enough from the auto shop to repay your initial investment with interest and...gratuity."

"Gabe!" She grinned in that way that'd stolen his breath when he was a post-pubescent boy looking to stick his dick into anything that would take it, and she was just his dad's pretty barista. "I'm so fucking happy for you! I thought you'd take at least a year to be in the black, but here you are! Crushing it." Darby flicked through the stacks of cash like an old pro but quirked a painted brow at him. "Bro, you know you can, like, just transfer this to me, right? Who even carries cash these days? Especially at your age?"

Gabe shrugged, punching his fists into his jacket pocket and pecking at a few rocks with the toe of his boot. "Old habits," he mumbled, realizing he'd never even thought about using traceable—if more convenient—methods of tender exchange. "Anyway... I'm headed back to Boston."

"Wait, what?" Darby's eyebrows shot up in surprise, and her face was a mixture of confusion and concern as she dropped the money on the picnic table and went to him. "Did someone die? How long will you be gone? Do you need me?"

He sighed, raking a hand through his hair as he tried to find the right words to articulate the turmoil inside him. It was harder than he thought. "It's not that simple, Darbs, but it's also not a big whoop. I'll handle it."

"Your family?" she asked, her voice softening with empathy.

"Gabe, you know we're here for you, right? You don't have to face this alone."

"Thanks, but this is something I need to do." Gabe's resolve strengthened; his jaw set with determination. He knew what he had to do, even if it meant leaving behind the people who had become like family to him.

"I get it," she said. "How long will you be gone? Need me to check in on the shop?"

Gabe took a step back out of slapping range before saying, "I put the shop on the market yesterday." He was going to donate the income to the further success of Gemma's shop. It was the least he could do.

Darby became incredibly still. She stared at him for long enough that he wondered if he should just turn around and go.

But no, he had to stay and take his lumps.

"Gabriel...you're leaving for good?"

Gabe looked at the sky so he wouldn't have to see her. So he wouldn't have to see himself reflected in her disappointment. "I have to."

She closed the space and punched him in the stomach. It landed softly, padded by his heavy jacket, but he pretended it hurt for her sake.

"No the fuck you don't, Gabe. Don't tell me you're being a piece of shit Kelly and running out on Gemma, who is half in love with you!"

And this was why he had to go.

Because no one would look at him and assume he had a *good* reason for doing anything. Because he wasn't a *good* guy from a *good* family with a *good* past and *good* tendencies.

Darby's eyes shimmered with unshed tears, reflecting the twinkling lights that adorned Brewbies like it was a fairytale kingdom.

A fairytale... That's all this ever was. Darby had found a Prince Charming, and he was happy for her. But he'd always known fairytales weren't meant for guys like him.

"You can't just leave, Gabe. What about Gemma?"

Her name hit like a lead pipe to the abdomen. "That was all pretend, Darbs. I told you that."

"Bullshit."

"This isn't *about* Gemma," Gabe insisted, his voice tight with suppressed emotion.

Well it was about Gemma, but not like Darby thought.

He glanced away, focusing on the fireflies that danced around them like tiny embers in flight. "It's Mikey. He's stolen my identity and committed fraud. If I don't go back to Boston and clear my name, I'll end up back in prison."

"Jesus, Gabe." Darby's hand flew to her mouth. "I had no idea. But dude, it doesn't mean you have to go back. You should stay here and seek legal help. I'm sure there's a lawyer in town who could—"

Gabe shook his head, flexing his tattooed fingers. "No. This is something I need to handle myself. It's my family, *my* mess."

"Is this really all about your brother, or are you just scared of getting too close to Gemma?" Darby's eyes narrowed, and her innate ability to read people shone through the veil of her worry.

"Both, maybe," Gabe admitted, his shoulders slumping as he stared at the ground. "But I can't ignore what's happening in Boston. You know that as well as I do."

"Maybe I can talk to your dad," Darby suggested. "He might be able to help."

Gabe shook his head, a dry chuckle escaping him despite the situation. "That won't work, Darbs. I, um... I hit the old man before I left. He'd probably let me rot before offering any assistance."

"Jesus," she muttered, again. "What the hell were you thinking?"

"Trust me, he had it coming," Gabe insisted, clenching his jaw at the memory. "But that doesn't change the fact that I need to go back and deal with this mess myself."

"Even if it means leaving Gemma?" Darby asked, her voice

barely above a whisper. Her fingers twitched on the tabletop, as if reaching out for a lifeline that wasn't there.

"*Especially* if it means leaving Gemma." The words tasted bitter on his tongue, but Gabe refused to let his own selfish desires tarnish the life he'd built in Townsend Harbor—or put Gemma in danger. "I can't drag her into my family's problems. She deserves better than that."

"Doesn't *she* get to decide that?"

"No!" Gabe exploded, literally kicking rocks this time. "No, the fuck she doesn't, Darby. What the fuck do you mean? *What?* You want her coming to my court dates with her craft projects? Getting searched to visit me in prison? Getting harassed by my piece-of-shit brothers, or worse, shaken down by my dad when there's no one to protect her from all that? No. Just no! Because she *would* is the thing. She'd fucking do it with a smile and cry about it later. Fuck that, Darby. Fuck that so *much*."

By the time he'd finished, he realized he'd driven Darby to collapse onto the picnic table bench. She wiped fat tears from her rouged cheeks.

He felt those tears in the soul he'd shoved back into its cold chrome container.

"Promise me you'll come back when you can." Darby's breath hitched, and her voice cracked with emotion. "Promise me this isn't the last time I get to see you."

Gabe sighed. "I don't know what happens next, Darbs. I can't promise anything. That's the fucking point."

She snapped, slamming her fist onto the table. "Do you really want to throw away everything you've built here? What if it works out? What if there is no jail time?"

Gabe took a deep breath, swallowing the lump in his throat. "I'm not throwing it away, Darby. I'm trying to protect it. Because it's always going to be something. You know that. Guys like me, we just... We were beat before we were born."

Darby stared at him for a long moment, her eyes searching his face as if seeking some hidden truth. Then, with a resigned sigh, she stood and reached for his hand.

Instead of taking it, he pulled her into a tight hug, feeling her tremble against him, inhaling the scent of her weird shampoo that kept her hair so bright. He committed it to memory—a reminder of the people he had come to care for in this sleepy bit of paradise.

Pulling away, Gabe gave Darby one last lingering look before striding out to his motorcycle. The sleek black machine gleamed beneath the moonlight, waiting to carry him back into the chaos he had tried so desperately to escape. He swung his leg over the seat, and the familiar sensation of leather meeting muscle anchored him as he turned the key and revved the engine to life.

As he adjusted his grip on the handlebars, Gabe's tattooed fingers flexed—the intricate Celtic designs a constant reminder of his heritage and the tangled web of family drama he had left behind. The weight of it all threatened to suffocate him.

With a final nod to Darby, Gabe rode off into the night, scattering fireflies like sparks in his wake.

TWENTY

U.F.O.

UN-FINISHED OBJECT

GEMMA PINCHED HER TEMPLES, WISHING SHE HAD A
pocket full of Advil or a vodka tonic. Maybe several vodka tonics.
All day, Bazaar Girls had been a zoo, packed to the rafters with
tourists. The annual Townsend Harbor fall festival brought out
the best in the town and the worst in its residents. Namely, their
shameless exploitation of eager festival attendees' insatiable need
to spend money on cheap crap.

Which Gemma had, luckily, stocked up on two weeks early
for once.

She rang up a customer's lavender sachets, felt pumpkin craft
kit, and goat milk lotion, forcing a smile. "That'll be forty-two
fifty."

The woman handed over a wad of bills, clutching her
purchases. "This is the cutest little shop. So charming!"

Gemma gritted her teeth. If she heard "charming" one more
time, she'd go full-on banshee.

The door chimed as another customer entered. Gemma
glanced up, ready to pitch wares that were about as homemade as
a toaster oven, when she spotted Lyra. Wearing a painfully chic
camel-colored coat and her trademark *can we hurry this up?* glare,
she eyed the final straggler hovering over the Boho Button Bin

that Gemma had slapped together with a contact-paper-covered shoebox and a vat o' buttons she'd purchased from Amazon.

Lyra sidled up to the counter, her lips pursed, buttery leather boot tapping.

"I'm sorry," the customer said, scooting over to make room. "Did you want to look?"

"What I *want* is to be paid a salary roughly equivalent to the old white men in my firm and to be laid often and well. Since neither of those things appears to be imminent, I'd like to be able to talk to my sister before the heat death of the universe. Think you could manage that?"

The woman's forehead creased. "I'm sorry?"

"I would be too if my chief thrill in life was digging through a shoebox of plastic notions while my husband browses fly-fishing reels down at Big Rod's Float Your Boat. Which is still open, by the way. Whereas my sister's craft store is not. And yet here you are."

"I beg your par—"

"Oh for fuck's sake." Lyra sighed, digging through her purse. "How much did you pay for this shit?" she asked Gemma. "Ten dollars? Twenty?" After slapping two crisp bills down on the counter, she picked up the entire box and wedged it against the woman's sternum. "Happy birthday."

Behind her schoolteacher glasses, the woman's eyes widened. "How did you know it was my birthday?"

"I didn't. It's an expression. Like fuck off." Hands on the startled woman's bony shoulders, Lyra steered her toward the door. Once she'd been ejected into the constant stream of foot traffic, Lyra locked it behind her and flipped the Open sign to the Closed side.

"Hi to you too," Gemma said.

"Do you have any alcohol?" Lyra shrugged out of her coat. "I need some alcohol."

Gemma would too, if she'd spent the entire day sitting through a slideshow of their parents' vacation pictures.

And here's your mother and I at the Museum of Maritime Technology. Did you know there are actually three different kinds of clove hitch knots used by the Royal Navy?

"You're in luck," Gemma said, coming around from behind the register. "I have an open bottle of Merlot from the last Stitch 'n Bitch club in the mini fridge."

"Perfect." Lyra headed for the stockroom, returning moments later with two glasses and the wine. She filled each glass to the brim and handed one to Gemma. "*Salut.*"

Gemma clinked her glass against Lyra's and took a gulp of the velvety red wine just as someone pecked on the window.

Glancing at Lyra, Gemma momentarily thought her sister might be in danger of sprouting horns and a tail, until she saw that it was Darby.

"I'll get it," she said, rising from the old Chesterfield to unlock and relock the door.

Darby breezed in trailing the ghost of coffee and cinnamon. When she spotted the wine glasses, her eyebrows rose. "Rough day?"

"Obligatory parental interaction," Lyra replied with a dramatic eye roll.

"Oh geez." Darby winced. "Want me to hide you in my attic?"

"If only," Lyra said. "Hiding anywhere in Townsend Harbor is pretty much not a thing."

About that, she was absolutely correct.

Though Gemma had surrendered her crown as Gossip Queen around the time Bazaar Girls' P&Ls began to bleed, she'd been privy to several accounts of Gabe and Harrison's dustup at the wedding reception.

In addition to the fallout between Lyra and Harrison. That Harrison had flown back to New York City alone had quickly spread from the driver of the lone cab company that provided shuttle service to SeaTac to Judy by way of the gas station attendant on Highway 20.

Gemma was just as surprised as any of them that Lyra had extended her stay. More so, maybe.

"In that case, you should definitely come to the fall festival tonight," Darby said. "You could at least drown your sorrows in fried Oreos and throw pies at Mayor Stewart."

Gemma scooted to the edge of her cushion. "Say what now?"

Darby tucked a hot-pink curl behind her ear. "How have you not heard about this?"

"Because she's been working absolutely insane hours when she's not hiding in her emotional support blanket cave watching *Star Trek: Lower Decks* to distract herself from sickening heartbreak," Lyra reported.

Hearing her workaholic sister diagnose Gemma thus elicited an odd surge of pride. Faced with a situation that made her want to curl into a ball and sob, she had been able to throw herself into work.

It was actually kind of refreshing.

Darby's plump pout turned down at the corners. "Well then, you are *definitely* coming tonight, because I'm pretty sure nailing Hair Plugs McBrotox with a Boston cream counts as therapy."

Gemma really wished Darby hadn't said Boston. She had been lowkey Google Maps-stalking Gabe's old neighborhood. Not that she'd expected him to magically appear in one of the Street View images or anything, but she still liked to look. Liked to imagine Gabe sauntering down the street in front of Kelly's Pub with his loose-hipped gait.

"Okay, fine," Gemma agreed. "But no way am I wasting a Boston cream on that shitbird. Basic-bitch cherry or bust."

"See, I'd have gone with pumpkin." The pointy toe of Lyra's wicked-looking pump jiggled against the coffee table's leg. "More aerodynamic."

"Why not try all three?" Darby suggested before stealing a sip of Gemma's wine and handing it back. "Because: charity."

"I like the way you think," Lyra said.

Now that Harrison was out of the picture—or at least rele-

gated to the occasional photo bomb in the background—Gemma
had definitely noticed small shifts in the foundation of their relationship. A conspiratorial look behind their parents' back. A
binge-show suggestion Lyra didn't quite hate.

"It's settled." Slapping her hands on the skirt of her swingy
pinup dress, Darby pushed herself up. "Meet at my booth at seven
thirty?"

"Sounds good," Gemma agreed, relishing anew her decision
not to sign up for a booth of her own, as she had every year for the
last five years.

And every year, she almost always lost out after having
invested way too much money on banners and swag, giveaways
and grab bags that probably ended up stuffed in a corner in someone's closet—if not in the recycling bin down the street.

What had really thrown Gemma was how much FOMO she
wasn't feeling. How satisfying it was to reach for a fuck to give
and come up empty-handed.

In fact, she'd been quiet-quitting all kinds of things lately.

The Historical Preservation Society. The Arts Commission. The
Library Advisory Board. Even the Wildfire Preparedness Commit-
tee, which had previously given her access to the unreasonably attrac-
tive volunteer fireman whose forearms made her joke about resorting
to clandestine acts of arson just so she could ride him down a ladder.

She wasn't *entirely* sure if it was depression or radical self-
acceptance but found neither scenario bothered her overmuch.

After locking the door, Lyra returned to the couch, but
perched on the edge of the cushion.

To business.

"So," she began, her voice level and even. "I wanted to
apologize."

Gemma shot her a sideways glance. "For what?"

Dropping her gaze to her lap, Lyra traced the impeccable
crease in her tailored trousers. "For this whole thing with Harrison, for starters."

Gemma lifted her glass and took a healthy swallow. "What about him?"

It was a question not to emphasize her ignorance of any potential issues, but to narrow it down to which one of an assload she was referring to.

"For not really understanding what you've been going through these last few months," Lyra replied, folding her hands in her lap. "When Dad first told me about Bazaar Girls struggling, I thought that maybe you'd just lost interest, so selling might actually be best for everyone."

Gemma winced but couldn't deny the validity of her sister's suspicion. It had happened before. It would most likely happen again.

"Anyway," Lyra continued. "I was going to fly out here alone initially, but he was doing his love-bombing Mr. Supportive thing, telling me he really wanted me to be able to be there for my family, and idiot that I am, I believed him."

The shadow that flickered behind her sister's eyes elicited a sympathetic catch in Gemma's chest. "You're not an idiot, Lyra. He's really good at what he does."

Lyra reached for her wine. "Once he got here, he started pulling all the usual shit. Hinting how we never go see his family. How he's wanted to take a vacation forever but had to use his days for Cady's wedding instead. And it's like even when I know these tests of loyalty are coming, I always fucking fail."

"I understand," Gemma said, leaning forward and putting her hand on top of her sister's.

"Anyway." Lyra furiously dashed a tear from the corner of her eye. "That day, when we came to your shop, I should have been on your side, and I'm sorry."

"You're *by* my side, Lyra. You have been from the beginning. That goes both ways."

A veteran of a relationship with a novice narcissist, Gemma knew that pushing too hard would only serve to slam shut the door she was attempting to hold open. If Lyra decided to boot Harrison to the curb, it would have to be on her terms.

But Gemma *could* hope, perhaps the fall festival might help swing things in her favor.

~

THE SEASONALLY THEMED BACCHANALIA OF CARNIVAL food and bizarre contests was in full swing by the time they arrived.

Strings of lights crisscrossed over the crowded midway, illuminating spinning rides, food trucks, and game booths. The air was alive with laughter, shouts from the various rides, and the heavenly scent of funnel cakes, corn dogs, and all manner of other fried items.

Gemma drew in a deep breath, letting the nostalgia wash over her. For a moment, her heartache faded into the background, crowded out by a powerful sense of nostalgia.

Lyra nudged her. "See, I told you this was a good idea."

"You were right." Gemma smiled at her sister. "As usual."

"I won't let it go to my head." Lyra's eyes sparkled in the colorful light. "So, what should we do first? Cornhole? Pick-a-Duck? The ring toss? Or do you want to jump right on the Zipper and goose our adrenaline?"

Gemma laughed. "How about we start with something less likely to induce projectile vomiting? Like the cake walk. Or—ooh! The fortune-teller."

She pointed to a neon sign advertising Madame Zelda's Psychic Readings.

Lyra made a face. "Seriously?"

Gemma clasped her hands and pressed them to her sternum in supplication. "Please?"

Lyra rolled her eyes. "Fine. But if she tells me I'm destined to be a cat lady, I'm blaming you."

"Deal," Gemma agreed, chuckling as they entered the tent and were greeted by a woman draped in flowing fabrics and layers of chunky jewelry. The air inside was thick with the scent of incense, and a single candle cast flickering shadows across the fabric walls.

"Welcome, my dears," the woman crooned, gesturing for them to sit before her. "I am Madame Zara."

Lyra's eyes narrowed. "I thought it was Zelda."

The woman sat up straighter in her chair. "That's what I said."

Glancing at her sister, Gemma received a very vivid *see?* look.

"Who would like to go first?" Madame Zelda asked, resting ring-choked fingers on a whole-ass crystal ball.

"I guess I will," Lyra deadpanned, but obliged and held out her hand for Madame Zelda to examine.

"Cross my palm with silver, child, and I'll tell you your fortune," Madame Zelda intoned in an overblown European accent of dubious origins.

Lyra rolled her eyes but dug in her bag and handed the woman a five-dollar bill. "Sorry. I'm fresh out of pieces of eight," she said dryly, offering up her hand.

"Ah, yes," Madame Zelda murmured, tracing a red, dagger-like fingernail along Lyra's upturned palm. "I see great change in your future."

"Really? That's so vague it could apply to anyone," Lyra retorted, glancing at Gemma. "You know what I see? A fire hazard. If that candle gets anywhere near those polyester curtains, this thing is going up like a tinderbox."

Madame Zelda's eyes narrowed as she pulled Lyra's hand closer, squinting at it like it was a menu she was struggling to read. "You have the gift."

"What gift?"

"The sight," Madame Zelda said gravely.

"Lady, I can't even pick the right line at the supermarket," Lyra said. "If I have a gift, it's the kind I'd return for store credit."

Madame Zelda's rheumy eyes widened, and the reflection of the candle flickered in one pupil. "Your gift is newly awakened," she said. "You have a strong intuition and the ability to see beyond the veil. Use it to help others, and it will bring you great joy."

"Or a repurposed army surplus tent at a county fair?"

"*He'll* make a believer of you," the psychic said.

"Is that he with a capital H?" Lyra asked. "Because if He's currently on the line, I have some more specific questions I'd like to ask."

The psychic's teeth were smudged with red lipstick when she smiled. "Your soul mate, of course." Her gaze landed on Lyra's gumball-sized engagement ring. "He is yet in your future."

Gemma made a mental note to tip Madame Zara/Zelda extra.

A flush crept up Lyra's neck as she jerked back her hand. "Thanks, but I think you may have me confused with someone else."

"The spirits do not lie," Madame Zelda replied cryptically.

"Well, maybe they exaggerate." Lyra sat back, her arms crossed over her chest in a protective gesture.

Madame Zelda turned her attention to Gemma. "And do you have a question, dear?"

Gemma cleared her throat. "I couldn't help but notice that you also offer channeling sessions for lost loved ones," she said, tracing one of the gold foil stars on the stiff faux-velvet tablecloth.

"I do."

"Could you maybe contact someone who *hasn't* passed on?" she asked, earning her a curious stare from Lyra.

"I cannot guarantee contact with any entity," Madame Zelda said. "But I will try my best, if you wish to proceed."

"She means she wants you to pay her," Lyra said.

Gemma's pulse quickened. She fished a twenty-dollar bill from her purse and slid it across the table.

Madame Zelda folded it and tucked it below the neckline of her tie-dyed caftan.

This was foolish, Gemma knew. And yet... If there was even the slightest chance she could get the assurance that Gabe hadn't given her, it would be worth it.

"The spirit you wish to contact... It is a man," Madame Zelda murmured, closing her eyes.

"Fifty-fifty shot," Lyra whispered.

"Someone you cared for deeply," the psychic added.

"Why would you be trying to contact them otherwise?" Lyra asked out of the side of her mouth.

Madame Zelda's eyes flew open. "My guides tell me that he is sorry for leaving you. He wants you to know he still cares for you, but he had no choice."

Gemma closed her eyes. It wasn't possible, and yet...the message was exactly what she needed to hear.

"Do you have a message you wish him to receive?"

"You can do that?" Gemma asked.

The brackets on either side of Madame Zelda's mouth deepened. "I can't, but my guides can. If his guides are willing, of course."

"And do his guides require a cash deposit as well?" Lyra asked.

Gemma kicked the leg of her sister's chair. "I just want him to know that I miss him. And that I hope he's okay."

Madame Zelda was silent for a long moment. Then she sighed. "His guides have received your message."

Gemma opened her eyes to find Madame Zelda gazing at her with a strange mix of pity and curiosity.

"You have a good heart," the fortune-teller said gently, "and a love worth fighting for. Remember that in the difficult days ahead."

A love.

She didn't need to be a psychic to know that was true.

Gemma had been falling for Gabe pretty much from the moment he'd first spun—quite literally—into her orbit on a bolt of hot pink aerial silk.

The fact that she hadn't told a single soul cemented the fact in her mind. Over the years, she'd gone through crushes the same way she'd gone through hobbies. Frequently, and with great zeal.

But what she felt for Gabe was too important to be the

subject of a knowing eyeroll or teasing wink. It had to be protected at all costs.

Even from her well-meaning friends.

Or siblings.

"What a load of sh—"

"Shrewd observations," Gemma said, quickly standing to cut Lyra off. "Thank you, Madame Zelda."

"You're most welcome, child." Madame Zelda rose and brushed aside the curtain, effectively ending the reading.

"*Child*," Lyra mocked in a breathy voice once they were out of earshot. "How infantilizing is that?"

Gemma nodded absently, chewing a cuticle as they strolled down the midway. Everywhere she turned, her imagination supplied vivid images of what it might have been like to come here with Gabe. The childhood memories she could share with him. The new ones they could make.

She'd always wanted someone to make out with while bumping through the darkness of the ancient haunted house. Someone to get handsy with on the Ferris wheel or roller coaster.

Lyra peered at her with concern as they made their way through the crowd. "You okay?"

Gemma shook her head. "Yeah. Just tired."

And thankfully, Lyra let it go at that.

"Remember when we were kids and you cried for an hour because you felt sorry for the fake prairie dogs getting knocked down at the shooting gallery?" Lyra asked as they approached the section allocated to unwinnable games with oversized stuffed animal prize

Gemma snorted. "In my defense, we were seven and they were very lifelike." She warily eyed the game's successor—several rows of bowling-pin-shaped clown heads with leering, square-toothed maws and cottony red hair gone matted with age. "*Those* can die screaming."

"Twice," Lyra agreed.

They drifted toward the food tents, lured by splashy signs

advertising smoked turkey legs, candy apples, elephant ears, deep-fried Oreos, and kettle corn. Gemma's stomach rumbled, reminding her she hadn't eaten since the coffee and muffin she'd grabbed at Brewbies on the way to work that morning.

She'd sort of been avoiding the kitchen.

"Want to split some loaded tater tots?" she asked Lyra. "I'm craving something greasy and covered in cheese."

"What my nutritionist doesn't know..." Lyra said, giving her a conspiratorial wink.

Paper trough of digestible debauchery in hand, they found a picnic table in the beer garden and dug into the small mountain of deep-fried potato nuggets smothered in cheese, bacon, sour cream, and chives.

"There you are!"

Gemma glanced up from a mammoth mouthful to see Darby bouncing toward them in the pinup-style bikini top she always wore when manning her coffee camper.

Bouncing being the operative word.

Lyra did a double take and dissolved into a coughing fit after bypassing the all-important chewing phase entirely and nearly sucking a tot directly into her esophagus.

"You guys," Darby said dramatically as she sat down. "Did you hear? Madame Zelda's booth caught fire."

"I thought I smelled smoke," Lyra said, dabbing the corner of her mouth with a napkin. "But just assumed it was the last of my self-respect. Is she okay?"

"She wasn't physically harmed if that's what you mean," Darby said. "But what's this I hear about you having foretold this unfortunate series of events?"

Lyra blinked at her. "Please tell me you're kidding."

Darby shook her head, her remarkable branding assets swaying with the motion. "She's over at the first aid tent as we speak, regaling everyone who will listen with her harrowing tale."

"Great." Lyra shoved the tray of tots away.

"Hey!" Looking past Lyra's scowling face, Darby motioned

Ethan over and scooted to make room beside her as he joined the table. The frosty pitcher of amber liquid he placed before them looked like something they'd serve in heaven's waiting room, if not the foyer.

No doubt catching Gemma's unabashedly hungry gaze, Ethan dealt out the stack of clear plastic cups and filled them.

"Thanks," Gemma said, before taking a sip of the crisp, hoppy ale.

Ethan's broad, plaid shoulders shrugged. "You look like you could use some."

She decided not to think about his comment overly much.

Don't ask about Gabe, Gemma told herself. *Do not ask about Gabe.*

"Heard anything from Gabe?"

Shit.

All traces of levity evaporated from Darby's face. "Not much. But he did stop by before he left town."

Gemma glanced at Ethan to see how this revelation landed, but the former sheriff seemed understandably preoccupied with eyeballing the area at large in hopes of catching someone ogling his girlfriend's tits.

Darby's expression had shifted from shock to something more akin to pity as she dropped her gaze and stared into her beer. "His family sure fucked him over proper this time, didn't they?"

"Sure did," Gemma agreed, not wanting to admit that she had no idea what Darby was talking about. "Especially that, um..." She snapped her fingers, pausing as if searching her memory. "What's his name?"

"Mikey," Darby supplied.

"That's right. Mikey." Gemma smiled through the foam kissing the cup's lip. "I just can't believe that he...um, did what he did."

"Right?" Darby's normally sensual purr bordered on shrill. "Imagine stealing your own brother's identity to go out joyriding in a stolen car. Buying God knows what with cards he took out in

Gabe's name. And after Gabe had been working so hard to build his credit back." She shook her head sadly. "He'd actually been doing well enough that he was considering buying a house here. He even went to look at a couple."

"He did?"

It was the most engaged Ethan had been yet.

Darby nodded. "That one up by the clock tower that has the widow's walk and wraparound porch?"

Gemma's heart lurched within her chest.

Gabe had been thinking of settling in Townsend Harbor permanently? Of buying a house like the one she'd described to them in the small hours in the basement's cool cocoon?

"I can't believe he'd throw away everything he's accomplished just to bail out that goat-footed asshat of an older brother," Darby said.

"This is bullshit." The leftover tots jumped with the force of Gemma's fist on the table.

"Leave that to me," Lyra said with a determined grin. "I have a plan."

"A plan?" Gemma echoed warily. "What sort of plan?"

"The sort that helps," Lyra said cryptically.

"Help with what?" Gemma demanded. "What are you not telling me?"

Her sister gave her a mysterious little smile. "You'll see."

Gemma's heart leapt at the words, even as her mind filled with misgivings.

And yet...if there was even a chance of helping Gabe, she had to try.

She sighed, bracing herself for what was sure to be an interesting night, and resigned herself to her fate.

Consequences be damned.

TWENTY-ONE
Titanium Nuts

RESISTS RUSTING AND CORROSION VS. OTHER ALLOYS

GABE'S HEART POUNDED IN HIS CHEST AS HE STOOD AT the defendant's table, sweat beading on his brow. The Suffolk County Courtroom was a grand and imposing space, with high ceilings adorned with delicate moldings and towering windows that let in an abundance of light. The judge's bench, raised above all else, served as a constant reminder of the power held within these walls. He hadn't slept a wink. How could he with the image of Gemma burning his eyelids every time he closed them?

He steeled himself as the bailiff announced the judge's entrance.

His hopes for leniency were shattered when an unfamiliar judge entered the courtroom, stern-faced and unyielding. Panic slithered down Gabe's spine, and his stomach churned with anxiety as he scrambled mentally to gather his defenses. This was not the judge he had expected, the one connected to his father. Gabe felt like a tightrope walker who had just realized there was no safety net below. Not with this sharp-eyed vulture settling onto the bench.

Judge B. Obermeyer. The name didn't ring a bell.
Shit.

Gabe's mouth went dry as chalk. Sweat prickled along his hairline as his hands curled into fists.

He was on his own here. No one to call in favors or make problems disappear. Not for the first time, it hit him, stark and sharp as a prison shiv—he might not get out of this.

Second chances? Not in one of the oldest towns in America. Not in the system they'd built for profit and punishment.

Gabe dragged in a ragged breath, feeling an ache in his chest as familiar as the worn leather of his motorcycle jacket. He'd survived worse. He could live through this. What choice did he have?

Gabe straightened his shoulders and stared the judge straight in his beady-eyed face. The old bastard could throw everything, including the courthouse chandelier, at him. It wouldn't make a lick of difference.

He was already in hell—might as well lock him up.

The judge peered at him over the rim of his spectacles. "How do you plead to the charges Mr. Kelly?"

"Not guilty, your honor." The words rasped from Gabe's throat.

"Very well." The gavel cracked like a gunshot as the judge turned to the DA. "Counselor, you may state your case."

Gabe braced himself as the prosecutor, an elegant woman in her fifties, rose, a smug twist to her lips.

She hated him. Or she hated his family. This was going to be ugly.

The doors banged open.

Every head in the courtroom swiveled toward the commotion, including Gabe's. His heart slammed to a stop.

Gemma?

But not Gemma. She strode through the aisle with a purposeful gait, clad in a charcoal power suit and a severe bun in place of her usual tumble of curls and relaxed millennial garb.

Lyra?

No. Couldn't be. He'd kissed that freckle under Gemma's right eye too many times.

Then she slanted him a look from under her lashes, a glimpse of warmth mixed with anxiety that sparked recognition.

All the breath whooshed from Gabe's lungs. His pulse rocketed as Gemma settled beside him in a waft of honeysuckle and trouble. He could feel the heat of her body, the magnetic pull of her presence. It had been weeks since they'd last been in each other's company, and their proximity now filled him with an intense longing, threatening to derail his focus.

"Apologies for the interruption, your honor." Her voice held the same brisk cadence as Lyra's, though her eyes gleamed with mischief. "I'm Lyra McKendrick, Mr. Kelly's legal counsel."

Wait. Had those mushrooms he'd thrown into his omelet this morning been the wrong kind? Because he had to be hallucinating.

The judge frowned, gaze shifting between Gemma and Gabe. "You're late, Ms. McKendrick. See that it does not happen again."

"Of course, your honor. Scheduling conflict. Sincerest apologies. I can assure you it won't happen again." Gemma arranged a stack of files before her, the picture of competence.

Gabe leaned close as she shuffled through what he now could see were blank forms for ordering weaving supplies.

Fuck. He was going to end up in front of a firing squad.

He put his head next to hers. "What the actual fuck are you doing?" he whispered. "You'll get yourself arrested."

"Relax." She didn't look up from the files. "I've been a twin my entire life. I've got this under control."

"This is crazy." He gripped her wrist beneath the table, feeling panic and fury tangling in a knot in his gut. "You can't just waltz in here and"—he looked around, lowering his voice to barely audible—"pretend to be a lawyer."

"Watch me." Gemma's eyes glinted like cut glass. "You didn't think I'd let you face this alone, did you?"

"Just promise me you'll get the fuck out of here if things go south," he said. "I'll cover for you."

Gemma's smile softened into something tender that made his battered heart skip a beat. She covered his hand with her own. "I'm not going anywhere, so there's no point arguing. Now shut up and let me do my job—er, Lyra's job."

"Do you two need a moment, Ms. McKendrick?" the judge asked testily.

"Nope, your honor, just catching Ga—my client up on some recent developments in his defense."

"Would you like to share those developments with the rest of us, or are we just wasting *your* time?" Yup. The judge was home-grown Boston.

"Again, your honor, forgive me. I'm ready." Gemma stood, and Gabe almost passed out. Could everyone hear his heart beating? Did the judge see him sweating bullets and shitting bricks and doing other stuff he couldn't control?

His terror for Gemma made him look like a guilty man.

"Relax," Gemma whispered. "I'm great at following directions, remember?"

He remembered. He remembered every word they'd whispered in the dark. Every time he watched the sun paint pretty colors into the corona of her dark hair. He remembered that people liked to listen when she spoke because she wasn't just smart—she was wise and she was kind.

"Trust me," she added. The first demand she'd ever made of him.

In that moment, as Gemma's eyes met Gabe's, he felt the weight of his future resting on her slender shoulders. It was a precarious balance, but one he trusted her to maintain. A silent understanding passed between them, and Gabe knew he had placed his fate in her delicate hands.

She winked and turned her dazzling smile on the judge. "Your honor, I'm ready to proceed. Thank you for your patience."

The judge grunted, mollified for the moment by the radiance of her smile, and nodded for the prosecution to begin.

Gabe settled in for the long haul, Gemma a solid presence at his side. His crazy, maddening, magnificent girl.

The prosecutor riffled through the papers on her desk before standing to address the judge. "Your honor, we have several documents here that prove that on several separate instances, Mr. Gabriel Kelly committed the acts of fraud, forgery, identity theft, and—"

"Objection, your honor." Gemma smoothly rose to her feet, cutting off the prosecutor mid-sentence. "The charges against my client are completely unfounded. I'd like to move for a continuance so we—I—can mount a timelier and more accurate defense."

The judge peered at Gemma over the rims of his glasses. "On what grounds do you base this objection, counselor?"

"On the grounds of this great and...historical city in which we find ourselves," Gemma said with absolute conviction.

A ripple of surprise went through the courtroom, followed by a frenzy of whispers and a couple of chuckles. Even the judge looked taken aback.

Gabe stared at Gemma, torn between horror and awe. Oh shit. She was going to go down for contempt.

"You being smart with me, young lady?" the judge asked, leaning dangerously forward.

"I'm being honest with you, judge." Gemma smiled, polite but pitiless. "As officers of the court, we are all obliged to be truthful, and...and the truth will be very evident any minute now. Aaaaany minute."

Fuck. She was losing ground already. What, she didn't have a plan beyond kicking the door down? That didn't seem like her at all. But there she stood, shaking in shoes that weren't hers. He could feel the panic in her lithe form, see it in the trembling of her skilled fingers.

Gabe burned to do anything, say something! But if he did, it would endanger Gemma further and uncover her deception to an increasingly irritated judge.

"Your honor." The prosecutor's voice dripped with disdain. "I think Ms. McKendrick is very new at her job. I'd like to move—"

"Move out of my way, is what you'll do," boomed a voice from the back of the gallery.

A voice that puckered every sphincter in Gabe's entire body.

Turning his neck, Gabe watched his father, Patrick Kelly, march Michael up the center aisle, shoving him forward. The air buzzed with a cacophony of voices, and Gabe felt as if the floor beneath him had become unstable, threatening to pitch him into an abyss. He couldn't tear his gaze from Michael's face, from the mixture of fear and defiance etched across his features.

Panic and confusion warred inside Gabe as he noticed Darby hovering nervously behind them.

"Order! I will have order in the court, or I will clear the gallery!" the judge bellowed, pounding his gavel against the wood like a relentless heartbeat. It took several attempts for the clamor to subside, and each strike of the gavel echoed through Gabe's chest like a physical blow.

His father and younger brother were both in their black power suits with green ties, rings on fingers and chains around their neck. Michael, a taller, leaner version of his father, even sported a glinting diamond that belonged in the Crown Jewels on his left lobe.

Patrick straightened, eyes hard as flint. "Your honor, I've brought the man responsible for the crimes my son, Gabriel, has been accused of."

A shocked gasp rippled through the gallery. Gabe stared at his father in stunned disbelief, heart pounding.

Gemma's hand found his, squeezing tight.

The judge peered over his glasses at Michael. "Is this not also your other son, Mr. Kelly?"

"Yeah, judge, your genius detectives picked the wrong Kelly kid. Gabriel's been out of the business for years. But don't feel bad, your honor—Michael was trying to pin his dumbass crimes on his brother like a little snitch, and your people fell for it. Happens all the time."

The judge banged his gavel again. "I don't care who you are, Mr. Kelly. You will watch your language in my courtroom."

True to form, Gabe's father lifted his big hands with perma-grease-stained nails and turned to the gallery with a teasing grin and a disrespectful pop of his nicotine gum. "Forgive me, your honor. I forget how friggin' sensitive you types are."

Gabe dropped his head in his hands. Holy fuck, he was going to have a heart attack when the two women he cared about most were punished because his dad thought he was a funny fuck.

Which the fact that everyone chuckled didn't help one goddamn bit.

Michael wouldn't meet Gabe's eyes, but he spoke up, voice shaking. "I stole Gabe's identity and credit cards. I purposely turned in a member of the family, and that is unforgivable. I'm the one who should be on trial here, not him."

A roaring filled Gabe's ears as the pieces fell into place. The weird calls and texts from financial institutions. The unfamiliar charges on accounts he had to keep closing. All this time, Michael had been behind it. The betrayal cut deep, reopening old wounds.

The judge addressed the prosecutor, who looked like she would rather spit nails than announce that the charges against Gabe would be dropped. But she did it, because she had no other choice.

As Michael was led away in handcuffs, Gemma wrapped her arms around Gabe. "It's over," she whispered. "You're free."

He held her close, emotions churning. Joy and relief warred with anger and sorrow, and the rage and panic of the previous weeks—his previous life—refused to release its hold. But Gemma was here, her presence stronger than any ghosts in his past.

They escaped the chaos, retreating to the marble atrium of the courthouse. Sunlight streamed through arched windows and skylights overhead. The open space was a stark contrast to the cramped courtroom.

Gabe leaned against a column, dragging a hand through his hair as he tried to find strength in his legs to hold the rest of him up. "I can't believe..."

"I know." Gemma smoothed the lapels of his jacket, her eyes soft with sympathy. "Your own brother."

"No. I can't believe *you*."

She blinked once. Twice. "Me?"

"I can't believe you'd fucking do something that..."

"Amazing?" Darby offered, her ninety-million-inch heels loud against the floors. "Incredible? Courageous? Badass?"

"Reckless. Dangerous. Terrifying."

"Hey!" Gemma pouted, "I had to do it, Lyra was going to stand up for you, but her connecting flight was delayed and only her luggage arrived in time. She told me all I had to do to get a continuance so she could look over the case, and when Darby said your dad and brother would be here, I just tried to buy you more time either way." She ran out of breath before all the words got out, but she managed.

Gabe stared at Gemma, his eyes tracing the contours of her face, which seemed to glow in the soft light filtering through the atrium's high windows. Her lips were slightly parted as if she were anticipating his next move.

He couldn't help it—he had to kiss her.

Gabe pulled her close, and their lips met, fusing together in a passionate exchange that spoke volumes of their shared relief.

"Thank God you're here," he murmured against her mouth, feeling the tension drain from his body.

"Of course I'm here," she replied, her voice breathy and low. "I want to be where you are, Gabriel Kelly."

Gabe let out a sharp breath and released her, gaping at a woman he was realizing he didn't know all that well. "This is crazy —you realize that, right? You're being crazy."

"I'm crazy about you." A smile curved Gemma's mouth. "And

you, Gabe Kelly, don't seem to mind my crazy as much as everyone else does. In fact, I think you love me for it."

He shook his head, helpless affection swelling in his chest, overflowing into his throat, crawling into his eyes with the threat of humiliating emotion.

He did love her for it.

For her passion and determination and reckless courage that so often led them into trouble. Trouble he wouldn't trade for the world.

So how did he say it? How did he tell her that he wanted everything she was and had to offer? That it had taken exactly no time for her to become the velvet rope that anchored his heart in place? The reason he still even had one, probably.

Did the words *I love you* contain all of that? Was that why he'd never said them to anyone alive?

"Gemma..." His stomach flopped around like a beached carp, and he had to concentrate on her luminous eyes, shutting out the entire world so he could work up the courage to say—

"Twins, huh? You lucky little fuckah."

Gabe spun to face his father, placing himself between Gemma and the devil.

The man's shoulders were wide and his chest deeper than most, his eyes crystal blue and cold as the Fortress of Solitude. He wasn't tall, but his charisma towered over men and women both, as did his pound-for-pound incredible strength and legendary ruthlessness.

Gabe was going to look like him some day. Of all the Kellys past and present, they resembled each other the most.

But Patrick Kelly was *not* going to be who Gabe saw in the mirror at that age. Not even close. He was going to wear friggin' sweaters and shit with little fucky patches on the elbows. He was going to teach their kids to maintain cars... Sure. But he was going to hug them, too. He was going to tell them he was proud. Keep them safe from predators. Teach them to be street smart like him, but also genuine and kind. To show up for the people they loved.

Like Gemma.

"She's my girl, sure, so you don't disrespect her, old man. I don't care who you think you are or what you think I owe you for showing up today, but you don't look at her sideways or—"

"There it is." For the first time in his life, Patrick Kelly's eyes shone with pride. "I didn't think you had it in you."

Gabe's teeth clacked together. *What the fuck is he talking about?*

"You know when you were a toddler, I thought you weren't mine because you were such a sweet little shit?" Patrick smoothed down his green tie and made a rude gesture at an older woman who clearly disapproved of his profanity echoing off the walls. "Your mother said she didn't want to raise you a Kelly because you weren't a natural-born killer like the rest of us, but looking in your eyes now, I can see it. I can see you're lethally fucking serious right now."

Yeah. He was. He'd slaughter his father in front of God and the entire Boston legal system if Patrick so much as whispered a threat in Gemma's direction.

Pat Kelly was many things, but he wasn't known for being cruel to women. That'd been *his* father. Story went, the man had killed Patrick's mother in front of him.

"What do I owe you for making Mikey fess up?" Gabe asked, readying for his dad to demand his pound of flesh. "You want to break my nose so we're even? You want a payout? I've got property to sell. What I won't do is another job for you, so don't ask."

Pat looked at him a long time while everything said and done between them filled the cavernous space. He lifted his arm to squeeze at the back of his neck, a gesture Gabe just realized he'd gotten from the old man.

Swallowing profusely, he looked over his father's shoulder at a point on the far wall. He didn't want to think about all the hours he'd spent tinkering with cars at the man's elbow. Didn't want the image of their nights after a good job sitting around with beer and a game, paying attention to nothing but his dad's stories that put them in stitches.

He didn't want to love his dad. Had grown out of wishing things were different.

And yet...

"I'm the one that owes you, kid."

Gabe's breath seized, and he looked up for the very real possibility that the entire world was ending. Pigs were flying. Hell was freezing over.

All the shit more likely than Patrick Kelly owing a debt.

"Maybe I should have let your mother take you with her. I don't know. Maybe then I wouldn't be still working through my penance for what Johnny and I did to that Father Shit Fuck back in the day—I'll be saying Hail Marys until kingdom come."

Gabe's jaw loosened with such astonishment that he forgot his own name.

Was... Was this... Was his father *apologizing*?

Nah. Apologies weren't something the Kelly family did. Ever. That would mean they actually had to admit they'd done something wrong, and in his family, that was a hanging offense.

Pat cleared his throat. "Anyway, uh, it's Mikey's turn to take his licks. He was sore at you for taking off, but you don't turn on family, and you *don't* fucking turn them in. Besides..." He glanced away, and Gabe knew he was looking at Gemma. "Last time you and I...talked...I got what was coming to me, so I did this to make sure we're square. Can't start a new life with an old charge."

Talked. That's what he called the permanent dent in his nose courtesy of Gabe's right fist.

Smoothing down his tie again, Patrick offered a tentative half-smile to Gemma, who tucked into Gabe's side and reached for his hand.

"Woman like that's hard to find," Patrick said. "Not many people would fucking fly across country and commit multiple felonies to get you off lesser charges. She's braver than half my workforce, and better to look at than all of them."

"Easy," Gabe warned.

"She must really love you."

"I do, Mr. Kelly. Your son is impossible not to love." The surety in Gemma's voice reached into Gabe's chest cavity and squeezed his heart until it might explode.

The perma-gleam in his dad's eye dulled for a moment as he looked at Gemma, but didn't seem to see her.

"I knew a girl like you once," he told her in a voice gentler than he'd used on his sons as infants. "Eyes all big and dark." He inhaled for an eternity, staring through Gemma and into the past. "Italian, she was. Purest heart God ever made. Not to mention the plumpest ass—"

"Don't." Apparently, his father being the Kelly form of vulnerable had reduced Gabe to a monosyllabic mess.

"What happened between you?" Gemma's impulsive question shocked each of the Kelly men.

"Well, kid, she asked me to leave town for her...with her, I guess."

This was the first time Gabe was hearing anything about this, and he didn't know what to do about Gemma and the man who had an actual body count discussing their broken hearts.

What was happening?

"You didn't go?" Gemma sounded like the very idea was the saddest thing she ever heard.

For the first time in his entire life, Patrick Kennedy Dermot Kelly lowered his eyes in shame.

Strange. Gabe never thought of his father as a man who could feel regret.

Pat's eyes flicked back to him, pinning him down. "Take her home, Gabriel," he said. "Don't come back here."

Home.

It was a word Gabe clutched on to as he watched his father walk out of his life.

Which was the kindest thing he could do.

Darby, who'd stood quietly by, looked stunned enough to

need neurosurgery to get her thoughts back. "What just happened?" she breathed.

Gabe shook his head, trying to figure out what to say. "I meant it."

Gemma's voice broke the moment, and Gabe turned to face her clear, brilliant eyes. "What?"

"I *mean* it," she corrected herself, her upturned face soft and full of hope. "I love you." Her lashes flickered. "I know you didn't want me to, but I can't help it. It's why I talked Darby into bringing me out here and going to your father."

"Yeah..." Gabe said darkly. "Darbs and I are going to talk about that."

He wished Darby could hear him, but her heels were already clomp-clomping toward the main entryway the moment Gemma made her declaration.

Gemma's gaze turned fretful. "You don't have to say it back if you—"

Fuck.

Gabe gathered her face in his hands, cupping the delicate weight of her skull between rough palms so he could make sure she heard him correctly. That she was paying attention only to him. Nothing and no one else.

His heart jackhammered against his ribcage. "Every morning I wake up with your name on my lips," he said, the words tumbling out too fast. "Every time I see you, my heart pounds so damned loud, I can't believe you can't hear it across the room."

A smile slowly curved Gemma's lips and her eyes softened.

"You have a gift, Gem," he said, his hands shaking. "A way of making people feel seen. Heard. Like they matter."

Like you made me feel. But he couldn't say that, not yet.

"You showed up when I needed you," he said instead, his voice rough with emotion. "You're my hero, Gem. You saved me when that should have been my job."

"You silly man." Gemma reached for his hands, her fingers warm and strong around his. "You saved me right back. With your huge, ridiculously amazing heart. Your ability to accept me as I am, even when I'm being completely impossible to live with."

A laugh escaped him. "Impossible?" He shook his head. "You're the easiest person to love I've ever known, Gemma McKendrick. The living with part..." He shrugged, unable to keep from smiling. "We'll figure that out as we go."

Her own smile could have set the moon aglow.

Still, Gabe realized he had something else to say. "I've never loved anyone, Gemma. I knew I didn't, so I never said it."

"It's okay... You don't have t—"

"I love you, Gemma McKendrick. I fucking love you. I'm going to have to learn to live with the fact that I got no right and did no good to deserve you, but from here on out, I'm going to do my fucking best."

To his consternation, Gemma was shaking her head. "No, Gabe. There is no *deserve* when it comes to love. It just happens to you when you find someone you can't live without." Reaching up, she smoothed his one unruly forelock. "I'm going to make it my life's purpose to give you the love you should have gotten from everyone else. There's a lifetime of love you need to receive, Gabriel Kelly, and that starts now."

"I don't want you to do that." He shook his head, bringing his face down to hers to touch noses. To share breath. "I only want your love. No one else matters."

"You have it."

She rose on her toes to press her lips to his, and Gabe deepened the kiss immediately.

Her hands curled into his shirt, holding him close as he wrapped his arms around her waist, anchoring her body to his.

He couldn't fucking believe it. This morning he was facing his version of the guillotine, and now? Now...

"I don't know about you," she whispered, brushing her thumb over the curve of his jaw. "But I'm ready to go home."

Townsend Harbor. The home he thought he'd never get to have was waiting for him.

"Hey, Gabe?" Gemma said. "Do you think we could go to the Common before we leave? Also maybe a museum? Dad's a huge history buff, and the Revolution is something he reads about all the time, and..."

Gabe stopped her mouth with another kiss, not hating the idea of saying goodbye to his hometown before he began their life in hers.

Pulling back, he looked down at the love of his life.

"As you wish."

TWENTY-TWO

W.J.P.

WORK IN PROGRESS

THE PUDDLE OF SUNLIGHT SPILLED ACROSS GEMMA'S dust-darkened knees as she sat on the wood floor, chewing her bite of pizza.

"Well," she said as she as she savored the sweet, salty tang of pineapple and prosciutto. "According to the experts, we're officially compatible."

"I coulda told you that." Sprawled beside her on the floor of their new apartment, Gabe was already enthusiastically devouring his third slice.

An impromptu picnic in celebration of their official cohabitation.

"No, I mean the ham and pineapple test," Gemma explained, taking another bite. "It's one of those watershed relationship things. If you'd have insisted on plain old pepperoni, we'd be doomed."

Gabe reached over and pulled a piece of packing tape off Gemma's shorts. "Baby, after what you did for me, I'd happily eat pickles on a brick if that's what you wanted."

"It was nothing, really." Though truly, her performance at the Suffolk County Courthouse had been an utterly insane gambit, and still made her a little weak-kneed to think about.

"Do you even know what the penalty is for impersonating legal counsel?" he asked, one dark eyebrow arched at her.

Gemma wiped her fingers on her paper towel. "According to section thirty-three of the one hundred and ninety-third general court of the Commonwealth of Massachusetts, the penalty for impersonating any number of individuals acting in an official capacity shall be punished by a fine of not more than four hundred dollars or by imprisonment for not more than one year."

Thankfully, she hadn't done the serious googling on the potential penalties until *after* her brief but apparently impressive performance.

Not that it would have changed anything.

Had she to do it over again, she would have made the exact same choice.

She just might have ended up vomiting into Lyra's Gucci briefcase before making her official entrance into the Suffolk County Courthouse.

Gabe's brow furrowed in retrospective concern. "I still can't believe you did that."

That made two of them.

"I'm considering that as one of the titles for my autobiography." She was only half kidding. The other half felt an irrational little jolt of pride every time she remembered the look on Gabe's face when he'd seen her. Abject horror melting away to something like wonder bordering on awe when she'd begun spitting out legal terms courtesy of her neurospicy brain's uncanny ability to master an entire subject in mere hours of hyperfixation. She'd been able to chameleon herself into crisis-driven capability driven by the reliable engine of impulsivity, all while proudly trotting out facts from her newly acquired knowledge base like so many show ponies.

And—lo and fucking behold—she'd actually managed to help the man she loved in the process.

Help him in ways that perhaps not even a responsible, even-tempered and consistent performer like Lyra couldn't.

Or *wouldn't.*

Not that Gemma could blame her. What with the tedious and complicated rules governing the caseload her sister was now handling from out of state.

And anyway, the beautiful irony that one sibling impersonating another could potentially be the antidote to problems created by one sibling impersonating another was just too delicious to pass up.

"Any other solid contenders? For the title," Gabe quickly added, most likely noticing the faraway look she often got when scampering through the complex Habitrail hamster tunnels of her thoughts.

"So far, I've got *Not Like Other Girls: but Really Though* and *Dude, Where's My Keys/Phone/Life?*" Picking a piece of pineapple off one of the remaining slices, Gemma popped it into her mouth.

"Not bad," Gabe said, seeing her pineapple theft and raising her a pink curl of prosciutto. "But how 'bout, *Tangled: Unraveling the Neurotypical Bullshit to Find Your Best Life.*"

"That's really good, actually." He'd even leveraged the Zoomer speak that made Fawkes's hooded eye tick when he came home to find Gemma and Cady "high AF" and binging the latest historical humpfest.

Which was wonderfully, soul-soothingly often these days.

Gabe shrugged. "It was that or *The Neurodivergent Guide to Punching a Motherfucker in the Face.* I feel like probably you're not the only one who could use some mentorship on the finer points."

Even as he said it, Gemma experienced a brief but exceedingly detailed sensory flash of the precise moment when his knuckles had connected with Harrison's nose.

Crunching cartilage and all.

"In the scrapbook of my life, that moment right there is getting a full-page spread," she said fondly.

"I'd like to give you a full-page spread right now, " Gabe said, trailing his deliciously rough fingertips over her knee. "But I don't think that'd help this situation we've got going on here."

A smile curled the corners of Gemma's lips as she surveyed the "situation" in question. A swarm of boxes spreading out in every direction, most of them opened and disgorging their contents in overlapping piles.

His stuff. Her stuff.

Their stuff.

The realization hit her all over again.

She, Gemini Cleo McKendrick, sweater vest-wearing neurospicy knitter, was moving in with Gabe "The Babe" Kelly.

Moving into an apartment all their own.

Technically, all *Elizabeth Billings'* own, but for the next twelve months at least, the third-floor apartment above Star-Crossed was legally and officially theirs.

"Charming" was the word Elizabeth had used when pitching the idea of their moving in.

Gemma preferred "quirky" or "eccentric," or perhaps even "delightfully odd." Already, she'd come to cherish the nooks and crannies where the building had been converted from whatever it had been in its previous life to this airy, high-ceilinged, window-lined Victorian era flat. She'd examined every inch of the elaborate crown moldings that curved around the pendant light fixtures and stretched out in elaborate scrollwork where the ceiling met the creamy beige walls. She'd fallen shamelessly in love with the fireplace's jade green glazed tiles and wooden mantel whose hand-carved lions appeared to be of the cowardly variety, their time-blunted fangs protruding from snarls that looked more like sheepish grins. She'd twirled beneath the stained-glass skylights spilling candy-colored strobes over a parquet floor that creaked and squeaked enthusiastic greetings as they moved room to room.

Which Gemma had been doing a lot since they'd signed the lease.

Standing in the foyer, she'd imagined the entryway table where she'd put her grandmother McKendrick's green glass vase and fill it with flowers from the farmer's market every week. In the galley kitchen, she'd already made mental macchiatos and imagined filling Gabe's giant metal thermos at the old craft cabinet they were going to turn into a coffee bar. Hell, she'd even mentally knitted the pillow covers for the pull-out sofa she intended to acquire for the guest room.

These kinds of feverish mundane fantasies were not unique.

Gemma had lived a thousand lives this way. Built entire *castles* not in the sky, but in the fertile soil of her mind.

But now, *now*, Gabe Kelly's brutally strong, beautifully skilled hands would help deliver her dreams into the material realm.

That, and keep her from brushing her teeth with antibiotic ointment like she'd very nearly done that morning.

"You're right," Gemma agreed, returning to their current organizational conundrum. "But at least Bazaar Girls is only an elevator ride and twenty-two paces away. Moving the yarn horde will free up a shit-ton of space."

"I don't know which part I like more," Gabe said, rolling himself into a seated position. "That Elizabeth Billings bought your dad's building without Harrison getting a goddamn dime, or that she leased it to you for eleven dollars a month to pay off an energetic debt from a past life."

They held a look that turned into mirrored schadenfreude-flavored grins.

The Harrison part, definitely. True to his word, her father had backed out of all talk about selling the building once Gemma had handed over her financials.

Until Elizabeth Billings oh-so-gently suggested that she, Gemma, and her father meet up for coffee—kombucha, in Elizabeth's case—sans Harrison to renew their discussion.

And there, with golden morning light streaming through the windows of the cluttered, cozy craft boutique that felt like an extension of her soul, Gemma watched as Elizabeth artfully convinced her father that selling the building would be energetically aligned with his plans for retirement.

Even more surprising, that her suit-jacket wearing father had actually bought it.

A real estate mogul in yogi's clothing that lady.

"So how does it feel to be out of your parents' place?" Gabe took a swig from the brown bottle of beer wedged in the boot he'd shucked off when they decided to take a break to devour a hasty dinner.

"Let me see," she drawled, glancing around with exaggerated effort. "Going to have to say pretty fucking fantastic." Gemma stole a sip of Gabe's beer to wash down the last bite of their carb-and-dairy-laden dinner. "But I do feel guilty that now Lyra's stuck there instead."

Gabe accepted the bottle back and drained the last few swallows before setting it aside.

"Listen here," he said, scooting closer to her. "If there's one thing I know, it's that if your sister set her heart on rebounding from that yuppie turd at the Batcave or Buckingham friggin' Palace, I'm pretty sure she could make it happen."

Gemma smiled as she tossed her crust back into the open pizza box. About that, he was absolutely correct.

"True," she said. "I mean, I'm ridiculously thrilled Harrison's out of the picture, don't get me wrong, but I just hate to see her so...bitter, you know?"

Only yesterday, Gemma had swung by to drop off some muffins on her way to Bazaar Girls but thought better of it when she'd witnessed Lyra flip off the sun before shuffling back inside with the paper under one arm and scowl welded to her pale, sleep-creased face.

"Lyra's smart and capable," Gabe reassured her, placing a hand on her knee. "She'll bounce back in no time. And who knows?" He pushed himself to his feet. "Maybe she'll decide she *wants* to stick around Townsend Harbor for a while."

Gemma extended her hands, and Gabe effortlessly tugged her upward.

"And do what?" Gemma crossed to the kitchen and

resumed unwrapping the plates her mother had donated to their cause. "Go into private practice? Aside from the dispute over Nevermore, the biggest legal scrape to happen around these parts was when Roy Dobson filed suit again Myrtle's new llama, Darrell."

"Point taken."

That Gabe didn't even inquire as to the circumstances that would cause the new and marginally improved curmudgeon-lite version of Roy to seek financial compensation from a three-legged pseudo ruminant was a testament to just how integrated he had become into the fabric of the community.

"I'll bet she could make a mint doing readings," Gabe said with a wicked grin.

"Don't let her hear you say that," Gemma said, biting her cheek to keep from laughing.

Lyra's ongoing battle against the virulent rumor that she was psychic had only intensified in the wake of several other uncanny calls.

Like last week's for example. Gemma had dragged Lyra from the basement to browse for herbs at The Shrub Hub when Judy had steered her utility cart full of fall mums over to them.

When asked whether Judy would be kissing her true love at midnight this New Year's, Lyra suggested that the gabbing county dispatcher would be better off kissing an electric fence.

Which, for reasons no one could possibly understand, Judy did.

And there, on the sprawling acreage off State Route 19, Judy awoke from her self-imposed romantic shock therapy treatment to find herself gazing up into the kind blue eyes of a free-range chicken farmer who she'd been spotted canoodling with at several conspicuous Townsend Harbor hangouts since.

"And don't even get me started on the dating pool..." Gemma said.

"That bad?" Gabe asked.

"It's like..." she paused searching for an appropriate image.

"You know those little plastic kiddie pools that are always full of grass clippings and probably toddler urine after the first hour?"

"Grass clippings or not, I sure wouldn't mind one of those right about now," Gabe said, peeling off his sweaty tank top to reveal his gorgeously sculpted, tattooed torso. "It's hot as balls in here."

"I'll call someone about the radiator today," Gemma said, stacking plates. "Elizabeth conveniently forgot to mention that the only thermostat is downstairs in Star-Crossed."

"Figures." Gabe balled up his tank top and pitched it toward the laundry closet with surprising accuracy. "Probably tell us eighty degrees is the optimal temperature for awakening our subtle energetic bodies or some shit."

Gemma's gaze lingered on his bare back, struck by the sheen of perspiration deepening the intricate patterns of his Celtic tattoos. "She might be right," she said, wrapping her arms around his waist as she nuzzled into his neck. "Mine's feeling pretty awake at the moment."

"When is Lyra coming by again?" Gabe asked.

A small but much-appreciated offering to Gemma's occasional time-blindness.

"Six." Her fingers found their way to the waistband of Gabe's jeans as she melted into his back. "Think we have time?"

"Please." Gabe turned in the circle of her arms and lifted Gemma onto the counter beside the half-unpacked boxes of dishes and bakeware. "Thirty minutes and no parents upstairs? I'm going to fuck your brains out and still have time to change your oil shower and shower."

"Actually—" Gemma sandwiched her elbows against her ribcage when Gabe started lifting the hem of her shirt. "We might want to invert that order. Between the ridiculous radiator and hauling the last of books upstairs, I'm pretty well brined at this point."

"Good." A glow nothing short of feral lit in the depths of

Gabe's eyes. "Because I'm about to replenish the shit out of my electrolytes."

As Gabe's mouth explored the curve of her neck, Gemma's eyes drifted again to the jumble of their combined possessions— hers too many, and his too few.

All the selves she'd tried to be holding space for the selves he'd never had the chance to become. The artifacts of two separate lives slowly merging themselves into a single, shared mess.

Mess.

For the first time in her relatively short, frenetic existence, that word neither bit nor stung. Maybe, because on this particular Saturday, with Gabe's mouth on her skin and the late afternoon sun dappling the ordinary clutter of half-empty boxes, Gemma saw the sprawling chaos for what it truly was.

The raw material from which any and every possible future could be formed.

And the man who'd helped create it required no apologies. No assurances. No promises that she would hide it away or tame it into an orderly if arbitrary form.

She could simply let it be. Let *herself* be.

Alive, and in love, and imperfect all at once.

About Cynthia

 Cynthia St. Aubin wrote her first play at age eight and made her brothers perform it for the admission price of gum wrappers. A steal, considering she provided the wrappers in advance. Though her early work debuted to mixed reviews, she never quite gave up on the writing thing, even while earning a mostly useless master's degree in art history and taking her turn as a cube monkey in the corporate warren.

Because the voices in her head kept talking to her, and they discourage drinking at work, she kept writing instead. When she's not standing in front of the fridge eating cheese, she's hard at work figuring out which mythological, art historical, or paranormal friends to play with next. She lives in Texas with the love of her life and two fluffy cats, Muppet and Gizmo.

I **love stalkers! You can find me here!**
Visit me: http://www.cynthiastaubin.com/
Email me: cynthiastaubin@gmail.com
Join my Minions: https://www.facebook.com/groups/
Cynthiastaubins/

Subliminally message me: *You were thinking of cheese just now, right?*

And here:

Also by Cynthia

Tails from the Alpha Art Gallery

Love Bites

Love Sucks

Love Lies

Love Binds

The Kane Heirs

Corner Office Confessions

Secret Lives After Hours

Bad Boys with Benefits

The Jane Avery Mysteries

Private Lies

Lying Low

Case Files of Dr. Matilda Schmidt, Paranormal Psychologist

Unlovable

Unlucky

Unhoppy

Unbearable

Unassailable

Undeadly

Unexpecting

From Hell to Breakfast

About Kerrigan

 Kerrigan Byrne is the USA Today Best-selling and award winning author of several novels in both the romance and mystery genre.

She lives on the Olympic Peninsula in Washington with her husband, two Rottweiler mix rescues, and one very clingy torbie. When she's not writing and researching, you'll find her on the beach, kayaking, or on land eating, drinking, shopping, and attending live comedy, ballet, or too many movies.

Kerrigan loves to hear from her readers! To contact her or learn more about her books, please visit her site or find her on most social media platforms: www.kerriganbyrne.com

Also by Kerrigan

To Seduce a Highlander

THE MACKAY BANSHEES

Highland Darkness

Highland Devil

Highland Destiny

To Desire a Highlander

THE DE MORAY DRUIDS

Highland Warlord

Highland Witch

Highland Warrior

To Wed a Highlander

CONTEMPORARY SUSPENSE

A Righteous Kill

ALSO BY KERRIGAN

How to Love a Duke in Ten Days

All Scot And Bothered